FEB 21

PRAISE FOR MELANIE DICKERSON

"*The Piper's Pursuit* is a lovely tale of adventure, romance, and redemption. Kat and Steffan's righteous quest will have you rooting them on until the very satisfying end!"

—LORIE LANGDON, AUTHOR OF
OLIVIA TWIST AND THE DOON SERIES

"Christian fiction fans will relish Dickerson's eloquent story."

—SCHOOL LIBRARY JOURNAL ON *THE ORPHAN'S WISH*

"*The Goose Girl*, a little retold fairy tale, sparkles in Dickerson's hands, with endearing characters and a charming setting that will appeal to teens and adults alike."

—*RT BOOK REVIEWS*, 4^{1}/2 STARS,
TOP PICK! ON *THE NOBLE SERVANT*

"Dickerson is a masterful storyteller with a carefully crafted plot, richly drawn characters, and a detailed setting. The reader is easily pulled into the story."

—*CHRISTIAN LIBRARY JOURNAL* ON *THE NOBLE SERVANT*

"[*The Silent Songbird*] will have you jumping out of your seat with anticipation at times. Moderate- to fast-paced, you will not want this book to end. Recommended for all, especially lovers of historical romance."

—*RT BOOK REVIEWS*, 4 STARS

"A terrific YA crossover medieval romance from the author of *The Golden Braid*."

—*LIBRARY JOURNAL* ON *THE SILENT SONGBIRD*

"When it comes to happily-ever-afters, Melanie Dickerson is the undisputed queen of fairy-tale romance, and all I can say is—long live the queen! From start to finish *The Beautiful Pretender* is yet another brilliant gem in her crown, spinning a medieval love story that will steal you away—heart, soul, and sleep!"

"Dickerson breathes life into the age-old story of Rapunzel, blending it seamlessly with the other YA novels she has written in this time and place . . . The character development is solid, and she captures religious medieval life splendidly."

"Readers who love getting lost in a fairy-tale romance will cheer for Rapunzel's courage as she rises above her overwhelming past. The surprising way Dickerson weaves threads of this enchanting companion novel with those of her other Hagenheim stories is simply delightful."

"Dickerson spins a retelling of Robin Hood with emotionally compelling characters, offering hope that love may indeed conquer all as they unite in a shared desire to serve both the Lord and those in need."

"Melanie Dickerson does it again! Full of danger, intrigue, and romance, this beautifully crafted story [*The Huntress of Thornbeck Forest*] will transport you to another place and time."

COURT *of* SWANS

OTHER BOOKS BY MELANIE DICKERSON

THE DERICOTT TALES
Court of Swans
Castle of Refuge (Available June 2021!)

YOUNG ADULT FAIRY TALE ROMANCE SERIES
The Healer's Apprentice
The Merchant's Daughter
The Fairest Beauty
The Captive Maiden
The Princess Spy
The Golden Braid
The Silent Songbird
The Orphan's Wish
The Warrior Maiden
The Piper's Pursuit
The Peasant's Dream

A MEDIEVAL FAIRY TALE SERIES
The Huntress of Thornbeck Forest
The Beautiful Pretender
The Noble Servant

REGENCY SPIES OF LONDON SERIES
A Spy's Devotion
A Viscount's Proposal
A Dangerous Engagement

COURT _of_ SWANS

MELANIE DICKERSON

THOMAS NELSON
Since 1798

Court of Swans

Copyright © 2021 Melanie Dickerson

Published in Nashville, Tennessee, by Thomas Nelson. Thomas Nelson is a registered trademark of HarperCollins Christian Publishing, Inc.

Thomas Nelson titles may be purchased in bulk for educational, business, fundraising, or sales promotional use. For information, please email SpecialMarkets@ThomasNelson.com.

Scripture quotations marked NLT are taken from the Holy Bible, New Living Translation, copyright © 1996, 2004, 2015 by Tyndale House Foundation. Used by permission of Tyndale House Publishers, a Division of Tyndale House Ministries, Carol Stream, Illinois 60188. All rights reserved.

Publisher's Note: This novel is a work of fiction. Names, characters, places, and incidents are either products of the author's imagination or used fictitiously. All characters are fictional, and any similarity to people living or dead is purely coincidental.

Library of Congress Cataloging-in-Publication Data

Names: Dickerson, Melanie, 1970- author.
Title: Court of swans / Melanie Dickerson.
Description: Nashville, Tennessee : Thomas Nelson, [2021] | Series: [A Dericott tale ; 1] | Audience: Grades 10-12. | Summary: In medieval England, after her seven brothers are falsely accused of murder and treason, eighteen-year-old Delia flees their cruel stepmother and becomes a seamstress at Westminster Palace, hoping to gain their release, with Sir Geoffrey's assistance.
Identifiers: LCCN 2020037090 (print) | LCCN 2020037091 (ebook) | ISBN 9780785234012 (hardcover) | ISBN 9780785234029 (epub) | ISBN 9780785234036
Subjects: CYAC: Brothers and sisters--Fiction. | Nobility--Fiction. | Knights and knighthood--Fiction. | False imprisonment--Fiction. | Stepmothers--Fiction. | Christian life--Fiction. | Middle Ages--Fiction. | Great Britain--History--Medieval period, 1066-1485--Fiction.
Classification: LCC PZ7.D5575 Cou 2021 (print) | LCC PZ7.D5575 (ebook) | DDC [Fic]--dc23
LC record available at https://lccn.loc.gov/2020037090
LC ebook record available at https://lccn.loc.gov/2020037091

Printed in the United States of America

21 22 23 24 25 LSC 5 4 3 2 1

Born to Alfred Raynsford, Second Earl of Dericott, and Lady Millicent Fairchild

- Edwin—February 3, 1359
- Gerard—January 21, 1361
- Berenger—March 15, 1362
- Delia—April 4, 1363
- Merek—January 10, 1365
- Charles—April 29, 1367
- David—March 19, 1369
- Roland—February 4, 1371

ONE

DELIA'S STOMACH FELT SICK AS SHE WATCHED HER FATHER marry Parnella. The lady who would be the new Lady Dericott was much closer to Delia's age of fifteen than to her father's.

Someone tapped Delia's arm. She turned and shook her head at her brother Berenger. He smiled and winked.

One good thing was that her brothers had all been allowed to come home for the wedding. Her older brothers, Edwin, Gerard, and Berenger, stood around her like a bulwark—although a temporary one, as they'd soon be returning to their training—while her younger brothers, Merek, Charles, David, and little Roland, gathered nearby in a rare show of quiet solemnity.

When the wedding was over, they all walked through the village from the church back to Dericott Castle. Parnella held her new husband's arm with one hand and her skirt with the other to keep it above the dust of the road. Her head was so high Delia wondered if she could see anything besides the sky overhead.

Mother had died seven years earlier, and though Delia missed her, she had enjoyed the attention of the servants, and she was very close to her brothers. Or at least she had been until a year ago, when Roland was sent away to train as a knight at the age of six, like all her other brothers. Now Delia would have a step-mother in the house and no siblings with whom to commiserate.

By the time they reached the castle, her brothers were rest-less and had begun teasing each other. Her new stepmother had glanced back at them once, her eyes narrowed and her lips pressed together. Delia tried to get her brothers' attention and held her finger to her lips to remind them to behave, at least until they reached home.

In front of the castle, villagers were singing and waving rib-bons tied to sticks and carrying cakes as gifts to the newly wedded couple. Parnella barely glanced at the villagers as they offered wedding cakes. They were poor farmers or villeins belonging to Dericott land, and the cakes were gifts they baked themselves. Delia thanked each one, letting them give her the cakes, stacking one on top of the other. The servants took them as she entered Dericott Castle.

Delia and her brothers waited for Father and Parnella to begin the wedding feast in the Great Hall. Her brothers started a mock sword fight using sticks.

Parnella entered and stood near Delia but refused to meet her gaze. Father leaned toward Parnella and said something, then left.

As he strode away, Parnella's attention turned to Delia's

brothers. None of them seemed to have noticed she was even in the room. They were yelling and laughing and bragging about who was the better swordsman as they parried and thrusted with their sticks. Parnella's face twisted into a scowl.

Parnella said not a word, only stared straight ahead. But when Father came back, she pointed toward the brothers, who were still fighting, and cried out, "Look at how they are trying to intimidate me with their violence!"

Father's eyes went wide. "Stop that fighting this moment! Can you not see you are frightening Lady Dericott?"

"They knew they were upsetting me, yet they persisted." Parnella took hold of Father's arm, cowering behind him. "This is supposed to be a happy day for me. Please, won't you send them away?"

Father's mouth fell open. Delia and her brothers exchanged wondering glances.

"And the girl too. All she does is stare at me. I know she is thinking malicious thoughts toward me."

She could only be referring to Delia. Her father's expression was a mix of perplexity and irritation.

"They will be gone soon, back to the households where they're being trained as knights."

"I don't care! It is my wedding day. May I not have some joy and peace on my wedding day?"

"I am sure my brothers and I meant no harm," Delia said as Roland and David moved closer to her.

Parnella glared at Delia and made a contemptuous sound in her throat.

"Do not worry," Father said to his new wife. "They shall cease. Let us all go to the Great Hall for the feast."

In the Great Hall, Delia and her brothers began talking quietly among themselves. They were quite subdued after their new stepmother's outburst. Indeed, Delia felt sick to her stomach every time she thought about Parnella's words. How could they show the woman they meant her no harm?

But as the servants brought out more and more elaborate foods, and as their new stepmother paid them no attention, Delia's brothers began to talk in louder and livelier tones. Delia thought to warn them not to get too boisterous, but Gerard was in the middle of telling a story and she did not want to interrupt him.

"Then the horse stumbled and Sir Bollivet fell forward, right into the muddy stream."

Her brothers all burst out laughing, Charles laughing the loudest and slapping his knee in merriment.

"What are you boys talking about?" Father demanded in a loud voice.

"Telling stories about our training," Edwin said.

Father looked so angry, Delia spoke up. "They aren't doing anything wrong, Father. Only telling funny stories."

"They were laughing at me!" Parnella's face was cold, her eyes intense and dark.

Her father talked in hushed tones, leaning his head toward his new wife, but she interrupted him. "So you will let them ridicule and intimidate me?"

"Of course not. I—"

"Then send them to their rooms. How can you allow it? Insulted and ridiculed . . ."

"Go to your rooms, all of you." Father's face was flushed, and not from the wine. "I am ashamed of you for treating your new mother thusly."

Delia and her brothers stood up and slowly walked toward the doorway of the Great Hall.

"No one was laughing at you," Merek said, looking directly at Parnella, his voice clear and confident.

"Oh!" Parnella drew back as if he'd struck her. Father glared at Merek.

When they were all out in the corridor and heading for the stairs, Berenger said, "I cannot believe that woman could be so audacious."

"It makes me worry for you, Delia," Edwin said, his eyes soft but intent on her.

"No, don't worry." Delia tried to look confident and reassuring. "I will win her over. She will understand that we have no grudge against her and do not intend to harm her. I'll just have to be sensitive to her feeling like an outsider."

"Sensitive? Even if you kissed her feet you could not please that woman," Gerard said.

Merek snorted. "If she bothers you, Delia, I'll come back and stand up for you. I'll tell Father he can't let that woman treat you poorly."

"She certainly doesn't seem very sensible," Berenger added.

Her younger brothers looked confused and sad.

"Don't worry." Delia bent to hug Roland. "All will be well."

Gerard and Berenger went to the kitchen while the rest of them gathered in Edwin's room. Gerard and Berenger came back with roast pheasant and sweet fruit pasties. They all ate and talked and laughed—though quietly.

"I am worried about leaving you here with that woman," Edwin said.

"I am sure I will be well." But as soon as she said the words, she realized she was not truly sure at all.

Delia hugged all her brothers that night, surprised that none of them protested or groaned in reluctance at her show of affection.

"Write to us, or send a servant, if you need us," Gerard said.

"Yes, we will take care of you," Berenger said.

"Write often about how you are faring," Edwin added.

If only they could stay home longer. But perhaps with them gone it would be easier to convince Parnella that any evil intention toward her from Delia or her brothers was completely imagined. And then all would be harmonious between them.

ALMOST THREE YEARS LATER, SPRING 1381

Delia listened through the crack in her stepmother's bedchamber door.

"You must do something," Parnella was saying. "As it is now, our son will inherit nothing. Those selfish sons of your first wife will treat him badly when we are both dead and cold in the ground. His life will not be worth living. They'll throw him out to starve."

Delia strained to hear how her father responded, but his voice was too low.

"You must! You are the Earl of Dericott. You can change it."

"I cannot change the laws of England. The king . . ."

Delia could not hear the rest.

Surely Father wouldn't listen to that woman's evil counsel. But he had been different since he'd married Parnella. He'd never been a particularly attentive or affectionate father. But now he was constantly accusing her and her brothers of some ill will or wrongdoing toward Parnella, ideas Delia was certain her stepmother was putting into his head.

And there was the matter of her half brother, Cedric. It was strange how Parnella guarded her baby. He was four months old, yet Delia rarely saw him. Parnella kept Cedric in her own bedchamber, with a nursemaid to watch over him. Delia longed to help take care of the child, to hold him and see him smile up at her. But when Edwin had come to visit and picked up the baby, Parnella actually screamed, as if Edwin were trying to harm the baby or steal him away. She snatched Cedric out of his hands and cried, "You are not to touch him! Not ever!"

Delia did her best to keep out of their way.

When she heard movement on the other side of the door, Delia hurried away before she was caught eavesdropping.

Lately Delia had been having a strange feeling of foreboding. She had tried very hard in the beginning to reassure her stepmother that no one wished her ill. In spite of that, her stepmother had treated her with contempt and criticism, to the point that Delia gave up trying to win her over.

These past few weeks her icy stares seemed bolder, and she often ceased speaking when Delia came near.

The priest would probably tell her to pray against any evil that might try to come against her family. He might tell her to love her stepmother more, for love covers a multitude of sins. And Delia had tried to do both those things, but she could not rid herself of this uneasy feeling.

SIX MONTHS LATER, LATE AUTUMN 1381

Delia hadn't been able to get the sight of her father's lifeless body out of her mind. He'd been dead for two weeks now.

She often thought of the conversation she'd overheard between her father and stepmother and the premonition of danger it had given her. When Wat Tyler's Rebellion began not long after, she'd assumed that was the reason for her unease. But after her father's fatal fall from his horse . . . the uneasy feeling was a constant current crashing over her.

At least her brothers had all been allowed to return home to mourn their father's death. She had seen them only occasionally, mostly on holy feast days, though she wrote to them often while they were away. Edwin and Gerard had already been knighted and were serving as guards at one of the king's castles. But Edwin would not return to his knighthood duties, now that he was the new Earl of Dericott.

Delia ran down the stairs of Dericott Castle, out the door, and the short way to the stable. In the distance she saw Gerard helping twelve-year-old David practice his archery skills. She smiled at how patient Gerard looked, showing David how to draw the string.

Although Delia was still mourning her father, she was glad to have all her brothers home, and Edwin would be staying.

Delia had been meaning to speak to Edwin about their stepmother's fears that her brothers would not care for their half brother. Of course, Edwin would never mistreat the child, but she wanted to tell him to be sensitive of his stepmother's feelings. Even though her stepmother had not had a good relationship with Delia or her brothers, she hoped Parnella would eventually learn she could trust them. Perhaps now that she had a child of her own she would be kinder to them.

Delia pushed away thoughts of her stepmother and drew in a long, contented breath at how good it felt to be with her brothers again.

The tiny, high-pitched sound of puppies drew her attention, and she headed toward the stable and Flora, her father's favorite hunting dog.

Flora lay in the corner of the stable in the bed Delia had made for her of old rags and blankets. Her puppies were piled around her, most of them asleep. Delia knelt on the ground beside ten-year-old Roland, who was holding a puppy in his lap. One of them was mewling and crawling around, so she picked it up.

Delia cuddled the pup to her cheek. Its fur was soft and warm in the cool autumn air.

Roland cradled the light-colored puppy against his chest. "This one is the sweetest. Look. She doesn't mind me holding her on her back, like a baby."

"She can sense that you are gentle and wouldn't hurt her." Delia smiled. Mother had died soon after Roland was born, but Delia liked to think she was carrying on for her, at least with her younger brothers. Thankfully, none of her brothers were brutish or unkind. They'd all inherited Mother's qualities of gentleness and strength, and the younger ones allowed her to tell them to put on an extra cloak or hood to keep warm and even welcomed her hugs and kisses—as long as their older brothers weren't watching.

Edwin came walking up behind them. Hearing people address him as Lord Dericott was strange, but Delia was so happy he would be home with her now. Edwin would enjoy his new duties and would have more time for reading and learning languages, which he enjoyed almost as much as he enjoyed training to be a knight. He was quiet but could be outspoken against injustice. She'd known him to get furious about unfair treatment he'd witnessed and take action to make it right.

He was only twenty-two years old, but he would be a good landlord for those living in Dericott.

"A healthy litter. All seven still thriving?"

"Yes, and this one is mine, Edwin. I want to name her." Roland held up the puppy he had been cradling.

"Very well." Edwin picked up the black one with a gray ear who had just started crawling over his littermates and waking them up. Edwin held the puppy in one hand and stroked its fur with the other. "This is a lively one."

"There are only seven puppies," Roland said, snuggling his puppy to his chest again. "But there are eight of us, if you include Delia."

"Thanks for including me." Delia winked to soften her sarcastic tone.

"Not enough to go around," Roland continued. "So someone will not get to name a puppy."

"I don't mind giving up my rights to one," Edwin said.

Roland glanced up at Edwin. "Perhaps Merek won't mind not getting to name a puppy. I don't recall seeing him out here petting them."

Roland, ever the peacemaker. Merek was, Roland seemed to think, the least likely of his brothers to care about naming a puppy. And he was probably right. Merek was two years younger than Delia's eighteen years, but he was commanding and hated when she tried to take care of him.

Edwin suddenly lifted his head, staring in the direction of the road that ran past Dericott Castle. He put the puppy beside its mother and stood to his full height.

"What is it?" Roland asked.

"Sounds like horses."

A lot of horses. She and Roland also replaced their puppies, laying them against their mother's belly, and hurried up the slight incline toward their home.

Delia glanced down at her dress. Normally, if they were expecting guests, Delia would be wearing one of her fine gowns, the brightly colored silk ones with embroidery of gold and silver thread. But today, as on most days, she wore one of her older, plainer frocks for taking walks in the woods and playing with puppies and running footraces with her brothers. Her hair was uncovered, not even plaited or bound, hanging in loose curls down her back and over her shoulders, "like a common serving wench," her stepmother had once said with a scornful twisting of her lips.

Perhaps Delia should not show herself until she knew what manner of guests she would encounter. The horses' hooves were headed toward them, having turned onto the lane that led to the castle instead of continuing down the road.

Edwin reached the front of the three-story castle made of light-colored stone, its towers stretching up another level or two. He stood in front of the door as Delia watched from around the corner.

A whole company of soldiers galloped into view, emerging from the tree-crowded lane. Edwin narrowed his eyes and stood with his shoulders tensed.

Where were the guards? There was always at least one or two of them around. And why did Edwin have that angry look on his face? Did he know why these men were here?

The soldiers were all wearing gambesons and their swords were strapped to their bodies in ready reach. They galloped right up to Edwin before slowing their horses to a halt.

Several of the soldiers got down off their mounts while the one in the lead, who appeared to be the captain, spoke down to Edwin from atop his horse.

"We are here by the authority of Richard of Bordeaux, King of England, to arrest the seven sons of the recently deceased Earl of Dericott for treason against the king and against England."

Before he finished speaking, the soldiers seized Edwin and began tying his wrists together in front of him.

Delia's heart pounded as she ran forward.

"Stop! He has done nothing wrong!"

"Go and find the others." The captain motioned outward with his hand.

Soldiers brushed past her and charged into the house.

Edwin would stop this. He was the Earl of Dericott now.

She turned to the dark-haired captain, who was dismounting from his horse. "What do you think you are doing? He has not committed treason!"

"I have orders to arrest the seven sons of the late Earl of Dericott. Who are you?"

"The youngest is but ten years old. You would imprison a ten-year-old boy for treason?"

The captain's expression faltered. He was quite young to be a captain, hardly any older than Delia. His eyes were bright blue, and were he not trying to take away her brothers, she might have said his features were handsome.

Not answering, he glanced around. She followed his gaze and saw several soldiers coming up from the stable with David, Gerard, and Roland. The soldiers pointed their swords at her brothers' backs.

Her breath left her in a gasp. She turned to the odious man. "Stop them!" She took a few steps closer to the captain. "Surely you would not allow your men to arrest children!"

"My orders are to arrest all seven sons." He didn't look at her, but his jaw appeared hard and a muscle twitched as he watched the king's guards force her brothers up the grassy slope toward them.

"But they haven't done anything wrong!"

He suddenly turned to her. "You must step away. Better yet, go in the house. This is not a matter for women."

"How dare you?" He must mistake her for a serving wench, as her stepmother had said.

He ignored her and strode toward her brothers. He went to little Roland and began tying his hands together.

She wanted to hurl herself at him, snatch her brother's hands out of his grasp, and fight him off. But he could easily clout her in the head and knock her to the ground. After all, if he believed she was only a servant, he likely would not hesitate to retaliate . . . But if he knew she was the boys' sister, might he not seize her too?

Just then two soldiers came out of the house with Berenger, her nineteen-year-old brother who had been sick in bed with a head cold. That left only Merek and Charles, who were out hunting pheasants.

Some of the soldiers had gone inside the castle, so Delia ran to see what they were doing. She could feel the soldiers watching her, but she ignored them. As she entered she saw guards questioning the servants.

"Where are the rest of the master's sons?" they demanded. The servants' eyes were wide and frightened.

"Stop scaring them!" Delia glared at the guards.

"And who are you?"

"Tell us where the other two sons are," another guard said as they moved menacingly toward her.

"Why are you seizing innocent boys?"

The first guard suddenly reached out and grabbed her arm,

squeezing it so hard she cried out. Every one of his fingers dug into the soft flesh of her upper arm.

"Unhand that woman!"

The guard turned and let go of her arm. The young captain stood behind him in the corridor.

"Sir Geoffrey, we were only trying to get information from her," the soldier replied.

The captain looked at her. "Are you hurt?"

"You should be worried about yourself. Arresting innocent boys, lords and sons of an earl. Who are you? What is your name?"

"I am Sir Geoffrey Grenefeld, captain of this guard."

Sir Geoffrey. How she hated him.

"And who are you?"

"I am their sister, Lady Delia Raynsford."

His eyelids flickered. He was obviously surprised.

"Forgive us, Lady Delia, for our lack of decorum, but we have our orders and will do our duty."

Delia gave him what she hoped was a look of utter disgust. She pushed past him, brushing him aside with her shoulder, then lifted her skirts and took the stairs two at a time to the second floor of the castle.

She ran to her stepmother's bedchamber and pounded on the door.

She waited, hearing nothing on the other side. "Parnella!" Finally, the door opened and her stepmother and the nursemaid stood staring at her.

"Why are the king's men taking Edwin and the others—even Roland? What is happening?"

Her stepmother wore a cold, emotionless look on her face.

Delia's stomach sank. Her stepmother knew what was happening and she wasn't going to do anything to stop it.

"Keep calm, Delia. You always were too flighty and foolish for your own good."

Parnella was a tiny woman, and Delia easily could have knocked her to the ground, and she suddenly wanted to, very much.

"Why are they arresting my brothers?" She asked the question through gritted teeth. Tears stung her eyes, but she would not show any weakness, not in front of her stepmother.

"Your brothers," her stepmother said in her haughtiest voice, "are guilty of murder and treason. Someone has reported it to the king and he has sent his men to seize them and take them to prison, as he should, as any monarch should do in this situation."

For a moment Delia couldn't speak. Murder and treason? Preposterous. And why did Parnella seem to have prior knowledge of these accusations?

"You know my brothers are not guilty of murder or treason."

"You will not speak thusly to me. Go to your bedchamber and stay there until the soldiers have left."

Delia turned away from the heartless woman and hurried down the corridor without speaking another word. But instead of going to her bedchamber, she went down the stairs and out the front door, only to see four soldiers escorting Charles and Merek out of the woods, their hands tied in front of them. Though they were younger than she was—Merek was sixteen and Charles fourteen—she normally thought of them as men. They were training to be knights, after all. But with the menacing soldiers surrounding them, they looked much younger.

Her heart trembled inside her as the soldiers forced each of her brothers onto one of the extra horses they had brought with them.

This was wrong. Unjust. How could they take her brothers away?

Roland's face crumpled as he sat atop his horse, his bound hands clutching the pommel of the saddle. Tears ran down his face. Her heart constricted, her arms aching to hold him and protect him from these awful men.

The rest of her brothers were stoic, but she knew they were afraid. Taken away to prison! They would be held in a dungeon somewhere, probably in the Tower of London. But these false charges would never be upheld. They would be cleared of any wrongdoing, of such ridiculous accusations.

Edwin's eyes met hers intently, then he said to Sir Geoffrey, "May I speak to my sister before we go?"

Sir Geoffrey did not break eye contact with Edwin as he answered, "No. I have a charge to take you straightway to the king."

"Heartless man!" she yelled at him.

His expression faltered as before. But then he looked away from her and raised his arm. "Let us be off."

And the soldiers obeyed this Sir Geoffrey, turning their horses' heads toward the road, drawing her brothers' horses by their lead ropes.

She wanted to call out to her brothers not to worry, that all would be well. These charges would never be proven or upheld.

They were innocent and would be released very soon. But her brothers would not have heard her over the pounding of the horses' hooves.

God, may you punish that Sir Geoffrey for his cruelty.

Delia's rage turned to pain as her heart seemed to break, a sharp pain building inside her chest. Who could possibly have accused her brothers? Who would have done such a thing?

But she knew.

Parnella.

TWO

DELIA WAS PILING CLOTHING ONTO A SQUARE OF CLOTH when her bedchamber door opened. She spun around.

"Mistress Wattlesbrook." Delia pressed a hand over her heart. "You startled me."

The older woman had been a servant in her household since before Delia was born.

"What will you do, my child?" She stretched a hand toward Delia's bed where she was gathering things to take with her.

"I am going to London." Truly, Delia did not know what she would do. She only knew she couldn't stay there and she had to do something to set her brothers free.

"I see." Mistress Wattlesbrook stared at her with a serious look on her wrinkled face. "You will need assistance. You have few relatives, as your father was an only child, but you have an aunt, your mother's sister."

"Is she a nun?"

"She is the abbess at Rosings Abbey. Did you not know?"

"I had forgotten." Delia rarely heard her aunt mentioned.

"She would help you, I believe. Go to her. As an abbess, she is not without power. Perhaps she would even speak to the king."

Delia's heart lifted. This was hope indeed.

"It is also possible that she won't help at all." Mistress Wattlesbrook stared at the floor. "She seemed a hard woman and appeared not to be close to your mother the one time I remember her visiting."

At this discouraging information Delia's heart fell further than it had lifted.

"But you must try." The older woman came closer and pressed a roll of bandages and a few small pouches of dried herbs into Delia's hand. "This one is for restful sleep, and here is some feverfew. Remember that it is good for fever, headaches, cough, and putridity of the lungs."

"You knew I was leaving?" Delia was reminded of other times when the old woman seemed to know things without anyone telling her.

Mistress Wattlesbrook did not answer but took hold of Delia's wrist and looked into her eyes. When she spoke, her voice was a raspy whisper.

"You must take care. There was a man, a stranger, here on the morning your father died. I saw him with my own eyes coming out of the stable. I have been suspicious that your father's death was not an accident."

"What? You think Father was murdered?" The blood seemed to drain from Delia's head.

She sank down on a cushioned stool nearby. The idea that someone might have killed her father was a shock that swept through her in relentless waves. He had never paid her much attention and was rather impatient with her when she tried to talk to him. But the thought of him being murdered . . . Her stomach felt sick, her head light.

Her thoughts went to the day Edwin returned after their father died. Edwin had been the first of her brothers to get home. Delia had seen him coming and met him in the stable. After embracing her longer than she ever remembered him doing before, he asked the head groom how their father had fallen off his horse. The groom replied that the girth on his saddle broke, but when Edwin asked to see the saddle, the groom could not find it or the girth. Edwin and Delia searched as well, but they were indeed gone.

"There is evil afoot," Mistress Wattlesbrook continued. "It is not uncommon among great folk like your father for someone to try to take his power and wealth. And your stepmother is the daughter of a baron. Where there is wealth and power, there is someone willing to do anything to take it." The old woman winked and laid her finger against the side of her nose, one of her habits.

What could Delia do? She knew nothing of fighting against people who wished her ill.

But that was not entirely true, was it? She had been fighting her stepmother's attempts to undermine her father's regard for her and her brothers for the past three years.

"You must be brave," Mistress Wattlesbrook said quietly, as

if she'd read her thoughts. "No matter what happens, be strong and courageous."

Mistress Wattlesbrook turned away and shuffled to the door.

"What do you mean, 'no matter what happens'?"

Mistress Wattlesbrook looked thoughtfully past Delia, not meeting her gaze. "We ask for thorns to be taken from us, trials to end, but sometimes God does not take them away. He walks us through them. So stay hopeful and believe for the best, but don't lose faith if the worst happens."

Delia's stomach twisted.

"Fare well, my dear. I shall be praying for you."

"Thank you," Delia said, her voice barely above a whisper.

But she would be strong. She had to be. Her brothers needed her, and she could not let them down.

Delia waited until she was sure the household was asleep and the darkness was deep enough to conceal her departure. Then she tossed her bundle of clothing out the window.

She could climb any tree her brothers climbed, and often did. She had climbed up the trellis outside her bedchamber window when she used to play with her brothers. But tonight would mark the first time she had ever climbed down the trellis.

The three-quarter moon glowing above was her only light as Delia stuck her head out of her window. She felt a little dizzy looking down, trying to see the ground below. Vines darkened the trellis, but she had no choice. She had to get away, and without her stepmother knowing. She would do whatever she had to do to save her brothers. After all, the penalty for both murder and treason was death, and the king's court had tried and executed many men since Wat Tyler's Rebellion had been quashed.

But her brothers had had nothing to do with the violent uprising, and they had been all together only once, for a few days over the summer, though it had been around the time of the uprising.

Delia still did not know much about what had caused so many men, and even a few women, to rebel against the government and murder some of the wealthiest men and the most influential leaders in England. It was said that the villeins had risen against their masters. But many of the instances of violence—burning down homes and beating and murdering foreign merchants—had been perpetrated by artisans and free men, people who didn't toil under an unfree serfdom. But certainly it had something to do with men feeling they'd been treated unjustly. In one county they'd killed the king's tax collector.

Delia remembered Edwin saying, *"If poor men are taxed beyond their means to pay, then the tax is unfair."*

Had Edwin repeated those sentiments in front of someone he shouldn't have? Or was their stepmother behind these accusations of murder and treason? If her stepmother was responsible for these charges against her brothers, then Delia would need to get away tonight.

She grabbed her tapestry bag with the rest of her things. Could she hold on to it while climbing down? Better to drop it and hope it didn't make too much noise when it hit the ground.

She sat on the windowsill and tied the back of her skirt to the front of her belt, making breeches of a sort. Then she threw one leg out to dangle from the window ledge.

She looked down at the blackness below her, her stomach dropping as she tried in vain to see the ground. No doubt the first step would be the hardest. She took a deep breath and let it out. "My brothers need me," she whispered.

She drew her other leg up and over the ledge, then held on with both hands as she supported her weight on her stomach and used her feet to search the trellis for a toehold. When she finally found one for each foot, she scooted her stomach off the ledge and searched for another toehold, one at a time, farther down until she was holding on to the window ledge with one hand and the trellis with the other.

As she climbed down, she kept her body pressed against the trellis to prevent it from unlatching from the stone wall. She imagined herself falling and hitting the ground on her back. The image made her lose her breath, and she squeezed her eyes closed.

"Think of something else," she whispered to herself.

Her favorite place at the stream near her home came to mind. She imagined the joyful sound of the water dribbling over the rocks in the streambed, the wildflowers growing amid the green grass and ferns, sunlight dappling everything with its cheerful light.

But then she wondered when—or if—she'd ever see it again.

She wouldn't think about that either. All that mattered was that she would go to her brothers and find a way to secure their release. She would not let them suffer if she could help it.

She wondered again what role her stepmother had played in her brothers' arrest. Her stepmother did have the most to gain from her brothers' death—for they would be executed if found guilty of treason. With Father gone, Edwin had inherited the title, the land, and the castle. Parnella and Cedric were dependent upon him now. But if all of Delia's brothers were dead, Cedric would become the heir.

If Father's death was not an accident, did Parnella have something to do with that too? She had nothing to gain from Father dying, did she?

Her foot slipped. She held on tight and searched frantically for another place to step. She moved one hand down, then the other, before finally finding another toehold. Slowly, her heart pounding, she glanced down. She wasn't even halfway.

It was much harder going down than up, and harder still in the dark. But she kept going. The leaves weren't as thick on the trellis closer to the ground, and she was able to go faster. Finally, she jumped the last two feet.

She took a deep breath and grabbed up her bags, tucking them under her arm, then walked, bent over and looking from side to side, toward the stables.

There was a guard in charge of the stables at night, but she hoped he was asleep. After all, no one had ever attempted to steal a horse from their stable. There was rarely any talk of robbers in their forests or on their roads. Even during the recent rebellion, everything was relatively calm and uneventful in this corner of England.

Delia crept closer to the stable, still not seeing any of the guards. She kept in the shadow of the nearby trees. Would she be so fortunate as to get away with no one seeing her?

Her foot crunched on a dry twig, making a loud cracking sound. She stopped and listened, holding her breath. A frog croaked down by the stream, but there were no other sounds, so she continued on.

She rounded the corner of the wooden stable. Only a few more feet to the door.

A tall figure emerged from the doorway.

Delia froze.

The man strode a few feet and stopped.

Her heart beat so hard she could barely breathe. Would he see her if she turned around and ran? Should she speak and try to pretend she was going on a nighttime walk?

The guard was Hugh, one of the less chivalrous of Father's guards. He'd once grabbed one of their kitchen servants right in front of Delia and tried to kiss her. When the servant screamed, he laughed and roughly pushed her away.

Delia's stomach twisted at the sight of him. But he wouldn't dare lay a hand on her. Or would he? She no longer had her father or brothers around to defend her.

Hugh held a mug in his hand, no doubt filled with ale or something stronger. He took a long drink, then sauntered forward, continuing to move away from the stable.

Delia watched until she could no longer see him, then walked quickly but carefully through the door.

The stable was dark, so Delia used her hands to feel her way to her favorite horse's stall. The mare snuffled, no doubt surprised to find someone opening her stall door in the middle of the night. But thankfully, neither she nor the other horses created much noise, and Delia was able to light a lamp and saddle her horse with ease, as if God's own hand were guiding her.

When she finished she blew out the lamp and hung it in its place. Then, just as she took hold of her horse's reins, footsteps sounded on the hard ground at the doorway of the stable.

". . . some ale hidden in the stable."

Another voice answered, but the words were unintelligible.

Delia shrank against her horse's side, her heart thudding so loudly she could barely hear. Would they see that the mare had been moved? Perhaps Delia could hide behind her in the stall.

She thought she heard them tapping a barrel, then the sound of liquid pouring out. How furious her father would have been had he known the guards were drinking his best ale in the night.

Laughter came from outside the stable. The men seemed to have moved away from the door, but how close were they? Could she leave now without being seen?

She waited and listened. Nothing. She moved toward the open doorway, pulling her mare by her bridle. Figures were moving in the distance. Her heart seemed to stop beating as she led her horse out of the stable, listening hard, then she moved a little faster and made her way through the trees on a shortcut to the road. She crossed a little stream, stepping on stones to avoid getting her feet wet. Her left foot slipped, forcing her to step quickly with her right, ending with both feet submerged to her ankles in the cold trickling water. She held back a groan.

Delia finally made it to the road and mounted. Leaning

forward, she managed to take off both shoes and tied them to the saddle horn before setting out down the road at a gentle pace that wouldn't make much noise. Finally. She was on her way to the abbey to see her aunt and that much closer to rescuing her brothers.

Delia's teeth were chattering long before she reached Rosings Abbey. The sun was just coming up when the group of gray stone buildings came into view.

Her shoes still weren't completely dry, but she put them on anyway, the cold leather molding to her equally cold feet. She must have been riding about six hours, and her arms were shaky and she felt sick to her stomach.

Two guards were standing near the entrance, and they acknowledged her with a nod. A servant, a young man who dragged one foot behind him, met her and offered to take her horse.

Delia had been riding astride, and when she dismounted, she suddenly found herself sitting in the dirt. She scrambled to her feet, clutching the saddle to steady herself.

"Are you well?" The young man stood holding her horse's bridle, his gaze on her face.

"I've been riding a long way, but I am well."

"Go in that door there and they will attend you."

"Thank you." Delia concentrated on walking in a straight line.

While riding for all those hours in the dark, she had fixed her mind on staying awake and keeping her horse on the shadowy road. Now she suddenly felt just how exhausted she was from being awake all night, weary and afraid she would not be equal to the huge task of saving her brothers.

A convent sister, who was wearing an enormous wimple, met her just inside the door and waved at her to follow. Delia walked behind the tiny woman as they wound their way down a narrow corridor.

"Please, pardon me, but I would like to speak with the abbess."

The woman stopped abruptly and turned toward Delia. Her eyes were drawn together, her lips pursed. But she did not speak.

"I am Delia, daughter of the Earl of Dericott. Abbess Beatrice is my mother's sister."

The woman stared at her another moment, glancing down at her dress, before nodding and continuing down the corridor.

Delia was exhausted, but the sooner she spoke to her aunt, the sooner her mind would be at ease. After all, Aunt Beatrice was family.

Perhaps she would not help her. Perhaps Delia was taking a risk even coming here to ask her aunt for help. No doubt, as an abbess, she was politically connected, and she would need to protect her relationship with powerful entities such as the king.

The nun led her through another corridor, turning two more times before coming to a door and knocking.

"You may enter," was the muffled reply from the other side of the door.

The nun turned to Delia and held up her hand, palm out, pushing down twice.

"You wish me to stay here?"

The nun nodded, then turned and went inside, closing the door behind her.

Delia waited, her heart starting to jump around inside her. In spite of her lack of sleep, she was wide awake.

The door opened and the small woman emerged. She looked at Delia, then held the door open for her, nodding and waving her inside.

Delia walked in slowly, blinking, as the room was lined with glass windows that let in the early morning light.

A woman stood at the far end of the room, her hands folded in front of her. She wore a flatter, less obtrusive wimple that wrapped around her neck up to her chin and hid every trace of her hair. Her face was wrinkled and her expression showed no sign of a smile.

When Delia reached the abbess, she bent her head and knelt on the floor before her.

"Stand up, child. Delia, is it?"

Delia arose quickly, which made her vision spin. A reminder that it had been many hours since she'd eaten.

"Yes, Your Grace."

"Did someone send you here?"

"No."

"Well, speak. Tell me why you are here."

Tears stung Delia's eyes. This cool, unfriendly greeting was not what she'd hoped for. Delia was her niece, but she may as well have been a poor farmer's daughter from the countryside begging for the abbess's favor. But the memory of her brothers being hauled away, of Roland as he sat atop the horse, his hands tied, tears streaming down his cheeks, quickly drove her own tears away.

"My brothers have been wrongly accused of murder and treason against the king and were taken to prison by the king's guard."

The hard defiance of her own voice surprised her.

Her aunt, however, betrayed no emotion whatsoever. She only stared, as if studying Delia's face.

"The last time I saw you," she said finally, "you were a baby. You cried for my entire visit."

Did she expect Delia to apologize?

"And who do you believe has accused your brothers of treason?"

"I don't know. But I think my stepmother may be involved."

Again, the abbess did not immediately speak or show any change of expression as she stared at Delia.

"My stepmother wishes her own child to be Father's heir, and with Father's death two weeks ago . . ." Her heart ached at the mention of his death, still so fresh and painful.

"Stop."

Delia leaned back, an involuntary reaction to the unexpected command.

"You should know that it is unwise to voice your opinions, at least until you are aware of the opinions of the person to whom you are speaking."

Delia's mind was racing. Would her aunt tell her stepmother that she had come here asking for her help? Would she end up in prison with her brothers?

"You are here to gain my help for your brothers, are you not?"

Delia's heart pounded in her throat, her thoughts whirling around in her head. But she focused on her brothers.

"Yes."

"Well, you are safe with me. I have no great love for your stepmother—I know a little of her—and your father was foolish to marry her."

Delia's heart ceased pounding so hard. Perhaps her aunt would help her.

"If she has done what you suspect and falsely accused her own stepsons for the sake of her child, then . . . it is a very cruel thing indeed for you and your brothers."

The tears pricked her eyes again.

"Now tell me what your plan is and how you wish for me to help."

"I am going to London to plead with the king for my brothers' release. I will tell him the truth about these accusations and beg him to let them go."

"And why do you believe this scheme will work?" Before Delia had time to answer, Beatrice narrowed her eyes and asked, "How old are you?"

"I am eighteen years old. But—"

"Do you know the king? Have you ever spoken with him?"

"No. I haven't."

"Then your plan is not a good one. You, a slip of a girl and so young. You know nothing of court politics. The king is but a boy himself, younger even than you. One day he is compromising with the leaders of this revolt and promising to enact the reforms they want; the next he is having them executed."

Delia was silent. Finally, as her aunt said nothing further, she said, "You are correct that I don't know anything about court politics. But I am going to London to see what I can do to save my brothers, even if it gets me beheaded." She set her jaw and met her aunt's stare.

The abbess frowned. "At least you have some gumption. But take my advice and don't try to speak to the king. If there is no real evidence against them, the king—or his councilors—are likely to postpone the trial, and therefore you will have several months to bide your time and hope that your brothers can find a way to prove they are innocent." She paused, still staring hard at Delia. "Tell me. Do you have any skill in embroidery and sewing?"

"I can sew and embroider. My tapestries—"

"Good. I know the mistress of linens for the king's palace in London, and I will give you a letter recommending you for a position sewing for the king's household."

What good would that do?

"You may not have heard, but the negotiations have been completed and our young king will soon take a wife—Anne of Bohemia. Go and work. Bide your time. When the king marries, she will need some ladies, noblewomen, as companions and to wait on her. I will send you letters, one for the king and one for his queen, recommending you to be the queen's lady-in-waiting. The queen will converse with the king in French, no doubt, as it is as familiar to the king as English, and more so for the queen. Do you know French?"

"Yes."

"Latin?"

"Not as well, but yes."

"Can you humble yourself? Can you take direction and do another's bidding?"

"Of course." She might be an earl's daughter, but her mother had been dead for ten years and her father had neither pampered nor humored her in any way.

"You will need to make sure your brothers have food—the meals the prison provides are meager. But otherwise you will need to keep quiet and not tell anyone you have seven brothers in prison for treason against the king. Can you do that?"

"I can."

"You cannot be one of those women who talks incessantly, who thinks she must confide her secrets in someone. You are not one of those women, are you?"

She shook her head, but honestly, she didn't know. She had never had any secrets except the feelings she had about her step-mother, and she had confided those only to her brothers and a few of the servants whom she trusted the most. She trusted her brothers with her very life. They were all good and honest. They listened to the priest, prayed to God, and loved each other. She could not have asked for better brothers. And now that she was their only hope of escape and freedom, she did not imagine she would jeopardize their chances by wagging her tongue to some stranger in London.

"See that you live meekly and quietly and do not attract attention to yourself, except as a dutiful and loyal subject of the king. And I will give you those letters."

"Thank you."

"And now, you need to sleep and rest. If your stepmother sends people here seeking you, I will not tell them you are here, nor that you ever were." She took a step closer to Delia, lifting a wrinkled hand to grip her shoulder. "I admire your determination to save your brothers. I can see the courage in your eyes. You needn't fear I would betray you. I know something of this new wife of your father's, of her character, and neither your stepmother nor her child could ever gain my loyalty."

"Thank you, Aunt Beatrice." She took a chance addressing her in the less formal manner.

Her aunt raised one brow. "I will be in prayer for you. Only God can help you with this king. He is a boy of fourteen, and it is most unfortunate that his father died so soon and left his young son with such shrewd and ruthless councilors, for a boy-king is only as powerful as his most loyal supporters. But if you are clever and courageous, perhaps God will give you favor."

Delia nodded, suddenly feeling the weight of her undertaking. But better to be exiled or beheaded with her brothers than to be dependent on the stepmother who had condemned them.

Three

Sir Geoffrey, the knighted son of the Duke of Strachleigh, watched closely as his prisoners—a few of them children—were forced to mount their horses and set out after a night of rest. Geoffrey saw the youngest one struggling, so he went forward and gave him a boost. The boy did not thank him, only stared straight down at the horse's neck.

"How old are you?" Geoffrey asked in a low voice.

The boy turned and looked at him. "Ten."

Geoffrey felt the now-familiar stab through his stomach. Could there be any honor in arresting children? Surely no ten-year-old boy could be guilty of treason, of collusion in Wat Tyler's Rebellion, or murder. The very idea was ridiculous.

But what could he do? He had to follow the orders he'd been given. But it angered him. Something was very wrong here.

He moved away from the boy and his brothers and strode toward his own horse.

Geoffrey wished he could at least tell the boy he was sorry, but he could not risk it. His men, nearly all of whom were years older than he was and much more experienced, though lower in rank and familial status, would think him weak and soft and would not respect him if he expressed any remorse or compassion for their prisoners' predicament.

"You'll surely get commended for bravery on this assignment, eh, Geoffrey?" This latest gibe came from a baron's son, Sir Tristan.

The fellow beside him guffawed.

Geoffrey refused to react. "Mount up," he said in his gruffest voice. "Let us be off."

The look on the sister's face still haunted him. How she must loathe him for his dishonorable act of taking her young brothers to prison, no doubt for some equally dishonorable reason. Someone must want the brothers out of the way so that they could seize their land or other inheritance. Geoffrey was well-acquainted with such treachery. Or perhaps it was for vengeance and someone was using the king and his power, his fear of losing control again, to get what they wanted. Wat Tyler's Rebellion had shaken the king and all the wealthiest men in England and put fear into their hearts. Before the events of the past several months, they never would have thought the poor serfs and farmers had the power to murder some of the most powerful men in England, or actually breach the Tower of London.

Geoffrey had been away visiting his sister, Amicia, when the uprising happened, so he had not witnessed the chaos, but he had been told the guards at the Tower had seen the mob coming and had not resisted them, but had let them through the gate.

Geoffrey had experienced the greed of the wealthy nobles and what they would do to gain what they wanted by immoral and cruel means, and he clenched his teeth at the thought of being used for ignoble purposes. For surely someone was imprisoning these brothers for their own gain.

He spurred his horse forward, taking the lead as he and his men rode toward London.

Delia had made her way to London, escorted by two of the abbey guards, who left her at the palace entrance. And now she stood before the mistress of linens and watched her read the letter her aunt had written.

She wore the dress her aunt had given her, the type of clothing she'd be expected to wear as an embroiderer in the king's household—a fine linen dress that was somewhere between a house servant's dress and a lady's. The abbess promised to soon send the fine clothing Delia would need to be a lady-in-waiting to the queen.

Mistress Maud looked up from the letter. "So Abbess Beatrice is your aunt. And you do not mind working—sewing and embroidering? The wages are not very generous."

"I do not mind. That is, I am eager to do the work. I enjoy embroidery." Sewing, not so much.

"You will be expected to work as hard as anyone else."

"Of course. I understand." Delia had heard that the women who worked as seamstresses and embroiderers were oftentimes illegitimate daughters of the royal advisors, courtiers, and other noblemen, or even paramours of said royal advisors. But her favorite housemaid, Julianna, who had once been Delia's nurse, had taught her never to judge others. "'Judge not that you be not judged.' You have lived a privileged life, but others have not. They have struggles and face things you will never have to face," she had said. What would Julianna say if she could see her now? Surely neither of them ever could have imagined Delia being forced to work as a seamstress, desperate to save her brothers from execution.

No, Delia could never judge anyone. She'd already imagined what could happen to her if she could not secure her brothers' release and she was left alone. Either she'd have to live in the convent, dependent on the graciousness of her aunt, or she'd have to make her own way. And most women she had heard about who were alone ended up in very bad situations.

Mistress Maud stood. "Come. I'll show you to your room. You can put away your things and begin working."

Delia followed her new mistress. Where were her brothers at this moment? Certainly they were not being treated as well as she was. Did they have anything to eat? Thankfully, her aunt had given her a little money to buy food. Were they warm? Did they even have a proper bed? She knew little of prisons, but she was aware they were hard, harsh, cold places with little food and no comfort. Just thinking of her brothers in a place like that made her stomach sink as an ache gripped her chest.

They made their way up so many flights of steps that Delia was breathing hard by the time they reached the top. The mistress opened a door and led her to the end of a narrow corridor, where a small window let in light, to the last door on the left. She stood aside to let Delia enter.

"You will sleep here with the other embroidery maidens. Choose an unmade bed and I will have someone bring you linens before the day is done."

Delia put her bags beside a bed in the corner. The mattress looked lumpy and thin, but she was reminded of where her brothers were sleeping. She could hardly complain about a lumpy mattress.

But perhaps her brothers' living conditions were not as bad as she imagined. They were the sons of an earl, after all. Perhaps they were being treated well.

She hurried back out the door where Mistress Maud was waiting for her, then followed her back down to her new life of embroidering for the king.

Geoffrey's men were released from their watch at daybreak. Geoffrey had been training the new guards, so he'd stayed with them through the last hours of their watch. Tired, his eyes burning, he made his way down from the tower and headed toward the kitchen to break his fast.

Had the seven sons of the Earl of Dericott even been fed the day before?

He clenched his teeth every time he remembered the moment

he reached Dericott Castle and saw whom he'd been sent to capture and bring back to London.

He told himself he wasn't to blame, that he was only doing as he was ordered. But he couldn't stop thinking about them. He wanted to ask questions to discover who had accused them and why, as it seemed unlikely that they were guilty of the charges. But no matter how careful and discreet he was, his queries could make their way to the wrong person, and depending on how powerful the brothers' accuser was, he could lose his head, literally, as many men had recently. Still, the prisoners held at the Tower were rich and powerful noblemen. Perhaps someone was taking care of their needs.

Although they were not his problem or responsibility, Geoffrey was angry that he had been used to arrest them, that he had anything to do with their imprisonment.

He saw himself in the brothers' faces. They'd seemed as innocent and ignorant as he had once been to the politics of England and its rulers. And he had also been the son of a man with a title. But one sudden accusation, one well-connected bitter rival, and Geoffrey had found himself without his birthright, stripped of the title he'd been destined for, and doing the bidding of cruel men who held more power than they deserved or could handle.

He was still chewing the last bite of his breakfast when he took a hemp bag and began filling it with pasties and bread rolls and small cheeses—whatever he could grab. If the guards were allowed to eat the king's food, why not his falsely accused prisoners? He twisted the bag closed and strode out of the kitchen toward the prison tower inside the Tower of London.

As he neared the door, someone else headed in the same direction, to the same door—a young woman. A moment later, her eyes met his.

She flinched, almost as if someone had struck her. She even stopped midstride and glared at him. That was when he realized who she was—the sister of the seven brothers.

What was she doing here? She must have traveled practically on their heels to get here so quickly.

Before he could think of what to say—or whether he should say anything at all—she set her jaw in a hard line and spun around, heading back the way she had come.

Were his eyes and mind playing a trick on him? Perhaps he was only imagining, because of his guilt, that the young woman was the Dericott sister. But her reaction to seeing him made him think she was indeed who he thought she was. She'd had the same expression on her face when he rode away with her brothers.

No wonder she had looked at him with hatred. He hated himself in that moment.

His heart again heavy, he headed for the stairs that would take him to the prison cells.

With the help of one of the guards, he found the brothers. They were housed together, all seven in one large cell—large for a prison cell, but it could hardly be considered large enough to be a suitable dwelling for seven people. He had the guard unlock the door.

He stood in the doorway and saw that the brothers were lying on the floor, sleeping—not surprising since the sun was barely up, and even if it was overhead, the window high above their heads let in only a bit of light. Then he noticed one of them—the oldest one—sitting with his back against the wall, his eyes open, watching Geoffrey.

The oldest brother stood to his feet, his gaze unwavering. "What do you want?"

"Just to know how you are faring."

"We are your prisoners. We are faring as prisoners normally fare."

"Edwin, is it?"

The other brothers were beginning to get up from their places on the bare floor, and he saw they had no blankets or even adequate clothing for the chill and damp. The night had been rather cold.

"Edwin Raynsford, the Earl of Dericott, and therein lies the reason I'm here. So why don't you tell your king to execute me and let my brothers go. There's no need to behead us all." He said the words sardonically.

"I am only a lowly guard captain. I have no power except to do as I'm told. I came to ask if you needed anything."

Edwin simply stared at him out of narrowed eyes. No doubt he didn't trust Geoffrey.

"And to bring you this food." Geoffrey held out the bag to him.

Edwin accepted it from his hand and said nothing.

As the rest of the brothers recognized Geoffrey, their expressions changed. The younger ones' eyes widened, while the older ones' narrowed.

He could hardly blame them for hating him. They saw him as the enemy, but they should have no fear of him. Their real enemy was someone powerful, and that did not characterize Geoffrey.

But what if the accusations were true and these brothers—the older ones at least—were guilty of treason? Geoffrey's position was not so secure that he couldn't be accused by association. But that was a cowardly, ignoble thought.

Geoffrey had nothing else for them, so he turned to go, then hesitated, his chest heavy at the thought of them sleeping on the cold floor with no blankets.

"We are innocent of these accusations," Edwin said quietly. "We never thought about treason for a moment in our lives, and we don't even know who it is we supposedly murdered." His expression seemed sincere.

Geoffrey nodded. But what could he do? He found himself saying, "If I can help, I will." He almost mentioned he thought he'd seen their sister on the grounds below but thought better of raising their hopes.

Geoffrey left the prison cell, let the guard lock the door back, and went down the stairs to the ground below. As he walked back to the barracks, he looked for the girl he'd seen. She'd been dressed like one of the sewing maids. Was she still lingering about?

She surely was not their sister. Their sister was a wealthy earl's daughter who lived in the country, away from society and city life. She'd probably rarely, if ever, been in London, and she certainly could not be a sewing maid in the household of the king. The job was beneath her.

And then he saw her, standing in the doorway to the White

Tower. When she noticed him looking at her, she stepped back and closed the door, hiding herself from his view.

Should he run and find her? Chase her down and demand to know who she was? No, he didn't want to attract that kind of attention to himself.

He rubbed his face, feeling weary to his bones. Time to go to bed. He did not have the energy to chase some maiden who, if he were able to catch her, would think he had lost his mind.

Delia watched Sir Geoffrey, that hateful man who took her brothers to prison, walk off toward the soldiers' barracks. When she was sure he was out of sight, she hurried toward Wardroab Tower, where she hoped she would find her brothers. She had very little time before she had to begin her day's work with the other sewing and embroidery maids, and because of the soldier, she'd just lost several minutes that she could have spent with her brothers.

She pushed open the heavy door. A guard just inside stepped toward her.

"No one is allowed in here. Prisoners and guards only."

"I wish to visit . . . someone who is imprisoned here." Abbess Beatrice's words came back to her, warning her not to tell anyone who she was or what she was doing there. But how else would she get to see her brothers? She had been sure they would allow family members to visit the prisoners, as they were the ones expected to bring food and other provisions.

"Your name?" The guard's expression never changed. "And the prisoner's name?"

"Delia." Would she have to tell him she was the daughter of the deceased Earl of Dericott? That the prisoners were her brothers? "I wish to see Edwin Raynsford, the Earl of Dericott."

The guard stared unblinking at her face. "Very well. Come with me." He led her down a damp corridor. The stone floor was covered in slime in places, and the ceiling dripped on her bare head.

Then they went up several levels of narrow stairs. She saw no one in the dark halls or on the stairs, which were dimly lit with candles on wall sconces, other than the guard who was leading her. She did hear a moan, loud and long, almost inhuman, but it faded away as they continued up a narrow staircase.

At the top, the guard turned down a corridor and stopped at the nearest door. He unlocked it, let her inside, then closed and locked it behind her. Her heart thumped hard at the sound of the metal lock clicking and shutting her in.

"Delia!"

Roland's voice pierced her heart as her littlest brother leapt at her and threw his arms around her. Delia hugged him close as her other brothers drew near.

"Delia." Edwin's voice vibrated with concern.

Roland let her go and wiped his cheeks with his hand.

"Are you all right?"

Roland just nodded and kept wiping his face. Her other brothers hugged and kissed her as well.

"What are you doing here?" Edwin said. "Were you arrested?"

"No, no. I came—" She stopped, glancing around. "Can anyone else hear me?"

"I don't know."

She kept her voice low. "I went to Aunt Beatrice and she provided a letter so I could get work at the Palace of Westminster as a seamstress. I wanted to see what I could do to help you escape."

"Delia." There was a gentle tone of rebuke in Edwin's voice. "You shouldn't have come. Escape?" He shook his head. "You need to go home."

Tears pricked her eyes, but she blinked them back.

"I'm sorry," Edwin said, his expression as sober as she had ever seen it, "but I don't want anything to happen to you, and it isn't possible to escape from the Tower."

"Better to be here than at home, do you not think?"

A muscle twitched in Edwin's cheek as he clenched his teeth. "I cannot argue." Then he hugged her, kissing the top of her head.

"You're safer here with us," Merek said with a glare. "We all know Parnella did this."

"I'm glad to see you," Berenger added.

"Are you safe, then? Where are you staying?" Edwin asked.

"I am staying at the palace. What could be safer than that?" She smiled up at her oldest brother.

He shook his head. "The king's court is not a safe place at all. You can't let anyone know who you are. You don't know who might be our enemy."

"But I'm not part of his court. I'm a lowly seamstress. And no one knows. The mistress of linens is the only person who knows

I'm the niece of Beatrice, the Abbess of Rosings Abbey, and she doesn't know I'm the sister of an earl."

She looked around the empty room.

"This is not where you sleep, surely?"

"It is." Gerard glared at the wall behind her head. "Falsely accused and wrongly imprisoned. Whoever accused us should have just killed us outright." Her twenty-year-old brother could be very passionate in his opinions sometimes.

"Do they feed you at all? Are you hungry?" Delia would find them food if she had to steal it from the kitchen.

"Just pottage and dry bread," Charles said.

Little David held up a bread roll. "Sir Geoffrey brought us food."

"Sir Geoffrey?" She recoiled as she said the name.

"Yes, he brought us some bread and cheese." Berenger looked surprised even as he said the words.

"He just left." Charles's voice was muffled, as he spoke with a mouthful of food.

"So guard captains bring you your food?" What a strange duty for a captain.

"I don't know why he brought us food," Edwin said.

"Probably felt guilty," Berenger said.

"He should die of guilt," Merek growled, crossing his arms over his chest.

"He is not our enemy," Edwin said. "He was only following orders, what any soldier must do. And bringing us food was a kindness. He had nothing to gain from it."

They all fell silent.

"Do you have no blankets?" A lump formed in Delia's throat. It was quite cold, and they'd not been allowed to take any extra clothing with them when they were seized. That certainly was not kind of this captain, Sir Geoffrey.

"No blankets and no pillows." Roland put his arms around himself.

"I'll bring you something just as soon as I'm able." Surely there was a storage room somewhere in the palace where such things were kept. She couldn't let her brothers shiver in their sleep on this cold stone floor.

"Don't do anything that will bring suspicion upon you," Edwin said.

Roland said, "We can sleep like the puppies to keep warm— on top of each other." He smiled as if it were a clever jest.

"We will manage." Gerard patted Delia's shoulder reassuringly. "Just keep yourself safe."

"Yes. We can stand anything as long as we know you're well, Delia." Berenger was closest in age to her, but he acted like a man twice as old.

When had her brothers become so mature and strong? A week ago they'd all seemed like boys. Now they were men who ignored their own terrible circumstances and seemed only to think of protecting her. But she'd prove that she could take care of herself and help them too. She had to.

Somehow she would. Whatever it took.

FOUR

GEOFFREY STRODE ACROSS THE GRASSY OUTER WARD, then through the gate to the Inmost Ward toward his duty station at the back of St. Thomas's Tower. The king was expected to wait at the great archway below the king's royal lodgings, which opened directly onto the Thames, to meet the ship that was now sailing down the river. The king's new bride-to-be, Anne of Bohemia, would be arriving sometime in the next month or two—no one knew exactly when. But today's arrival was to be other important people—a Medici and other dignitaries and advisors from Italy—coming to speak with the king and his councilors.

Geoffrey scanned the area for anything suspicious. Guards were stationed at their usual places, but today's events were important enough that a few extra guards had been sent from the Palace of Westminster to make sure nothing went wrong.

It was still early morning, and there seemed to be no one

about. He moved toward the door to check inside. He was greeted by another guard, someone from his own company, who assured him all was well and quiet, so he went to get something from the kitchen to break his fast.

He pulled on the door to the kitchen, and it flew open. A woman cried out as she fell into his chest. He grabbed her arms to make sure she didn't end up on the floor. She gasped, and her eyes widened as she stared up at him. Her headscarf fell off and let loose a cascade of dark hair down her back and onto her shoulders. It was the same woman he'd seen the day before, the one who looked like the young Dericott lady. She was very pretty.

She pulled back, her hands balled into fists, but he pretended not to realize she was trying to get away from him and tightened his grip on her arms.

"Who are you?" he asked.

She rasped, "Unhand me."

"Are you the daughter of the Earl of Dericott?"

Her mouth tightened and she pursed her lips. "I am a sewing maid for the king."

It was her. He was almost certain. Why wouldn't she admit who she was? Was she a spy? Perhaps he was mistaken about her brothers being innocent of treason. Perhaps they were a family of traitors.

"What are you doing here, now, if you are a sewing maid? Why aren't you working?"

"Am I not allowed to leave the sewing room? Are you my jailer?"

"Such vitriol." He raised his brows at her. "I am no one's jailer. I am only a soldier in the king's service."

It was unchivalrous of him to keep holding on to her, and taunting her was beneath him. The sparks in her eyes made him want to get closer. But since he was not—and never wished to be—a harasser of women, he let her go.

She stepped away.

"If you are not the earl's daughter, then why do you look at me with such hatred?"

"I-I did not," she said. "You are daft."

She had spirit to call him daft. He was a foot taller than she was, and he was not only a captain, but a knight and the son of a duke. Spirit or . . . the privilege of an earl's daughter.

"You are the sister of the seven sons of the Earl of Dericott. Don't deny it."

"What business is it of yours? You—"

She stopped herself from whatever she was about to say. But he had his answer.

"Were you able to visit them? I could direct you to where they are being held."

Her expression softened a bit. "I saw them."

He studied her face, her eyes, as she was finally looking at him with less spite. She was quite a beauty, with her thick, wavy hair, dark-blue eyes, full lips, and small nose. How old was she? He would guess about eighteen.

She was dressed like a palace servant or seamstress, but . . . "You are not a sewing maid."

"I am." She glared, her eyes sparking again.

"Why are you here instead of at the palace?"

"I came to . . ." Her cheeks turned pink and she refused to finish her sentence.

Then he noticed her apron was tied up like a bundle with something inside. She had come to take food from the kitchen for her brothers.

What was she doing here sewing for the king? It made no sense. A seamstress was a lowly job, one taken by unmarried women who had no wealth or position, and it was certainly not a job for an earl's daughter. But perhaps she was planning something nefarious.

"Thank you for bringing food to my brothers," she said quietly.

So they had told her of his altruism. "It was my pleasure."

She seemed to love her brothers. An admirable quality. But were they enemies of the king? If he could gain her trust, he might discover what she was about.

"I would like to help if I can."

"Why do you want to help them?"

"Several of them are very young, and I have no wish to see anyone treated ill."

She stared him in the eye, then huffed out a breath. She glanced away, then back again. "If you truly wish to help them . . . they need blankets."

"I will see what I can do."

"And I'd like to knit them sweaters, but I have no yarn." Her voice was soft and lilting now.

"I will find you yarn. But how can I get it to you?"

"I am not sure. You would not be allowed in the servants' quarters."

"I could have it delivered to your room." He was suddenly aware that he was leaning toward her. He stopped and moved away.

She bit her lip.

"Will you allow it?"

She stopped chewing her lip and met his eye. "Very well."

Why did his heart leap at her acquiescence? She could be a spy, and he should remember that.

He nodded. She took another step away from him.

"Be careful," he said. "This is not a safe place for you to be."

She gave him a questioning look, tilting her head to one side. But she nodded and continued on her way, hurrying across the green. Her small frame seemed even smaller among the various tall buildings of the Tower of London, but her shoulders were squared, her head tilted in a determined way that said, "I can do anything I set my mind to."

Perhaps even break her brothers out of the Tower of London?

Such a thought was ludicrous. No one was able to escape the Tower, and it seemed even less likely that a slip of a girl could do it. But something told him that this particular girl could surprise him.

Early the next morning Delia went to find the market to look for blankets for her brothers.

Her heart had beat hard against her chest when she'd encountered Sir Geoffrey the morning before, but she'd kept her head high, not wanting that hateful captain to know how much he frightened her—especially now that he knew who she was.

Her stomach sank as she remembered Aunt Beatrice's words about not telling anyone who she was or why she was there. But Sir Geoffrey had recognized her. It wasn't her fault.

The sky was quickly lightening with the coming dawn as she hurried past all the buildings that belonged to the Tower of London. She'd always heard about the White Tower—the enormous castle keep next to the River Thames in London—but she hadn't realized there were so many other buildings inside the curtain walls that comprised the Tower. There were gates and inner gates, an Outer Ward, an Inner Ward, and an Inmost Ward, a Tower Green, gardens, and many buildings of various purposes. There was even a menagerie of exotic animals, gifts to the king from faraway lands—lions and tigers and other animals never seen in England before—and the walls were riddled with towers. Some of the towers were used as lodgings for the kings and queens, and she wondered if King Richard himself was staying in one of them now, since there seemed to be more guards here than when she had come before.

Several people, including the king's mother and the Archbishop of Canterbury, had taken shelter inside the Tower of London during Wat Tyler's Rebellion. And yet, as intimidating as it appeared, the fortress had been breached. The men-at-arms guarding the Tower of London had not prevented the rebels from entering through the gates and harassing the king's mother. The mob had even seized and executed the archbishop, beheading him on Tower Hill. No doubt this was one reason the number of guards patrolling the "impregnable" Tower had been greatly increased.

If only she could speak to the king, could plead with him to release her brothers. But for the moment she needed to get to the market, where the mistress said she might purchase some blankets.

She had found the storage area where the blankets were kept, but she couldn't take any without being seen. The thought of stealing them had filled her with too much guilt anyway, so she decided to buy some instead with the small amount of money her aunt had given her. Besides, she had to save all her gumption for whatever laws she would have to break to save her brothers.

And what terrible bad fortune, running into that odious captain of the guard who arrested her brothers. Perhaps Sir Geoffrey was not a bad person. He had visited her brothers and brought them food. They told her how kind he had seemed. But she'd seen the suspicion on his face yesterday morning, felt the way his hands had gripped her arms and refused to let go.

She would not trust him. Any man who could arrest young boys could not be worthy or good. And he was more than a soldier; he was a knight and the captain of the guard. And therefore he must be a nobleman's son, with privilege and power. But a man's birth did not make him noble of heart.

His face—his blue eyes, brown hair, and perfect features—was burned into her memory. It might be easier to hate him if he weren't so handsome. But a handsome evil man, surely, was more dangerous than an ugly one. They could get away with more. And her reaction to him proved her point.

She found herself on an unfamiliar street and her stomach churned. Would she be able to find the market?

After wandering around for a while, she found a kindly looking woman and asked her where the market was. With her direction, she found it, then a vendor selling blankets. They only had five, but thanks to Aunt Beatrice, she had enough money to buy them all. That would have to do for now.

Staring at the few coins left hollowed her out. What would she do when she ran out of money? She had taken food for them from the Tower kitchen, but she could be caught and ordered to stop. Her brothers would starve to death if they ate only the meager allowance of bread and pottage, and they weren't even given that every day. She needed to be able to buy food for them.

Her mind cast about for someone she might turn to. Aunt Beatrice had helped her get this far, but she was far away and did not seem eager to do more than what she had offered. Delia was alone, a strange feeling after growing up with so many brothers, having often looked to Edwin, Gerard, and Berenger to take care of her anytime she needed help. How strange that she was now their only hope.

And if she failed? If the king beheaded them, as he had done to many others, as traitors to the Crown?

Her heart sank and a heavy weight settled onto her shoulders. How could she go on without her brothers? She'd be all alone. And she could never go back to her stepmother. She'd rather die than ask her for food or shelter or anything else, even if she turned out not to be the one who had falsely accused her brothers.

Delia forced those thoughts away as the vendor laid the blankets across her extended arms. Why had she not thought how awkward it would be to carry so many blankets?

"Do ye have them all? Not going to drop them, are ye?"

"No, I have them." Delia smiled, struggling to look much more confident than she felt. Then she headed back toward the Tower.

The blanket on top began slipping toward the dirty street. She let go with her left hand and grabbed at the blanket. With one arm under and one arm over, she grasped tightly to her overlarge bundle. She must look strange, walking down the street, her head barely showing above the great stack of blankets.

Winter was coming, and these woolen blankets would help keep her brothers warm on the cold nights. Her brothers needed her, and her heart lifted at being able to help the people she loved—the only people in the world who loved her.

After getting a few hours' rest, Geoffrey stood guard at St. Thomas's Tower, watching as the Dericott girl struggled to carry a stack of blankets in her arms. She was walking through the gate, but none of the guards were offering to help her. Unchivalrous cads. They were not sworn to noble behavior as knights, but they were men, weren't they?

Geoffrey left his post and stalked across the Tower Green toward her, his hand on his sword so it wouldn't slap his back with every step.

"Lady Delia."

She looked startled when she peeked over the gray wool in her arms and saw him. But she did not reply.

"May I help you with your burden?" He reached for them before she could answer, taking all but one. Only when he started walking with them toward her brothers' prison cell did she say quietly, "Thank you."

"It is an honor to assist you, Lady Delia." He remembered then her need for yarn and that he had promised the day before to get some for her.

"You should not address me as . . . as that." Her expression was a mixture of fear and assertiveness. "No one else knows who I am. I'm here only as a servant."

Was that not suspicious? How better to spy on the king and his councilors than to hide one's identity and work as a lowly sewing maid in the king's palace?

"I am only here to try to help my brothers," she went on, as if to explain why she wished to keep her identity a secret. "My aunt told me I shouldn't tell anyone anything about myself, that it was safer not to." She sounded out of breath and her voice trembled just a bit.

Should Geoffrey keep a closer watch on this earl's daughter whose seven brothers were accused of treason? Perhaps he should gain her trust, and he could better do that by pretending not to be suspicious of her.

"How shall I address you, then?" He pointed in the distance. "'Yon maiden!' 'Servant!' 'You there!'"

She raised her gaze to the heavens, but a smile graced her lips as she glanced back at him.

His heart did a strange little lurch. Who was manipulating whom?

They continued on their way to the tower where the brothers were being kept. They climbed the steps in silence, and when they reached the cell, he opened the door himself, as the guard had given him the keys.

He pushed open the door with his foot, still holding the blankets in his arms, and let Lady Delia go in first.

"I brought you some blankets." The smile on her face was much brighter than the one she'd given him. The brothers' faces brightened too when they saw her.

"Thank you," Edwin said. If they were guilty of scheming against the king, then Edwin, as the oldest, was their leader.

The smallest one took the blanket from his sister and hugged it to his chest.

"I was only able to get five."

"It is enough," Edwin said.

"We can share," the little one said.

As Edwin took the blankets from Geoffrey's arms, he looked him in the eye and said, "Thank you, Sir Geoffrey."

Lady Delia began talking with her brothers in low voices, asking how they were faring. Geoffrey decided he should excuse himself, so he caught Edwin's eye, nodded, and let himself out the door. He waited on the other side with the key so that he could lock it when she departed.

There was no way in or out except the staircase below, with another guard at the only door leading out of the tower, so he felt safe going down to talk to the guard. But when he was halfway, he heard the door upstairs open and close. He started back up, but when he reached the top, she was standing in the dark corridor, her shoulder propped against the door, her face in her hands.

The sound of soft weeping arrested his attention. He took another step and saw that her shoulders were shaking.

He'd been sent away from home at the age of seven. He'd never spent much time with women, and a weeping woman was not part of his experience.

The weeping stopped and time stretched out as she continued standing with her shoulder against the door and her face in her hands. He could move forward, rattling the keys, and pretend he hadn't noticed she was crying. But if she looked up and caught him standing there staring at her . . . that would be awkward.

She looked so forlorn. He ached to hold her, to pull her to his chest and let her cry in his arms.

Strange, unexpected, unwise thought.

He advanced toward her and rattled the keys. She startled, pushing herself off the door and wiping her face with her hands, keeping her back to Geoffrey.

It took him only a moment to lock the door.

"Are you well, Lady Delia? Is there something I can do for you?"

She sniffed and shook her head, her face downturned. "I am well, thank you. I only—" She shook her head again and started toward the stairs. He walked beside her, letting her precede him, but as she reached the top step her foot slipped and she stumbled, teetering dangerously.

He grabbed her.

"Oh!" She was staring up into his face as he held her. "I—my foot—I must have stumbled." But then her eyes broke contact with his and she looked down again.

He gently pulled her upright, letting her get her feet underneath her. She did not flinch away from him, and he pulled her close, until her forehead rested on his chest.

"Forgive me." She kept her hands between her chest and his.

"There is nothing to forgive." He tried to make his voice as gentle as possible. He didn't want to frighten her or make her feel threatened in any way, and he most certainly did not want her to push out of his arms. His heart swelled at the way she felt—so soft and vulnerable. He just wanted to keep holding her.

If Lady Delia was manipulating him, purposely playing on his sympathies . . . He'd worry about that later.

"This is all so unjust," she said quietly. "I am so thankful to you for bringing them food and being friendly to them." She took a deep breath and blew it out. "My brothers are so brave, and I must be brave as well."

She took a step back, so he loosened his hold. She swayed. "Steady, now." Geoffrey took her arm, holding her elbow as she moved down the steps. She allowed him to keep his hand on her as they slowly descended.

She was so young and seemed so alone.

"If you ever need anything, come and find me. One of my men can fetch me."

She looked up into his eyes. The blue depths of hers were shimmering, and the tiny smile was back. "You are very kind."

Again, he felt that tug inside his chest. Had he already won her good favor? Or was she just manipulating him? As they reached the bottom of the steps and he handed the keys off to the guard, he found himself staring into her eyes in the overcast light of a cloudy morning.

"Good day, Sir Geoffrey."

"Fare well, Lady Delia." There was nothing to be done except to let her go. Either she was an innocent, caught up in the evil done to her and to her innocent brothers. Or she was a temptress and a traitor to the king, bent on the king's overthrow and demise. Only time would tell.

FIVE

DELIA SAT WORKING IN THE SMALL SEWING ROOM WITH fifteen other women of various ages, though most of them were young. Her mind wandered and roamed while her fingers flew through the task of sewing silk pillowcases for the king and his guests.

As she recalled her encounter with Sir Geoffrey earlier that morning, she felt the mortification wash over her in a fresh wave. How could she have let him see her upset and crying? She only hoped he hadn't been standing there watching her, that he had just walked up and didn't realize she'd been sobbing.

Seeing her brothers confined—these courageous, active brothers of hers—and how they were reduced to barely surviving off occasional provisions of bread and pottage . . . She couldn't bear it. She had hurried away so they wouldn't see her crying over the sheer injustice and cruelty of their situation.

It hurt even more that she could do so little to help them.

Would the queen arrive in time for Delia to beg for her help? If she did, how would Delia obtain evidence to show that they were innocent? She'd have to prove that someone else had committed the murder they were accused of, that her brothers were loyal to their king. She needed money and influence and power, but she had none of those things.

She was being paid so little to sew, and she had been scolded severely for arriving late to the sewing room earlier that morning. Tears stung her eyes at being accused of sloth.

But the reprimand had been worth it. How good it had been to see her brothers again and to embrace them, to know they were not despairing and were still unharmed. She had heard the stories of other prisoners who had been tortured in unthinkable ways in the dungeons of the Tower of London.

At least she'd been able to buy her brothers some woolen blankets. She still needed to get some yarn. Though Sir Geoffrey had promised her some, he might not come through. If he did not, she was not sure she had enough money to buy yarn, certainly not enough to knit sweaters for all seven of her brothers. Tears pricked her eyes at the thought of being able to help only some of her brothers. But somehow she would find a way.

Delia was standing in the doorway of her mother's sickroom. "Mama? Can I help? Mama?"

Her mother turned her head slowly on her pillow. Her eyes stared right through Delia, so bright and clear. Mama opened her mouth, as if to speak, but then the servant rushed into the room, knocking Delia to one side with her hip as she brushed past her.

Delia couldn't see around the servant's wide frame as she stood by Mama's bedside, so Delia moved to the other side of the bed. Mama turned and looked at Delia again, then lifted her hand as if reaching for her.

"Shoo!" the servant cried. "Your mother is sick. Can you not see that? Go away and play with your brothers. Go on, now."

Instead of obeying, Delia reached out for her mother's hand. "I'll help you, Mama."

"Come!" The servant picked her up from behind and carried her out just before Delia could reach her mother's hand.

"Mama!" she screamed.

Delia awoke, her heart pounding in her chest, to a dark room filled with the sound of deep and even breathing. Around her, the other sewing maids were sleeping in their small beds. She crossed her hands over her chest, trying to slow her own quick breaths.

It was only a dream. Truthfully, Delia had been too excited about her new baby brother, begging the servants to let her help bathe and change and care for him, to even realize how sick her mother was. The servants had indeed kept her from her mother in those days when she lay dying, but the events in the dream had never taken place. Her mother had never reached out to her, nor had a servant carried her out of the room. No, Delia's mother had died without Delia ever seeing her after the baby was born.

Tears chilled her temples as they flowed from the corners of her eyes. If only she'd known her mother was sick. Maybe she could have helped her in some way.

"I'm so sorry, Mother," Delia whispered under her breath.

Her mother had been gone these ten years now. Delia had been comforted by her brothers, her sweet, protective, loving brothers. But now those same brothers were in danger. What would happen if they were executed for treason? If she couldn't save them?

Her stomach felt hollow and her chest heavy. How could she bear the shame and anguish if she failed her brothers?

She turned onto her side, wiping the tears that had pooled at her hairline by her temples. She prayed silently, letting her lips move as Hannah had done when she'd prayed in the temple asking God for a child. Delia begged God over and over not to let her brothers be executed, to free them from the Tower, to give them justice. *God, You are a God of justice. Where is Your justice in this?* Why was God allowing their enemies to triumph over them?

But she felt no relief, no less fearful after her anxious prayers. Did God even care that her brothers were in trouble?

Cast all your anxiety on Him because He cares for you.

Was that not in the Bible?

Delia squeezed her eyes shut and tried to remember more passages from Scripture. She'd been made to read the Holy Writ often enough by her tutors, both in Latin and in the English Scriptures that had been translated by some monks in a nearby monastery. But her heart was so heavy, she just wanted to be assured that God would free her brothers.

God cared for her, but what did that mean? Did it mean He would give her what she wanted and needed, which was for her brothers to be freed? It couldn't mean that, since she had needed her mother, but God had allowed her to die. So what did it mean?

She wanted to believe that good things would happen to good people, that the wrongs in their lives would be made right, that their enemies would never triumph over them, that they would never be treated cruelly. But since it couldn't mean that—bad things happened to good people, both in the Holy Writ and in the lives of people around her—it must mean that even if someone were to be cruelly treated and even murdered, God would still care. He would be with them till the end, just as He was with the martyr Stephen who was stoned to death. He had looked up and seen a vision of Jesus and heaven even as he suffered and died.

God, please don't let my brothers die. But if they do, give me the strength to bear it.

She prayed this silent prayer until she fell asleep.

Delia finished the embroidery on the hem, neckline, and sleeves of the dress for the king's cousin and ward, a girl around his own age by the name of Evangeline. The dress was a gift for her birthday. At least, that was the whispered rumor among the other seamstresses. Delia was honored to have been chosen to embroider something for a member of the king's family. Would the young ward be pleased with the embroidery? Would she like her new dress?

Delia looked up as she exhaled a deep breath. Her shoulders ached, unaccustomed to hunching over and sewing all day every day, but she was satisfied she had done her best on the embroidery and it had turned out very symmetrical and beautiful.

Madame Celine, who was in charge of supervising their work, made her way over to her. "I hope you did not soil the fabric." She took the dress from Delia's hands and stared hard at it, as if expecting to find a stain or dirt of some sort.

"Does the embroidery look well enough for the king's ward?"

Madame Celine turned her sharp look on Delia. "Don't be impertinent. And don't flatter yourself." The rather short, round woman turned on her heel and left the room with the dress draped carefully over her arms.

What should Delia do now?

She glanced around. The other women were working on various sewing tasks, and she was supposed to take whatever was left on the table, but the table was empty.

She pulled from her bag the sweater she had been knitting for Roland and some of the yarn that Sir Geoffrey had sent to her.

At least, she assumed the yarn had been sent by Sir Geoffrey. No one else knew she was looking for yarn. It had arrived as they were all getting ready for the day's work the previous morning, and the other women had gasped and exclaimed over the abundance of the fine wool yarn.

"Where did you get so much yarn?" one young seamstress about Delia's age had asked.

"A friend sent it. It's for my brothers—that is, I'm knitting them sweaters." She hadn't told anyone her brothers were imprisoned in the Tower of London.

The other sewing maids just stared at her. Finally, one said,

"The last thing I want to do when my day's work is done is knit sweaters."

"It is the truth, is it not?" another woman said. "My hands are aching by the end of the day, and my shoulders too."

"All I want to do is soak my hands in warm rose water and close my eyes," said another.

And then the conversation was diverted from Delia's yarn as they all turned away from her and talked among themselves. Delia breathed a little sigh of relief that they hadn't asked her any more questions about her brothers or the yarn.

Now that she seemed to have no more embroidery work to do at the moment, she took out her knitting needles and started on Roland's sweater. She hoped it would keep him warm this winter. A cold wind had swept in the last two days, making Delia shiver under her thin blanket on the little bed that made her back hurt unless she lay on her side.

Delia tried to keep her knitting needles quiet. They clicked together in the quiet room, but since no one seemed to be noticing that she was working on her own project instead of the king's, and since Madame Celine had not returned to give her a new assignment, she simply knitted and let her mind wander.

Why was Sir Geoffrey being so kind to her? Did he have ulterior motives? Regardless, she was grateful for the yarn. She could at least thank God for it, even if Sir Geoffrey had impure motives. What would he say when she saw him again? Would he demand payment of some type? She did not think he was that kind of man, but her servants had taught her not to be naïve or too trusting of men.

"A man never does anything without expecting something in return," Matilda had warned her.

"Men are ever scheming," Sophie, the scullery maid, said.

"They want one thing, and one thing only, if you're a woman." Cook nodded ominously at Delia, then pointed her ladle at her, as if to emphasize the point.

"But Lady Delia is a lady," Cora said, wiping her hands on her apron. "No man would dare lay a hand on her."

"Not so," Matilda said with a sober pursing of her lips. "I used to work for the Earl of Shrewsbury and his daughter—" Matilda looked right and left, then leaned forward, lowering her voice. "She was violated by that vicious Rupert, who just became the Viscount Dashwood. He thought he could do anything he wanted just because he was the son of the king's closest advisor. No woman is safe, especially if she has no father or brothers to protect her."

Delia's stomach sank as she remembered their words now.

She would have to be careful not to need rescuing. And if anyone tried to attack her, she would get away and run. She was not too ladylike, having grown up climbing trees and exploring the woods, hunting and fishing with her brothers. If need be, she could throw a few punches as well, though she could hardly imagine the man who could not punch her much harder than she could hit him.

She suddenly looked up from her knitting to find Madame Celine glaring down at her.

"What are you doing?" Her voice was cold and raspy, her eyes tiny and black.

"There was no more work to do, so I was knitting."

"Knitting? Did I say you could knit? Does the king wear clothing knit from common yarn? He is not paying you to knit for some man you wish to entice."

Delia's cheeks burned and her breaths started to come hard and fast. How dare this woman accuse her of something so crude? It was on her tongue to retort that the sweater was for her ten-year-old brother, but she bit back the words, not wishing to dignify this woman's undignified accusation.

"You will stay one hour after everyone else has finished for the day. Do you understand? One hour. You will sew what I tell you and only what I tell you." Madame Celine dumped a load of heavy fabric in Delia's lap. "Now get to work and hem these curtains."

Delia caught a glimpse of one of the other sewing maids bending low over her work, her eyes wide but focused on what she was doing, her needle moving up and down very quickly. The maiden beside Delia was also bending low, keeping her eyes on her work, but she was grinning, and she let out a snort. She then coughed and cleared her throat.

Delia felt her jaw clenching as she quickly put her knitting back in her bag and took up her sewing needle. She began hemming the heavy curtains that would hang on the beds in the king's palace.

Would all the other sewing maids hate her and snicker at her now? Her cheeks still burned. But why should she care what any of them thought of her? She was not ashamed of what she was doing. What could be more important than helping her brothers?

When she was done with her work, she would go back to her bed and knit until she fell asleep.

And Delia would soon be able to work out the plan she had discussed with her aunt. King Richard's new bride would arrive, and Delia could present herself to Her Grace as a lady-in-waiting. Then she could speak to the new queen about convincing the king to set Delia's brothers free. And when her brothers were free, they would find a lovely place where no one could hurt them, where her stepmother would never find them, and they could live happily, taking care of each other.

She would leave this place and never see any of these people again.

Six

Delia had one afternoon off per week, besides Sunday when she was required to attend church, and today was the day. She quickly left the workroom, gathered some knitting supplies, and hurried to the market to buy food for her brothers.

After buying bread, dried fruit, cheese, and even some cold meat, she headed to the Tower.

She caught herself searching the Tower Green for Sir Geoffrey. How foolish. She did not wish to see the man, did she? Besides, if she did see him, she'd have to thank him for the yarn, but without making him think she was grateful enough to do some kind of favor for him. He was still a stranger to her. She knew nothing of his family, and the only thing she truly knew about him, besides the fact that he could sometimes seem kind and thoughtful, was that he had taken her brothers away to be imprisoned.

She approached the tower where her brothers were being held. A man-at-arms who looked to be around thirty years old stopped her at the door.

"What is your business here?" His cheeks and eyelids were puffy, as if slightly bloated, and his eyes were red-rimmed, but otherwise he might be considered handsome.

"I wish to visit the Earl of Dericott and his six brothers."

His gaze swept her from head to toe and back up. "Are you a relative of theirs?"

She froze. What should she say? Sir Geoffrey was the only guard who knew she was their sister. Still, anyone who saw her visiting would probably assume she was a relative, or sent by relatives, so she said, "I am."

"Are you their sister?" He quickly added, "You need have no fear of me. Come. I shall take you to them."

She frowned at his presumption, but he seemed kind enough. "How did you guess that they were my brothers?"

"You do resemble them."

As they made their way up the stone staircase, he looked over his shoulder at her. "I am Sir Elliot of Allendale. And what is your name?"

A slight chill went down her spine. This stranger did not need to know her name. But he already knew who she was. "Lady Delia," she said, purposely adding her title to put a small bit of distance and formality between them.

"It is a shame your brothers are locked away. Seven of them, is that right?"

Delia did not answer.

"Are all of your brothers in prison? Or do you have more?"

She almost said, "Yes, all," but then she remembered Cedric, the baby whose future Parnella was trying to secure by getting rid of Delia's brothers. Again, she felt a slight chill. "Why do you wish to know if all my brothers are in prison?"

"Forgive me, my lady, if I seem impertinent. I am a curious soul, and I only wished to know in case I might be able to help you. It seems such a shame for all your brothers to be in prison, awaiting the king's justice."

Justice? Delia had to bite the inside of her cheek to keep from retorting that justice could not be further from her brothers at this moment. A cruel fate was possible for them, even beheading, but that would be the opposite of justice.

After taking a deep breath, she said, "My brothers were falsely accused."

They had arrived at her brothers' cell. Sir Elliot stopped and stared down at her. "Lady Delia, if there is anything I can do to help you and your brothers, I pray you will ask me. I would be very pleased to help."

She gave him a half-hearted smile but said nothing. Why would he want to help her? He did not know her, and as a knight and man-at-arms in the service of the king, he could not help her in the event she had to take extreme measures and break them free by some trickery or violence.

Finally, moving very slowly, he took out the key and let her in. She had to brush against his arm to get past him through the door. He must not have realized he was standing so close.

Her brothers had such strange looks on their faces when she entered the room that her heart jumped into her throat.

"What is it? Is something wrong?"

She went first to Roland, who was wiping his eyes with his

sleeve, and wrapped her arms around him. Roland didn't answer, just hugged her, burying his face in her shoulder. Delia gazed over his head at Edwin.

He frowned. "We were just told that our trial is set for a week from today."

Delia's vision went a little blurry, her knees trembling.

"But don't worry," Edwin said. "We knew we would have to face the charges eventually."

"This will give us a chance to speak on our own behalf," Gerard added.

But this was too soon.

Delia's heart seemed to stop beating. She would not have a chance to talk to the queen—who had not even arrived yet in England. And that had been her entire plan, to convince the queen to help them, to ask her to ask the king to save her brothers from these treason charges.

They needed more time.

Delia hadn't realized until this moment how much she'd hoped the trial would never happen, how she had depended upon God providing a way for them to be exonerated of these ridiculous charges without having to be tried in the king's court.

But she could not allow herself to show any hopelessness. She had to encourage her brothers.

"We will pray. God will give you the words to speak. And no one could possibly believe you are guilty of treason. It's ludicrous. We will tell the truth and make sure they know how treacherous our stepmother is."

Edwin had something close to a scowl on his face. "You cannot come to the trial."

"Why not? I am your sister. I'm a witness."

But Edwin was shaking his head, Gerard was crossing his arms over his chest, and Berenger was frowning at her.

"I will be there. I will tell them—"

"No. You must not even let anyone know you're our sister." Edwin's voice was firm.

She fought the panic rising inside her. "But people already know—Sir Geoffrey, the mistress of linens at the palace. And the guard who escorted me up the stairs knows. He guessed I was your sister."

Edwin looked concerned. "I don't like that anyone knows, but that is only three people. You can still hide and be safe."

"I don't want to hide." Her face was tingling and the blood seemed to have left her head.

"Don't come to the trial. We can't have them accusing you too," Merek said.

"We want you to stay safe, Delia." David gave her a pat on the back. The twelve-year-old was still only as tall as her chin, but he was as brave as any knight.

Roland swiped at his nose with his wrist but said nothing.

Tears pricked her own eyes, then she frowned. She could be as brave as her brothers.

"I will not let anything happen to you. I will find a way to get you out of here. I swear it."

"Don't swear," Charles said softly.

The rest just looked at her sadly or stared past her at the wall.

"I can. I can get you weapons. Or I can steal the key to the door from a knight. Mistress Wattlesbrook gave me some herbs that will put a man to sleep. I brought them with me. I can give it to the guards and I can get you out. You know I'm as brave as you."

Roland sniffed. "Delia killed that poisonous adder with a stick when it came at me."

Edwin smiled at Roland. "Delia is very brave. She is our sister, after all." He winked. "But we will throw ourselves on the mercy of God and pray that He provides a way out so that Delia will not have to put herself in harm's way."

"Did you at least find out what you are supposedly guilty of?" Delia asked.

All her brothers looked grave again. Edwin spoke up.

"We are supposed to have killed a coroner in the village of Wycrofton in Bedfordshire by stirring up some rustics, encouraging them to burn his house down. We supposedly did this because we hated the king."

"Have you ever even been to Wycrofton? Any of you?" She looked at her brothers' faces.

They shook their heads.

"I rode through there once a few years ago," Berenger said.

Edwin's expression was tense. "It is difficult to address such an accusation, since no part of it has even a hint of truth."

"I'd like to meet the man who would accuse us." Gerard grabbed at an imaginary sword.

"I'd like to separate his body from his head," Merek said through clenched teeth.

"Trial by combat—that would be my preferred trial." Berenger looked ready to fight. Her brothers were all such good fighters, they'd surely defeat anyone who challenged them.

But there would be no trial by combat, and they knew that. And Delia would do whatever she had to do to take care of her brothers. They would not be harmed if she could help it.

Delia looked at her oldest brother. "Edwin, you were always good with words. I will procure some parchment, a pen, and ink for you, and you can write a letter to Aunt Beatrice, as well as the most powerful men you know, and ask them to intercede with the king on our behalf."

He nodded, but he did not look very hopeful.

She stayed the rest of the afternoon with her brothers, knitting while they talked, carefully avoiding the subject of their trial as they relived favorite memories from their childhood. They spoke of things she hadn't thought of in years, of hunting with their father, of memories with their mother that made her feel warm inside. She listened intently, committing the events and their words, as well as her brothers' smiles, to her memory. And all the while her fingers and hands worked the needles. By the time the sun had gone down, she had finished Roland's sweater.

"The first of seven," she announced as she pulled the sweater over Roland's head.

"Thank you, Delia. It fits perfectly." He smiled at her. He was trying to be as brave as his brothers, but she could see the tears in his eyes.

"It looks good on you." She only wished she could finish all the sweaters before the weather turned colder. But it was already the beginning of December and their trial was in seven days. The fear of what could happen made her shut down any thoughts about it.

"Yours is next." She smiled at David.

"You should go before it gets any later," Merek said.

"I wish I could escort you back to the palace." Edwin's jaw tightened.

"I will be well. No one even notices me. I'm just a sewing maid." She smiled.

She embraced all her brothers one by one, then Edwin walked with her to the door. He frowned and said softly, while the others were talking among themselves, "Don't worry about us, and no matter what, do not put yourself in danger."

"You can't stop me from trying to help you all, Edwin."

"Listen to me." His eyes were intense as he stared at her. "You will hurt us more if something happens to you. We can endure anything as long as we know you are safe."

Delia threw her arms around her oldest brother and buried her face in his chest. A tear leaked from each eye as she forced back a sob. But she would not add to his burden.

"I will stay safe." She pulled away, opened the door, and left without looking him in the eye.

The guard who had offered to help her—was his name Sir Elliot?—was standing outside the door. Had he been there all this time?

"I hope you found your brothers well."

"They are very well, I thank you."

Delia hurried down the hall, hugging her bag of yarn and knitting needles to her chest. Sir Elliot followed her.

"Forgive me if I'm being intrusive, but I heard your brothers will be tried in the king's court soon."

"Yes." Delia's heart sank all over again. And she remembered her brothers' and her aunt's words of warning.

"It is a terrible time for you, I am sure. I would like to help you, Lady Delia."

"I do not know how you could help me." Unless he wanted to give her the key to her brothers' cell in the middle of the night and provide a place for them to hide.

"Oh, you underestimate me, my lady. I can help."

"Why would you wish to help me?"

"Because you are in distress. And your brothers' lives are in grave danger."

Could she trust this man? They had reached the bottom of the stairs and were standing in front of the door. She waited for him to open it.

"Do not forget. I can help you, my lady."

"And what would you require in return?"

"Only your trust, as I can see you are an excellent woman."

Should she be suspicious of his smile?

"There is something you can do." Delia had nearly forgotten. "Would you bring my brothers some parchment, a pen, and some ink? For writing letters?"

"It would be an honor to procure those things for you, Lady Delia." He placed his hand over his heart. "I would be honored to prove to you my loyalty in that way."

"I thank you." Truly, she was very thankful. Perhaps her aunt would use her influence to help them. Or one of the other powerful men among her brothers' acquaintances would be willing to speak for them. Would this be the way God used to set her brothers free? Or at least to delay their trial?

"When will you visit your brothers again? I will try to be here."

"I am not certain." She couldn't bear to wait a whole week, when she'd have her afternoon reprieve from work, especially since they were facing a trial in the king's court on the next day.

She turned away to leave.

"Remember. I can help you. Do not forget."

Delia glanced over her shoulder. What a blessing it would be if she could trust this man to help her, but after the treachery of whoever had falsely accused her brothers . . . Her stomach clenched at the thought of taking this man at his word and of him turning out to be treacherous. After all, his reason for wanting to help did not ring true. Or was she just too mistrustful after her stepmother turned out to be so heartless?

She would just have to pray that God would reveal the truth to her.

As she hurried across the Tower Green toward the gate that would lead her back into London and to the palace, she glimpsed someone approaching her.

Sir Geoffrey strode toward her with a sober look on his face.

"I saw you talking to Sir Elliot. What was he saying to you?"

"Good evening to you too, Sir Geoffrey."

Was Sir Geoffrey asking her that because he wanted to know if they were plotting to break her brothers free? Would he thwart them? Would he have her arrested?

"Forgive me. How are you faring, Lady Delia?"

"Very well. How are you?"

"Well, I thank you. But . . . how well do you know Sir Elliot?"

"Not at all. I just met him today."

"And he was behaving well toward you?"

"Yes. He offered to help me. I asked him to provide my brothers parchment, pen, and ink so they could write letters, asking for help. He told me to let him know if I ever needed anything else."

Sir Geoffrey's jaw tensed as he stared past her. "Forgive me if I am speaking out of turn, but I would warn you about Sir Elliot. He is a bit of an aggressor."

"An aggressor?" Delia raised her brows at him.

"When it pertains to fair maidens."

"Fair maidens?" Delia noted the uncomfortable look on Sir Geoffrey's face, the way he was shuffling his feet and clearing his throat.

"Forgive me. I know you don't have a protector here in London, and I wanted to let you know . . . That is, if you need my help for any reason . . ."

"Now you sound like Sir Elliot. But how do I know who to trust?" She put her hands on her hips and stared hard at him.

Sir Geoffrey was frowning. "I see that what I said was unwelcome. Forgive me. But I . . . did hear that your brothers will be tried in one week."

"Yes." Fear stabbed her stomach as the news swept over her again. Her shoulders felt weighed down.

"Do you have any witnesses who can defend your brothers, men of influence who would vouch for their character?"

"My brothers were pages and squires for powerful men—or at least the sons of powerful men. I'm afraid, however, that they might not learn of my brothers' trial in time to come to their defense. And they might not be willing, as no one is safe from this king's court and its executions." She said the last part softly, almost in a whisper.

"That is true. I'm afraid most would be afraid of turning the king and his council against themselves." Sir Geoffrey's face brightened, his eyes growing wide and hopeful. "But if they could say they were with your brothers when they had supposedly committed the crimes they are accused of . . ."

Delia sighed and shook her head. "They were all home for our father's funeral. The only people who saw them and could vouch for their whereabouts were me, my father's servants and men, and my stepmother. And she would benefit more than anyone from their execution, so I could not trust her to be truthful." Delia swallowed the lump in her throat. "She is the only person of noble birth besides me, and therefore the only person who would be believed by the court."

"Do you have no relatives who would stand up for you? Someone who would go to the king to attempt to get them pardoned?"

"I have an aunt who is the abbess at Rosings Abbey, the one I mentioned my brother is writing to. I do not know if she would be able or willing to help in that way, but Edwin is asking her, begging her, to speak to the king for us."

"Do you have someone, a courier, to carry his letter to your aunt?"

"I don't." Why hadn't she thought of that? She was so accustomed to having servants around to take care of such things.

"I will find a courier for your brother."

"Thank you." Her heart seemed to press against her chest.

He nodded. "Just be careful about trusting Sir Elliot."

"So I can trust you, the man who seized my brothers and imprisoned them, but not Sir Elliot?" She raised her brows, but he was looking down.

"I am sorry I was used for such an ignoble purpose. I had no choice, as I myself have no power in this king's court. I was only following orders."

She knew it was true, but . . . "It's difficult not to blame you, just a little bit."

He let out a long breath. "I wish you would forgive me."

"I do." She was suddenly sorry for teasing him. "I do forgive you."

"I would never do anything dishonorable, not purposely, and I had no idea that most of the men I was sent to arrest were not men at all, but children."

He'd never do anything dishonorable. Did that include helping her brothers escape the Tower if they were convicted of treason and sentenced to death by beheading? He would surely consider that dishonorable.

"It is unfortunate their trial is being conducted so soon. I thought your brothers would at least have more time, that the trial would not take place until the new year."

"I did as well." Delia had counted on them waiting until she could make friends with the new queen. "I don't know how they will be exonerated. We need time to prove they are innocent. If only I could find who actually committed those crimes . . ."

"Everything is politically motivated here. The truth rarely has any bearing in these matters." Sir Geoffrey's voice sounded bitter, and he chewed the inside of his lip.

"Is there no hope that the judges will see through the fraudulent charges?"

His eyes were sad as they met hers. "It is possible; however . . . if someone powerful wishes your brothers dead, whether they are innocent or not will matter little or nothing to the judges."

Tears stung Delia's eyes, due as much to the compassionate look on his face as to his words.

"But that does not mean God will not intervene in some way," he said quickly. "God can do anything, and we will pray for a miracle."

"Of course." But Delia's stomach sank anyway. Had she not prayed for a miracle when her mother was sick? What was purer than the fervent prayers of an innocent child praying for her mother? And yet her mother had died. Why would God come through for her and answer her prayer this time, if not then? But she felt almost blasphemous for even having that thought. Wouldn't God be angry with her for her lack of faith?

"I must go. I want to get back to the palace before it is dark."

"Of course. Will you allow me to escort you back?"

"No, thank you. Good night, Sir Geoffrey."

"Good night, Lady Delia."

As she started toward the gate, she caught a glimpse of Sir Elliot looking at her. He nodded, and she nodded back at him.

Who could she trust? Only God knew.

SEVEN

IT HAD BEEN TWO DAYS SINCE DELIA HAD SEEN HER BROTH-ers. Had Sir Elliot procured the necessary materials for writing a letter? Even if he had, would they be able to send the letter? How would they hire a courier?

She didn't finish her work until after dark every evening, as the days were so short now, and she was not allowed to leave during the day. When she rose every morning, it was also dark.

She had slept poorly, awake long before dawn, worrying about what would happen to her brothers. She might as well arise and go see if she could visit her brothers before she was required to appear in the sewing room. She didn't think they would mind if she woke them.

But the women who would not have to get up for another hour or two would mind if she woke them. So Delia dressed in the dark and moved as soundlessly as she could through the room of sleeping sewing maids and out the door, closing it carefully behind her. Once she reached the outside gate of the palace, she put her sturdy wooden clogs over her slippers and ventured out into the still-dark, pre-dawn world.

She did not encounter anyone on the way to the Tower of London except for a few guards and some drunk men stumbling and laughing together. They called out to her from the other side of the street, but Delia kept her head down and walked as fast as she could.

Finally, she was approaching the Tower gate when she remembered the gate was locked. The guards would not appear until after dawn.

How foolish she was! Should she wait, hoping she could at least see her brothers quickly before she had to leave to get back in time? Would she be harassed by drunk men like those she'd just seen on the street? The only other thing she could do was go back to the palace, but she'd much prefer not to walk back through the London streets until after the sun was up and more decent, ordinary people were milling around and going about their business.

Delia approached the gate. She had her knitting supplies with her, so she could at least work on David's sweater.

The path leading up to the gate was paved with cobblestones that were smooth and clean, so Delia found a nice corner and sat down with her back against the stone wall. She took out her knitting and began twisting the yarn around the needles, working the yarn into David's unfinished sweater.

A swan swam on the slow-moving River Thames in front of her. Was it her imagination, or did the large white bird look dejected? Its head was bowed low as it let the current take it downriver. Then it turned and moved toward the shore, getting out and shaking its feathers rather half-heartedly. On the shore, among the grasses and reeds, were other swans, all of them huddled together. They barely acknowledged the newcomer, looking up at it, then going back to their huddling.

Delia tried to count them. If she was not mistaken, there were seven sitting on the ground, almost in a circle, and the one that had just come up out of the water made eight.

Were the swans sad about the coming winter? Were they huddling for warmth? Or for companionship?

Delia continued knitting, glancing up now and then at the swans, who barely moved as the gray light around them grew gradually brighter.

"Lady Delia?" Sir Elliot was standing over her.

"Good morning." She stopped knitting and stared up at him.

"You seem in need of assistance, my lady."

"I was waiting for the gate to be opened so that I can visit my brothers."

"The keeper of the keys should be along shortly. May I keep you company until he arrives?"

Sir Geoffrey's words of warning came back to her. *"Just be careful about trusting Sir Elliot."*

But Sir Elliot had been perfectly chivalrous so far. Perhaps Sir Geoffrey was jealous, as Sir Elliot was rather good looking, with his green eyes and blond hair. Although Sir Geoffrey was at least as handsome.

"You may." She looked down at the nearly finished sweater in her lap.

Sir Elliot started sliding down the wall until he was sitting beside her on the cobblestones. He kept his hand on his sword and adjusted it to rest against his thigh as he stared into her eyes.

Delia gazed back at him, noticing the bushiness of his eyebrows and a small scar on his cheek. But there was something about the way he was looking at her, the tilt of his smile. *"He is a bit of an aggressor when it pertains to fair maidens,"* Sir Geoffrey had said.

Sir Elliot leaned toward her and said softly, "I was able to procure the parchment and pen and ink for your brother to write a letter."

Delia felt a slight lift in her chest. She gave him her complete attention. He was staring at her lips now.

"Thank you. You are very kind to do that service for my brothers and me."

"And I am willing to help you further. You have a friend in me."

"Again, you are very kind."

He leaned toward her, staring into her eyes even more intently. "I know things seem frightening for you and your brothers now, but you can look to me for help. You will need a friend, and I can be that friend. I can even help your brothers escape, if it comes to that."

"You would do that? That is so kind and brave of you." Indeed, she hoped he was being sincere, but . . . "Forgive me, Sir Elliot, but it seems strange that you would be willing to risk yourself in such a way when you hardly know me or my brothers. And I have no wealth with which to reward you."

"I assure you, my lady, I do not need wealth. But it is true that men cannot be trusted . . . as a rule." He frowned and nodded, staring at the ground for a moment. Then he fastened his gaze on her face again. "The truth is that you have captured me—your plight with your brothers, the sweetness of your manner, and . . ." He paused, then sighed. "You are so beautiful. It may seem strange in so short a time, but you have captured my heart, indeed, from the first moment I saw you."

No one had ever spoken in such flattering terms to her. She quite liked it. But at the same time, as he had admitted, the level of his ardor after knowing each other so briefly was strange. She shouldn't trust such a proclamation. And she knew she was still just a girl, with no experience at all with men. Her servants' warnings came back to her, about not allowing wily men to turn her head. No, it did not seem wise to trust him—especially in light of what Sir Geoffrey had told her about him.

But she was also not ready to reject his offer of help outright. The threat of her brothers being executed was too great.

"I am flattered, Sir Elliot."

"It is not flattery. It is the truth." He placed his gloved hand over his chest.

"I am still praying that God will make a way to clear my brothers of the false accusations during the trial. According to the Holy Writ, the truth will set them free."

"Yes, of course. Some are inclined to hope for intervention from above. But you should consider that if they convict your brothers of treason, they will set an execution date and may even move your brothers to the dungeon to await their fate. And then the guards will be doubled or tripled, and it shall be nearly impossible to free them."

She had not thought of that.

The sound of marching feet filled her ears as Sir Elliot scrambled to stand. He stood at attention as a man dressed formally in a bright-red uniform approached, surrounded by guards, and marched in a stately manner toward the gate. They moved past Delia and Sir Elliot, and the formally dressed man with the impressive hat stopped at the gate, took out a key, and unlocked it. He went inside, along with half the guards, while the other half stayed at the gate.

Sir Elliot reached out a hand to Delia and helped her rise. She stuffed her knitting into her bag.

"Will you allow me to escort you?" Sir Elliot stood quite close.

"Yes, I thank you."

They passed through the gate, the guards barely glancing at them.

The farther they walked, the closer Sir Elliot seemed to walk beside her; he actually brushed her arm with his hand a few times.

When they reached the tower where her brothers were kept, Sir Elliot opened the door and let her in. As they climbed the stairs, he leaned so close she could feel his breath on her hair.

"I am your slave, Lady Delia. Do not forget that I have pledged to help you and your brothers, and that I have already done as you bid me by bringing them the parchment and ink." His gaze seemed heated as he stared at her face, focusing on her lips. "Do not forget."

When they reached her brothers' door, he just stood there. Would she have to ask him to unlock the door?

"I . . . thank you, Sir Elliot. Your kindness and generosity are duly noted."

He finally unlocked the door. She quickly pushed it open and had to brush past him to get inside, then closed the door on his face. For some reason she felt relieved to get away from his intense eyes and the way he leaned toward her.

Her brothers were lounging about the room, the younger ones still asleep. If only she were able to buy beds for them. How terrible that they had to sleep on the cold stone floor. Should she ask Sir Elliot to procure beds for them? But, Lord willing, they would not be in this terrible place much longer. Surely they would be set free, if there was any justice at all.

Her four oldest brothers all greeted her quietly and embraced her in turn. She probably only had half an hour before she'd have to leave them and return to her sewing duties at the palace.

"What brings you here?" Edwin asked.

"I couldn't sleep." She wished she could tell them she had spoken to the king about them and convinced him to exonerate and release them, but she still had no idea how to get anywhere near the king. "Were you able to write and send the letters?"

"I was, and Sir Geoffrey found couriers for them. I wrote one to our aunt at the abbey, as well as one to my benefactor, the Marquess of Cavenbury, although I hear he is not in favor with the king and his councilors. If I'd had more parchment I would have written to every nobleman whose sons we have trained with, but I don't know how much good it would have done anyway.

Probably none of them would be willing to risk their position or the good graces of the king and his closest advisors."

They all looked rather downcast. Delia searched her mind for something uplifting she might say.

Edwin stared at her. "I have thought about what you must do if the worst happens. You must go to Aunt Beatrice and ask for her protection."

"I do not wish to join the cloister and be a nun. Besides, the worst is not going to happen."

"It does not look reassuring, Delia. I am sorry to say it." Edwin spoke in a solemn tone.

"I am not completely without allies. I will find a way to get you all free, if the worst happens and the trial does not go well."

"Who are these mysterious allies?"

"I know a guard who has promised to help me, and Sir Geoffrey has also promised to do what he can."

"Sir Geoffrey would not endanger his own career or his own life to help us. He is a kind man, but you can be sure there is a limit to a man's generosity and helpfulness."

"Sir Geoffrey might not, but there is another guard who has taken an interest in us."

"Who?"

"His name is Sir Elliot. He says he will help."

"Darling Delia, you cannot trust every man—he is a stranger! When did you meet him?"

"The last time I came here to visit you."

"And you have seen him since then?"

"Not until this morning. But he declares he is in love with me."

"Men do not fall in love that quickly. You must be careful. You are beautiful, but also very vulnerable. You have no one to look after you and protect you. Evil men will try to take advantage of you."

"I am not so daft. I will be careful."

"I do not think you are daft. But I do not trust this guard. The next time I see Sir Geoffrey I will ask him about this Sir Elliot."

"And why do you trust Sir Geoffrey so much?"

"He has been kind to us. I trust him—more than anyone else in this king's court." Edwin's expression hardened. "Why? Do you have any reason to mistrust him?"

"Sir Geoffrey? No, but . . . if he's as dutiful and honorable as he says, then he will not hesitate to escort you to your execution—knowing you are innocent!"

"Our execution would not be his fault." Edwin looked sad. "But perhaps God will save us. Nothing is too hard for God. He can save, whether by many or by few."

Edwin knew the Scriptures better than any of them. He was a good hunter as well as a mighty swordsman and jouster, but he was also quite studious, having studied the Holy Writ for himself using their grandfather's Bible. Edwin seemed to draw comfort from the words in the Holy Writ, but for Delia the words rang hollow right now, when she was so afraid of what was about to happen. God never promised to save them from being wrongfully executed, only to be with them and to take them to heaven if they were.

They talked for a little longer, then Delia told them she must leave.

David and Roland hugged Delia. Roland cried but waved Delia away when she tried to hug him again. He wanted to be brave like his brothers.

Delia said no more to Edwin about Sir Elliot and his offer to help, but when she left, she was more determined than ever to accept assistance wherever she could get it to set her brothers free.

Sir Elliot was waiting for her outside. He hastily locked the door and turned to her. "You poor dear." He put his arms around Delia.

Delia felt herself stiffen. She had not expected him to embrace her. What should she do? She patted his back awkwardly. When he pulled away, his face was angled toward hers. Would he try to kiss her? She looked down, turning her head away from him and moving toward the stairs.

"I must return to the palace and to my work," she said. "Madame Celine will be furious if I am late and not sitting in my place when she brings us the day's tasks. She has scolded me once already, and I cannot afford to lose my position. I must hurry."

She used her chatter to fill up the time it took to walk down the stairs, then Sir Elliot followed her out of the tower.

"I will escort you to the palace. The streets are not safe for a woman walking alone."

She was not entirely sure she should allow him to walk with her. After his amorous embrace, she worried he might try to kiss her, and she didn't want her first kiss to be with a man she hardly knew. She wasn't sure how to tell him no, so she nodded and walked by his side, folding her arms as she carried her bag of knitting in front of her. Once they had passed through the Tower gate and were out of the Tower vicinity, he spoke.

"You are not afraid of me, are you, Lady Delia?"

"No, of course not." She smiled as if the idea were silly.

"I know you are hoping all will go well at the trial, but if it doesn't . . ."

"If it doesn't, I shall take you at your word, and I will be very grateful for your help." There. She'd said it. She could not allow her brothers to be executed.

"I am so glad." He reached out and squeezed her shoulder, but rather than reassuring her, the action gave her an unpleasant feeling that lingered after he removed his hand.

Delia quickened her pace.

"Why are you walking so fast?" He chuckled, a derisive sound. "You don't have to worry. If anyone attacks, I will protect you."

"I know. But I need to get back before Madame Celine finds me missing." It was true, after all.

Sir Elliot said nothing more, and when they arrived at the palace gate, Delia moved even faster and reached for the door.

"Ask one of the other guards at the Tower for me if you need me and do not see me."

"Thank you very much, and for escorting me." She glanced over her shoulder at him, then quickly entered the palace gate before he could reply.

Eight

GEOFFREY HAD EXCHANGED HIS SOLDIER'S GARB FOR WHAT he hoped was clothing that would help him blend in with the rest of the people in the king's court.

It was the day of Lady Delia's brothers' trial. Geoffrey stood at the fringes near the wall, trying not to attract attention as he watched the seven brothers, the young lords of Dericott, being led into the large hall.

The fourteen-year-old king's expression was tense, his eyes wary as he sat between two of his councilors—one of whom was Geoffrey's uncle, Baldric.

Geoffrey shrank back, hiding in the shadows of the room. He'd known his uncle would probably be attending today, but he hadn't been prepared for the gnawing feeling in the pit of his stomach at seeing the man who had betrayed Geoffrey's father as well as Geoffrey and his sister. The man who now held the title of Earl of Yelverton. At least the king had not granted him Geoffrey's father's title of Duke of Strachleigh.

The look on one advisor's face was of arrogance and indolence, his fat eyelids drooping as if he'd eaten too much and was now plagued with indigestion. The councilor on the king's other side was Uncle Baldric. His face showed shrewdness, his eyes narrowed as if to threaten anyone who looked at him. Heat boiled up inside Geoffrey and he looked away. He wouldn't think about his uncle. Not here, not today. He would focus on Lady Delia's brothers. Geoffrey said yet another prayer under his breath that God would not let them be wronged the way he had been.

With all the men either milling slowly about, stopping to talk with one another, or hurrying to whisper something in someone's ear or to deliver a missive into the hand of another, the trial did not appear to be starting just yet.

Was Lady Delia there? He hoped not, for she would surely stand out as the only woman in the room. If he were her brother, he'd have forbidden her from attending the trial, and as her brothers seemed to care for her, they had probably done so. Still, she was quite brave, so he looked around the room, searching for her dark hair and feminine form. But after a few moments he was satisfied she wasn't there.

Next, he studied her brothers' faces. The three oldest brothers were stoic as they stared straight ahead. The youngest two were wearing sweaters their sister had made from the yarn he had gifted her. Their expressions were more wide-eyed as their gazes darted around. Poor things. To be so young and on trial in front of these heartless men. The only man among them with any virtue at all was quite probably the young king, and he had less power than anyone else in the room, other than the Lords Dericott.

Geoffrey's mind went back to Lady Delia and the day before

when he'd been standing guard on top of the White Tower. Geoffrey had caught a glimpse of Lady Delia headed toward the building where her brothers were kept.

Her expression had looked grim. Little wonder, as she awaited her brothers' trial. And unfortunately Sir Elliot was the guard standing at the door as she approached.

Geoffrey was too far away to make out anything they were saying, but Lady Delia stopped and conversed with the guard, who leaned suspiciously close to her. Geoffrey's stomach roiled as the man-at-arms touched her on the shoulder and leaned even closer, as if he were whispering in her ear. What was he saying to her? Would the innocent girl become his next victim? Or was she plotting something with him, a willing participant? The next moment they both disappeared inside the building.

Geoffrey watched and waited as the sun rose, shedding more light across the Tower Green. A minute later Lady Delia and Sir Elliot emerged. Lady Delia appeared to be wiping her face with her hand. Sir Elliot stood quite close to her. She shook her head rather emphatically and moved away from him at a fast walk toward the gate. Sir Elliot did not follow her.

His chest ached as he pondered their relationship. Most likely Sir Elliot was trying to portray himself as a lovesick fool who only wished to help her, but his motives, of course, were less than honorable. But the thought that Delia might not be as innocent as she appeared was just as troubling.

He didn't like thinking ill of the girl. Not only was it un-chivalrous, but if he was honest with himself, he had been trying to suppress feelings for her that went beyond simple remorse for being the one to arrest her brothers. And he couldn't stop thinking of his own sister being put in the same predicament as Lady Delia, should he be falsely charged with a crime. If only he could find a way of clearing his dead father's name and getting his, and his sister's, rightful inheritance back from his uncle.

Two of Delia's older brothers bent and said something to the two youngest ones. The younger ones faced straight ahead with a renewed look of courage as the judge called the court to order.

Someone stood to read the charges against Delia's brothers. Geoffrey was surprised to see that John of Gaunt, the Duke of Lancaster, was in charge of the proceedings. He'd been feuding with Henry Percy, Earl of Northumberland, and the two had disrupted a recent parliamentary meeting. John of Gaunt had been almost as unpopular with the people as he was with Henry Percy. But he was the Lord High Steward, so it was his duty to preside over this trial of peers.

"Treason against the king and against England," he said, reading from a scroll of parchment, "for rebellion against the Crown, for supporting vandals who burned down the house of the king's coroner, Sir John Stanley, in Bedfordshire, and for demanding the death of His Royal Highness King Richard the Second."

A troubled look came over the face of one of the younger boys. The older brothers never changed their expressions, but one of the middle ones—Geoffrey thought his name was Merek— scowled defiantly.

"The accusers," the arrogant-looking John of Gaunt continued in his deep, monotone voice, "are John Albright of Bedfordshire and Andrew Goddard of Hertfordshire."

A flicker of confusion flashed across a couple of the brothers' faces. No doubt the real accuser was someone much more powerful, and they probably did not even know who this John Albright and Andrew Goddard were.

The first witness was called. He walked with a halting gait and spoke with a coarse and uneducated accent. "I heard the Dericott lords—the seven sons of the deceased Earl of Dericott— tell some young men they would give them ten farthings if they set Sir John's house afire and made sure it burned to the ground."

When he was questioned, the witness could not tell any of the names of the young men who had listened to the entreaty and had carried out the act of burning the coroner's house. He was asked if the Lords Dericott had spoken against the king or threatened his life. The man nodded his head.

"They said they was getting together a mob to go with them to London and storm Westminster. They was going to drag out the king. Then they would stab him and cut his head off."

Delia's brothers stared hard at the man, their expressions either angry or disbelieving, except for the youngest. His mouth worked, his lips pressing together then parting, as he seemed to be fighting back tears.

The court official called up the second witness, who came forward and made similar accusations. Both men were well-dressed but seemed uncomfortable, this one often pulling at his shirt. He also rubbed his hand down his face and across his mouth between statements.

The pompous-looking fellow who was questioning them, not John of Gaunt but some other man, continued. "Now, when you say the Dericott lords, do you mean all of them? Or only some of them?"

A stupid look came over his face as his gaze seemed to fix on the ceiling. After a few moments, he answered, "All. All seven of them."

"All seven of them made these statements?"

"Yes, all seven of them."

Edwin appeared to be seething, his face turning red and his chest rising and falling. Another brother was balling his hands into fists. Surely no one would believe this nonsense. Their story was obviously an invention, something these men had been told to say.

The brothers were asked to stand when their name was stated in order to answer questions. Edwin's name was called first.

"Are you guilty of the charges set before you by these witnesses?"

Edwin stood and replied, his voice strong and steady, "We are not guilty."

"State your name and answer only for yourself."

"Edwin Raynsford, Earl of Dericott, and I am not guilty. I never saw these men before. I never spoke against the king nor encouraged violence against the coroner's house. Before I became the Earl of Dericott, I was a knight in service of King Richard, and I am wholly and completely not guilty of these charges."

Each brother was asked to answer the question for himself. And they all answered in the same fashion as Edwin, stating they were not guilty of any of the charges laid out against them, with varying degrees of defiance and stoic indifference.

When it came time for the youngest to answer, he seemed to

take a deep breath, and his eyes filled with tears. He cleared his throat, then said, "Roland Raynsford. I am not guilty of these charges." He rubbed his eyes with his hand.

"Very well. You may sit."

Next, the arrogant man who had questioned them consulted with John of Gaunt and the king and his advisors. The king did not open his mouth, but appeared to be listening to the others.

As Geoffrey watched the men's faces, including his uncle's, his neck and forehead grew hot at the lack of compassion, the coldness that was evident in the manner and movements of these powerful men who were deciding the brothers' fate. Of course, he knew exactly how much his uncle cared for justice and truth.

They talked for several minutes. Another man came over to consult with them. Meanwhile, the rest of the room began to murmur among themselves.

Finally, the king opened his mouth and spoke a few words. If only Geoffrey could hear what he was saying, but he was too far away.

The other men all seemed to be talking at once. The king seemed to shrink back a little into his chair. He was so young, after all. And apparently his courage was limited to facing down mobs and listening to their demands while risking his physical person, not challenging his councilors.

The men spoke several more minutes. Finally, they all looked at the king. He looked resigned and spoke only a few words. The councilors nodded and looked at each other, nodding again. Then the pompous man asked the room to give them their attention again.

He asked Delia's brothers to rise to face their verdict.

The boys stood. The youngest, Roland, looked as pale as new snow.

John of Gaunt, Duke of Lancaster, spoke, standing straight and tall. "On the charge of treason against England and against the king, by order of His Royal Highness King Richard, you have all been found . . . guilty." He then named each of them, declaring them individually guilty.

"Your sentence, by decree of the law of England, is death."

Little Roland did not move, only stared with his mouth slightly open. Two of his brothers came on either side of him, putting an arm around him, while another put an arm around the second youngest, David. They did not speak. How could any words repair this? Geoffrey himself felt sick, heat rising to his head as he clenched his teeth with suppressed fury.

"The sentence will be carried out one week hence at noon on the Tower Green."

A quiet sob could be heard coming from one of the brothers as the older ones surrounded the younger two.

Poor Delia! How would she take the news? Who would tell her?

As Geoffrey left the courtroom, he wondered how he might get word to her. Even though he did not relish being the one to report the terrible news, he couldn't bear the thought of her hearing it from someone who felt no empathy or compassion for her.

His heart ached, and he relived the false accusations of his uncle all over again—his uncle who had maligned his good father while he was still grieving Geoffrey's mother's death. Due to his uncle's scheming, when his father died his uncle had taken everything—or rather, the king's court had given him everything, all of Geoffrey's inheritance.

When their father died, Geoffrey had no choice but to keep silent and send Amicia away to the Continent to a convent to keep her safe. He had quietly searched for evidence to clear his father of wrongdoing, but so far had been unsuccessful. And now, two years later, at the age of twenty-two, instead of becoming the Duke of Strachleigh, he was but a knight serving as a guard captain at the Tower of London.

As he left, someone placed a hand on his shoulder. He turned to see who it was.

Sir Elliot. "Have you seen Lady Delia?" he asked with a distracted look on his face.

"No, I have not."

"I went to look for her where the sewing maids work, but she wasn't there. She'd asked for an hour off."

She must have been somewhere nearby waiting to hear her brothers' verdict, or she was back at their place of imprisonment. But he didn't want Sir Elliot to find her before he did.

"You will let me know if you see her?" Sir Elliot pinned Geoffrey with a look.

Geoffrey couldn't lie, so he said, "Why do you need to see her?"

"You are quite the inquisitor." Sir Elliot raised his brows. "I just want to offer her my assistance, as a friend."

As a friend? Geoffrey did not trust that sentiment for a moment. He knew too much of Sir Elliot's dealings with maidens.

"I don't know where she is, but I'm sure she will be found." Geoffrey nodded and turned away before Sir Elliot could ask him again for his help in finding her.

Geoffrey went back into the hall to avoid Sir Elliot, but he was anxious to find Lady Delia himself. He wanted to go to Wardroab Tower to look for her, but Sir Elliot would probably beat him there.

With people milling all about, Geoffrey closed his eyes for a moment and prayed silently, *God, help me find her.*

As he opened his eyes, he thought he heard someone crying. To his right was a narrow corridor. He turned and walked into it, finding a tiny alcove. A woman was facing the wall, bent over, her hands over her face. She was softly sobbing, her shoulders shaking. She gasped for air, then let out another sob.

Geoffrey recognized the dress and the figure as Lady Delia.

What should he say? Should he touch her shoulder, or would that startle her too much? How she must still hate him, especially now, for the role he had played in her brothers' terrible situation.

His chest ached and his stomach twisted at her obvious distress. But of course she was distressed. Her seven brothers whom she loved and had intended to save had been condemned to die. But he also couldn't just continue to stand there watching her cry and not say anything.

"My lady."

She straightened but did not remove her hands from her face or turn around.

"Forgive me for disturbing you. Is there anything I can do?" In truth he had no idea how he could help. He couldn't offer to fetch her mother—her mother was dead. He couldn't offer to escort her home—she probably felt as though she had no home. Her bed was a cot in a servant's dormitory. He couldn't offer to save her brothers—that would be a false promise, since he was only a soldier and could be killed if he interfered in any way with their fate. And if he was killed, what would happen to his sister? Their uncle had made certain she had no protector except Geoffrey.

Much like Lady Delia.

She kept her back to him, and though she shook her head, she continued to cry. Would she hate even the sight of him?

He could not just leave her there. He imagined that Amicia would cry just as hard if he were sentenced to die.

A group of guards walking in tight formation passed their little alcove.

There must be something that can be done. Geoffrey glanced up to heaven. Had God placed Delia and her brothers in his path just to break his heart because he could not help them? Surely God did not wish for these innocent men and boys to be wrongly executed, leaving their sister all alone to fend for herself.

His thoughts were churning. If he could get an audience with the king . . . or with one of the king's councilors . . .

But there was precious little time. Only one week before the execution.

Delia's sobs seemed to be subsiding a bit. She was wiping her face with a cloth.

Geoffrey placed a hand on her shoulder. She took a deep breath.

"It is a harsh blow, but we must keep our hopes alive."

"What hope is there?" She turned and looked up at him with red-rimmed eyes that were filling with tears again.

"There is still a week to try to reason with the king."

"The king? Do you know the king? Would you be able to talk to him?"

Delia's face brightened as she gave him her full attention. It broke his heart all over again. And he'd be breaking hers now if he failed.

"I do not know him, but I can try . . . can try to get an audience with him. I was the oldest son of the Duke of Strachleigh." He rarely told anyone that, but if there was any benefit in the connection, Geoffrey intended to make use of it now.

"The king will at least know of you, then. If you could speak to the king and reason with him, tell him that my stepmother is behind this . . ."

"I will do my best, but I cannot promise I will succeed. I am nobody now, just a man-at-arms in the king's service." And his father had been wrongly accused by one of the king's closest advisors.

"But the king can do anything, and if he is certain that this is wrong, perhaps he will pardon my brothers, or at least postpone their execution."

"Perhaps. But it will be a miracle if I can get to him and speak to him."

"I will pray, then. I will pray most fervently. But please try." She looked up at him with such fearful hope, he could not have refused if he'd wanted to.

"I will."

"Thank you." She grasped his hand and squeezed it. "I do not know why you are being kind to me, but I am grateful." She barely got out the last word before she pressed her hand to her mouth, tears slipping from her eyes.

He couldn't help himself. He embraced her, gently drawing her close, and she pressed her face to his chest.

This . . . this was good. Just holding her. He breathed in, inhaling the smell of her, which was flowery and warm and soft, then let it out. Was he as bad as Sir Elliot?

No, he was nothing like Sir Elliot. That man used young maidens and then discarded them, rejecting them and breaking their hearts. Geoffrey hated all such dishonor.

He could tell she was crying again. He softly patted the back of her shoulder.

"Don't worry, Lady Delia. All will be well. All will be well."

"Forgive me." She sniffed rather loudly and pulled away enough to wipe her face again.

"Nothing to forgive."

"I must get back to my work." She took a deep breath and looked into his eyes. It was dark in the little alcove, but her blue eyes shone bright.

"Will you be all right?"

"I have no choice in the matter." She shook her head. "I will be strong, as strong as my brothers."

"You are quite strong, Lady Delia. Your brothers would be proud."

"Breaking down and crying outside the court? No, I do not

think they would be very proud of me today. But I was very proud to be their sister. Did you see how brave they were? Even little Roland and David." Her lips trembled, but she pressed them together and took a breath, as though to dispel any tears.

"Yes, they were quite brave. Like true noblemen."

"So much more noble than their accusers." Delia's jaw hardened. But then she shook her head slightly. "I must go. Thank you for your offer to speak to the king, Sir Geoffrey. I shall be praying for you night and day."

"Thank you, my lady."

"Both for success with the king and for God to bless you for your kindness."

"God will surely hear your prayers. And I shall be praying as well, for you and your brothers."

"God bless you and speed you." She clasped his hand again, her small, slender fingers soft inside his.

She brushed past him on her way out. His heart beat fast as he watched her go.

God, please don't let me disappoint her.

Nine

Delia's hands shook, but she was breathing easier now that the weight of the boulder had been off her chest a little. Sir Geoffrey would try to speak to the king. He said he couldn't promise her anything, but hope bloomed inside her anyway. And Sir Elliot had also vowed to help her. Surely, between the two of them, God would work to save her brothers.

Madame Celine would be angry with her for taking the time away from her work. *Please, God, let her not dismiss me.*

The memory of her brothers' guilty verdict washed over her again, bringing fresh horror and the same sinking feeling. How could this be happening? *God, please don't take my brothers away from me.*

"Running about the streets of London?" Madame Celine greeted her as she walked in and made her way to her seat.

Delia opened her mouth but closed it again, unsure what to reply.

"If only we could all be so free with our time." Madame frowned and rolled her eyes as she turned away.

Delia returned to her seat, picked up what she had been working on, and moved her needle in and out of the fabric. As monotonous as the sewing was, it did not keep her mind from dwelling on her brothers, the ridiculously unjust judges who had condemned them, and her fear of having to watch the only people she loved die in one week's time.

To steady herself, she began to pray silently while she worked, praying for her brothers to be saved. Soon she was praying more calmly, naming each brother, and praying for Sir Geoffrey, as she had promised.

Sir Geoffrey. Even though he'd never offered to help her break her brothers out of their tower prison as Sir Elliot had, she felt safer with Sir Geoffrey. But if Sir Geoffrey could not convince the king to pardon her brothers, she would definitely take Sir Elliot at his word and allow him to help her set her brothers free.

She would do anything for her brothers.

By the end of the workday, Delia was so tired she was nodding forward, falling asleep in the middle of a stitch. So many nights she'd lain awake the past week, worrying. And the strain of the trial today, hearing her brothers condemned to die . . . She was weary to her bones.

Madame Celine clapped her hands. "Put away your work and you may go."

Delia rubbed her face. She just had to stay awake long enough to walk down the corridor to her bed.

"Not you." Madame Celine stood beside Delia's stool.

Delia stared up at the woman's red cheeks and nose. She smelled of strong spirits, the kind her father used to drink on occasion.

"You will stay an extra hour to make up for running off today."

"But . . . I had urgent business."

"Urgent business? What business could you possibly have that could be considered urgent? You were meeting some man, no doubt. But I assure you that if you start showing that you are with child, you will be dismissed immediately."

Delia's back stiffened. She tightened her jaw. Some of the other sewing maids were turning to stare and listen.

"I did not meet a man." But what could she say? There was no explanation she could give except the truth, and Aunt Beatrice had warned her not to tell the details of her situation.

"Then what? What were you about?"

"I went to see if my brothers needed my help."

"Why would your brothers need *your* help?"

"It is a complicated matter."

Madame Celine's eyes narrowed and her mouth twisted, her nose wrinkling as if she smelled something sour.

"Please forgive me." She lowered her head to try to appear humble and apologetic. "I am very sorry for leaving work today. I will not miss work again."

"No, you will not, or you will be dismissed." Madame Celine grunted. She stood there, unmoving. Finally, she said, "And you will make it up now by working an extra hour. Now get to work."

Delia picked up the fabric and her needle and Madame Celine turned away from her.

Delia was so exhausted—even more so after the tense moments with Madame Celine—her knees trembled even as she sat there. Her vision blurred and her stitches were uneven, but she kept putting the needle and thread in and out of the fabric. She would not let Madame Celine know what she was feeling. She would push down every emotion. Delia would continue sewing and pretend she had no feelings at all, and no one as coldhearted as Madame Celine or those cruel judges at her brothers' trial would see her break.

She sewed, stabbing the fabric with her needle.

She had let Sir Geoffrey see her cry. And Sir Elliot as well. But they were kindhearted men, not cold and hard and harsh like Madame Celine. Or her stepmother.

Thank You, God, for Sir Geoffrey and Sir Elliot, kind souls willing to help me. Thank You for sending them, and thank You that You are going to save my brothers. You will not let them be killed. Such a thing would be more than I could bear.

Delia's shoulders ached and her neck seemed as heavy as a stone. Her eyes burned and her fingers hurt from all the times she had stuck herself with the needle, but she kept sewing, determined not to show any weakness.

When Madame Celine left the room, Delia rolled her shoulders, then her head, trying to relieve the pain and stiffness. But then she went back to sewing, not knowing when Madame Celine would return.

"You may go now, miss," Madame Celine said pertly when

she returned a few minutes later. "I don't want to hear you asking for time off again."

Delia stood, gathered her things, and nodded.

She stumbled a bit as she left the room. She had just enough strength to hold her head high as she passed Madame Celine. But inside she felt more humbled and beaten down than she had ever felt in her life. Her brothers, the most precious people in the world to her, had been sentenced to death, the humiliating death of a public beheading, for crimes against the king and England.

She'd been putting her hope in Sir Geoffrey and Sir Elliot and their promises to help her. But how likely was it that they would be able to save her brothers? And in such a short time?

It would be nearly impossible.

Delia did her best to preserve a façade of dignity in front of the other sewing maids in their bedroom. She did not even care enough to go to the servants' kitchen and retrieve her dinner. She just undressed and crawled into bed, then closed her eyes and lay facing the wall, trying not to let the pain overwhelm her and steal every last bit of her hope.

"Pardon," a quiet voice said.

Was this person speaking to her? Delia waited, not wishing to face anyone at the moment.

"Pardon me, but I brought you something from the kitchen."

Delia could no longer pretend she didn't know the woman was speaking to her, so she rolled over and was faced with the soft brown eyes of one of the sewing maids. She was holding out a cloth in both hands, and on the cloth was an assortment of cheese and pasties, nuts and dried fruit.

Delia sat up and accepted the bundle. "That is very kind of you." She managed to speak through her constricted, aching throat. "I thank you."

"I hope all is well with your brothers. Forgive me, but I heard you say your brothers needed you." The young woman sat on the bed beside Delia's. She was petite, with honey-colored hair and pale skin.

Delia's stomach rebelled at the thought of eating, but the girl sitting across from her looked so kind, she suddenly wanted to eat what was in her hands, if only to show her gratitude for the girl's kindness. So she lifted the small wedge of cheese and took a tiny bite, then took a walnut and a raisin and ate those also. Before she knew it, she was nibbling away at all of the food while the girl talked.

"I'm Margery. Many of the sewing maids aren't very friendly, but don't worry. Most of them don't stay long. You have a kind face, so I think we should be friends."

Delia still had the heavy shoulders and hollowed-out middle that had come upon her when she'd stood outside the parliament room and heard that her brothers were found guilty and would be executed in one week. But there was a strange balm in Margery bringing her food and telling her she wanted to be friends.

"I thank you. Yes, I would like to be your friend." A tear leaked from the corner of Delia's eye, but Margery did not seem alarmed.

"Good." She talked on while Delia ate her food, about when there were sweetmeats in the kitchen and which cooks were the friendly ones. She told Delia which sewing maids were friendly and warned her about those who were prone to violence. "Stay away from Johanna. I have personally seen her slap someone on two different occasions."

When Delia had eaten the last of the food, Margery said, "I can see you are very tired. I shall let you go to sleep now. But I will see you in the morning."

"Thank you." Delia did her best to smile. As long as her brothers were still alive, she had hope they would escape. And having another friend made it a little easier to hope.

Geoffrey made it to the palace so early the next morning that he arrived before the changing of the guard. He waited until the fresh guards replaced the ones who had been there all night, then saw his friend Sir Robert, who had trained with him years before. He was now a knight, like Geoffrey, but he guarded the Palace of Westminster, and Geoffrey rarely saw him.

After greeting each other and exchanging small talk, Geoffrey asked, "If I wished to speak to the king, how would I manage it?"

Robert tilted his head to one side and stared at him. "Finally going to complain about what your uncle did to you and your sister, then?"

"Perhaps." Geoffrey shrugged. He could not let Robert know what his true purpose was, could he?

"If you wish to go through his councilors, you should probably approach Lord Chelsey. He would take a bribe more easily than the others."

"But he is also friends with my uncle."

"Oh yes, I hadn't thought of that. In that case . . ." He crossed his arms and appeared to be deep in thought.

"What if I wished to have a chance encounter with the king, something the council and advisors would not be privy to?"

"You mean a planned chance encounter?"

"Precisely."

"I suppose if you . . ."

"What?"

"I'm thinking." Robert stood with his head raised, looking up at the sky.

"Would I be able to sneak into his bedchamber?"

"Not likely. His personal guards are always nearby, and they might run you through before you had a chance to explain what you were doing there."

"Could I speak to him while he's taking his meals in the Great Hall?"

"That is possible." Robert nodded. "That is probably the most likely way to get to him. Do you think you could slip into the Great Hall, past the guards there?" He nodded at the doorway nearest them.

"I think so. But will his councilors be there with him?"

"Yes, and you will not be able to talk to him without them listening, not in the Great Hall."

Would it be worth it to talk to him if they could not speak privately? If it was his only chance to talk to the king, he would have to take it.

Geoffrey thanked his friend for his advice and information. They stood talking until Sir Robert's commander came by.

Geoffrey walked to the Great Hall. Two guards stood at the door. But the king probably would not make an appearance in the Great Hall for several hours, and only if he was scheduled to eat in there that day. He often ate in his private rooms, or so Geoffrey had been told.

Trying not to draw attention to himself, Geoffrey left to pace the streets, to think through what he should say, and to pray quietly where no one would pay him any heed.

TEN

DELIA MADE HER WAY TO THE TOWER OF LONDON. SHE passed the menagerie of exotic animals that were kept chained and tied for people to come and gawk at. It made her sad to see these animals imprisoned here. They should be out in the wild where they belonged, just as her brothers should be going about their lives instead of imprisoned in Wardroab Tower.

Now that they'd been condemned to die, had they been moved to the dungeon?

Sir Elliot was standing guard at the door.

"Poor, dear Lady Delia." Sir Elliot shook his head, his brows low over his eyes. "I looked for you after the trial but did not find you. You must be so afraid."

"Yes."

He clicked his tongue against his teeth. "I will help you. I will not forget my promise."

"Perhaps the king will pardon them and there will be no need to . . . do what you had suggested."

A guard was passing by at that moment. He turned and looked quite boldly at Delia. She wanted to scold the soldier for looking at her that way, almost as though he suspected her of something improper. Instead, she looked demurely at the ground.

Why did he look at her like that? Was it because she was talking with Sir Elliot?

"A pardon from the king? How would you be able to get that?" He gave her a hard look, almost as if he was annoyed. But why?

"A guard has offered to try to talk to the king for us. He might be able to convince him to pardon my brothers."

"A guard? Who?"

"Does it matter?"

"I just thought I might be able to assist him."

She remembered what Sir Geoffrey had said about Sir Elliot and was reluctant to tell him. "Do you know the king well enough that you could talk to him for us? If the two of you went together, or even separately, to ask the king for a pardon, perhaps—"

"You would need to tell me who the other guard is."

She didn't want to tell him, but he was being very persistent. Surely there was no harm in telling him. They were, after all, both knights, men who were supposed to be honorable. "It is Sir Geoffrey. Would you go to the king with him?"

"Sir Geoffrey." His mouth twisted into a snide smile.

So Sir Elliot disliked Sir Geoffrey as much as Sir Geoffrey disliked him. But then Sir Elliot looked at her and his expression became more sober.

"Did Sir Geoffrey say he knows the king? Claim he could get an audience with him?"

"I don't believe so. He only said he would try to talk to him."

Sir Elliot pointed his finger at her. "Just remember, the king is very difficult to get to. His advisors . . ." He lowered his voice and leaned very close. "They keep a tight rein on him."

"That is what I have heard as well. But isn't it possible Sir Geoffrey could get them to see the truth? Are all advisors corrupt?"

Sir Elliot shook his head sadly. "They only look out for their own interests."

Delia's heart sank. But perhaps Sir Elliot was wrong.

"What else did Sir Geoffrey say he would do for you?"

Delia stared at Sir Elliot's face. He did not look pleased. Was he jealous? It seemed strange that he would not welcome Sir Geoffrey's help.

"I am only asking to see if you think he would help us plan your brothers' escape."

"Oh. I don't know. He never said he would help in that way, but he did not say he would not help, either."

"The truth is . . ." He heaved a sigh before going on. "Sir Geoffrey isn't just a commonplace soldier. In fact, he was set to be the heir to his father, who was the Duke of Strachleigh, but his father was stripped of his title for crimes he committed."

"Crimes?"

"I don't remember the particulars. But it caused his family great embarrassment. And Sir Geoffrey lost his inheritance. He will never be anything more than a knight, a man-at-arms."

If this was true, then how did Sir Geoffrey ever hope to sway the king and his advisors? The king would probably only know of Sir Geoffrey in connection with his father, who had supposedly done something very bad. But that was unfair. Sir Geoffrey was not responsible for what his father had done, any more than Delia and her brothers were responsible for their father marrying a cruel woman.

"Forgive me. I see that you were unaware." Sir Elliot sighed and frowned. Then he took hold of Delia's hand. "I would not disparage poor Sir Geoffrey for any amount of gold, but I just don't want to get your hopes up. The other thing you should know . . . I don't know all the details, mind you, but Geoffrey's uncle was involved in getting his father stripped of his title, and this same uncle is one of the king's advisors. His uncle was sitting right beside the king at your brothers' trial."

Delia felt the blood drain from her face. Sir Geoffrey's own uncle had condemned her brothers? His father had been stripped of his title, so he must have been accused of doing something nefarious, and his uncle had condemned her brothers, who were obviously being wrongly accused. What did this mean?

Her head began to ache at her temples. "I don't understand." The words came out just as her throat closed up.

"It is a complicated situation, I am sure." Sir Elliot seemed to be trying to console her, rubbing her hand with his thumb. "But if Sir Geoffrey's uncle took part in getting his father's—and therefore his—title and lands stripped from him, and since his uncle is a close advisor to the king, how did he think he would be able to get an audience with the king? And even if he did . . . well, let us just consider that the past incidents involving his father and therefore his name will not reflect well on Sir Geoffrey. Unjust or not, it is the way the world works."

She did not doubt it.

"But it is also possible," Sir Elliot went on, "that Sir Geoffrey and his uncle are on good terms, and in that case, why did Sir Geoffrey not go to his uncle before the trial and beg for his favor on behalf of your brothers?" Sir Elliot seemed lost in thought as he shook his head slowly.

A wave of sadness washed over her, proving she had put a great deal of hope in Sir Geoffrey's ability to talk to the king. Had he said he would talk to the king knowing he would not be successful? What were his motives?

She had no way of answering these questions now. And she was here to see her brothers. She would not assume the worst.

"We must pray for God to give Sir Geoffrey favor, to give my brothers favor."

"Yes. Of course. But remember, I am here to help you, Lady Delia." Sir Elliot stood so close, still caressing her hand as he pressed his arm against hers. "Your plight has touched my heart."

Delia's skin prickled and she took a tiny step away from him. "I thank you, Sir Elliot, for wanting to help me and my brothers. May I see them now?"

"Of course." He finally let go of her hand and led the way inside and up the stairs to her brothers' cell. Outside their door stood a guard who had never been there before. But of course they would increase the number of men guarding them, now that they were condemned to die.

Sir Elliot greeted the extra guard with a nod and a grunt, then unlocked the door.

She slipped inside quickly. As she looked at her brothers' faces, her whole body seemed to ache from holding back her emotions, holding herself together. But she couldn't break down in front of them. *I have to be strong*, her mind chanted. *Be strong. Be strong.*

The brothers all came toward her as one and hugged her quite soberly, with no words spoken by anyone. Sobs rose inside Delia's throat, but she choked them down. She could not invite her brothers' pity when they were the ones facing death.

When she pulled away and gazed into their faces, they were all so sad that she said, "Do not give up hope. Sir Geoffrey is trying to get you pardoned, and Sir Elliot has promised to help you escape."

Edwin looked concerned. "I don't want you to put yourself in danger for us, Delia."

"What makes you think you can trust this Sir Elliot?" Gerard asked.

"And what do they want from you?" Berenger asked. "We warned you before, you cannot trust strange men."

"They don't want anything from me. They just want to help, because they know you have been falsely accused."

"How do they know we are innocent?" Merek asked. "Bring that Sir Elliot here so we can meet him. Anyone who truly wants to help you will be willing to meet us." Merek was ever her protector, even though he was two years younger than Delia.

"Sir Elliot sometimes guards the door to this tower and holds the keys. He says he will help you escape if you cannot get a pardon from the king. Sir Geoffrey is trying to talk to the king." But the uneasy feeling gripped her throat again at the thought that Sir Geoffrey's family connections to the king—and therefore his motives for offering help—were confusing.

"Then we won't be beheaded?" David asked. His young face looked so bright and hopeful, Delia felt a stab in her chest.

Roland and David slapped each other on the back and started a mock sword fight, slashing and lunging with imaginary blades.

Edwin spoke quietly to Delia while the other brothers were talking among themselves. "It cannot be very likely that Sir Geoffrey will be able to convince the king to give us a pardon."

"Perhaps not, but Sir Elliot has said he will help you to escape."

"But how well do you know this Sir Elliot? When he brought me the implements for writing those letters, he had a look about him. I can't explain it, but it was a false look. I had the impression he was not genuine."

"Not genuine?" Delia shook her head at her brother, ready to rebuke him for thinking badly of someone who was helping him. But then she remembered the times when she herself had felt uncomfortable with Sir Elliot, when he seemed to lean a little too close or touch her shoulder too often.

"And why would he help us?" Edwin went on. "If he is caught helping us escape, he could be executed along with us."

"I don't know him that well, but—"

"Delia, you are very young and men will take advantage of you. You're so innocent."

"Who is taking advantage of Delia?" Gerard suddenly drew nearer.

"No one. No one is taking advantage of me." Delia crossed her arms over her chest. "Either Sir Elliot will help us or he won't, but I will make sure you escape. I will not allow you to . . ." Delia could not bear to speak, or even think, the words.

"We already have a few ideas of how we can get out," Merek said.

"You do?"

"We can overpower the guard who unlocks the door," Berenger said.

"He is only one, and we are seven," Gerard said. "And then we can get past the guards at the gate."

Delia looked hopefully up at Edwin.

"That is only one of the problems," Edwin said. "We will have to sneak out of the building and out of the gate, and hardest of all, we have to find somewhere to hide once we've escaped."

Delia's heart sank. Yes, they must have a place to hide until the new queen arrived. Then perhaps Delia could manage to convince her to get the king to pardon them.

"Aunt Beatrice is our only hope." Delia clasped Edwin's arm. "If you could get to the abbey, surely she would hide you there."

"It will be difficult to travel so far, all seven of us, without getting caught."

Delia's stomach twisted at the thought. "Perhaps you could hide in a barn or an abandoned house until I could manage to find a cart, and then I could smuggle you out a few at a time."

Edwin frowned. "It is possible, I suppose. But escaping is the first order of business."

"My idea was to go out the window using a rope." David smiled, looking proud.

Roland joined the conversation. "I think Delia should bring us swords wrapped in blankets. Then we can fight our way out." Her youngest brother slashed the air with his hand.

"We do need weapons," Merek said.

"I will see what I can get." Delia was feeling a bit lighter now that they were discussing realistic plans. She might be able to steal a few knives from the kitchen. Or perhaps she could ask Sir Geoffrey and Sir Elliot to get them a sword or two. Would they do that if it meant one or more of their fellow soldiers might be killed?

Her brothers would not go to their deaths without a fight. And she had never known of anything that her brothers could not accomplish, especially the older ones. The thought that she would be able to help them made her heart swell. She suddenly felt a wave of hope that was stronger than her fear.

Escaping would be dangerous for all of them, but to stay here would mean certain death. And if she could not secure their pardon, they would have to leave England forever to avoid living their lives in hiding, ever in fear of being captured.

Of course, the best thing that could happen would be for Sir Geoffrey to convince the king to pardon and release them. She had been praying for that very turn of events with every prayer she was able to send to heaven. For her brothers were bold and courageous, which also meant they could be quite reckless with their own lives.

Yes, she needed Sir Geoffrey to secure a pardon. *Please, God, please let it be so.*

ELEVEN

GEOFFREY WAS AT THE PALACE, WAITING AND WATCHING for an opportunity to speak to the king, well aware there were only five more days before Delia's brothers were set to be executed.

He waited for the guard at the door outside the Great Hall to walk away, as he had watched him do every so often. Then Geoffrey dashed as quietly as possible to the door, slipped inside, and stood there, letting his eyes adjust to the torchlight, which mixed with the dim light coming through the windows, as the sun was hidden behind thick clouds.

The king was sitting at the head of the table on the raised dais, and Geoffrey's uncle Baldric was to his left.

The two guards standing against the wall were staring straight at Geoffrey. He had to look as though he belonged here, had to look nonthreatening. But how could he approach the king or get anywhere near him without the guards pouncing on him?

The young king was also surrounded by older men—his

councilors—and although Uncle Baldric had not seen him, two of the others were already staring suspiciously at Geoffrey.

He started toward the king, striding quickly, his hands by his sides in as benign a way as he could manage. The two guards took a step toward him, their faces grim.

Geoffrey quickened his pace. Only a few more steps.

The guards grabbed him by his arms. He let his body go limp and did not put up a fight. "Your Grace," he cried out. "A word, I pray you!"

All eyes were on Geoffrey as each guard locked one of his arms with theirs. They jerked him backward, nearly knocking him off his feet.

Voices rose. The guards slowed and halted. The king, a skinny figure with pale hair, stood up.

"Bring him to me. I wish to hear him." His surprisingly thin voice was that of a fourteen-year-old boy, yet that boy was the king.

The guards now pulled him forward, toward King Richard, who fixed Geoffrey with a hard stare. As soon as the guards released him, Geoffrey knelt on the floor and bowed before the king.

"Rise and state your name. Are you a soldier in my service?"

"Yes, Your Grace. My name is Sir Geoffrey Grenefeld, and I thank you for hearing me."

His uncle was staring hard at him, equal parts fury and fear in his countenance. He looked as if he wanted to speak, but he said nothing.

"A knight?"

"Yes, Your Grace."

"Speak, then."

"I am the captain who was sent to arrest the seven brothers, the oldest of whom is the Earl of Dericott. Forgive me, for it is not my place to question anything done by my superiors, but I am concerned that these seven brothers are innocent, that someone wanted to take their lands and title that they would rightfully inherit and grant it to someone else, and so they invented these charges against them."

"This is an outrageous accusation." Uncle Baldric glowered but refused to meet Geoffrey's eyes.

"The younger ones are only children—twelve and ten years old. How can they be guilty of treason?"

"Witnesses heard their treasonous words and saw their evil deeds. They were put on trial and they were found guilty." Uncle Baldric turned to King Richard. "You cannot change the verdict. The populace will take it as a sign of weakness and we will have another revolt on our hands, and this one will be worse than the last. You must recall how ruthless the rebels were. You must—"

"That is enough. I am the king, am I not?" The king turned piercing eyes on Geoffrey. "If they were innocent, their friends and family should have offered up some evidence of their innocence."

"They were at their father's funeral when the incident occurred. And they have no living relatives except their stepmother and a very young half brother."

The boy-king gave Geoffrey a slight frown. "My councilors have vouched for the validity of the witnesses and their testimony, and it is my duty to uphold the law and trust their judgments," he said again.

"Take him away," Uncle Baldric said, waving his hand at the guards.

"Wait. Your Grace, can you at least postpone the execution? Until evidence can be found? Please, delay the execution!"

Geoffrey caught a glimpse of the king looking uncomfortable while his uncle sneered, before the guards dragged him the rest of the way out of the Great Hall.

And just that quickly, his audience with the king was over. He had failed.

Delia sat on her stool embroidering the pillowcase with the king's coat of arms, positioned beside the future queen's family coat of arms. The colored threads seemed to mock her as she wove them in and out of the fabric.

"That looks very well indeed," Margery said while looking over her shoulder. "I wish I could embroider as well as you."

"You are very skilled," another maid said, also glancing at Delia's work.

"Thank you." Delia smiled, and they all concentrated on their tasks as Madame Celine came back into the room.

Delia continued the tedious work on the pillowcase, which would show the alliance of King Richard II and his new bride, Anne of Bohemia, who had been Delia's dearest hope of securing a pardon for her brothers. But the queen would come too late.

The trial had come too soon. And the execution was only four days away.

But all was not lost. Hope bloomed inside her again at the thought of their planned escape. Was anything too hard for God? He could help them escape. All would be well. Besides, she couldn't cry tears of despair. Tears were useless, and she could not stain the precious silk of the pillowcase with her salt drops. She would never hear the end of Madame Celine's tirade if she did.

And there was still hope that Sir Geoffrey had succeeded in talking with the king.

It was rather amazing that she could sit here calmly putting needle and thread to fabric, sewing decorations onto pillowcases for a king who probably did not even notice them. Should she not be spending every possible moment with her brothers? She should be helping them plot their escape, finding a place for them to hide, gathering weapons and food and disguises.

She would get paid today, a week's wages. She could simply take her pay and never come back to work. But where would she stay?

She could sleep with her brothers in their cell. After all, no one here knew who she truly was. If she could help her brothers escape, then she could wait for the future queen to arrive and wed the king. Delia could don her more extravagant gown and use Aunt Beatrice's letter to gain access to the queen and then beg for her help.

Should today be her last day as a sewing maid?

Her mind felt cloudy, her thoughts uncertain. She had to think and consider whether this was the wisest thing to do.

But being with her brothers, planning their escape, was all she wanted. She had enough money to buy food for several more days at least. She would collect her pay today, then tomorrow she would take her things and go.

Delia finished her day's work after the sun had gone down and all was dark outside. She went to Margery and whispered, "I'm leaving. Will you please tell Madame Celine I will not be back?"

"Of course." Margery smiled, but it was a sad smile. "I am sorry you cannot stay."

"Thank you for being so kind."

"God be with you," Margery said.

"And with you," Delia replied.

She had taken her most valuable possessions from underneath her bed and packed them inside a cloth bag. Hugging it to her chest, she walked quietly out of the room and down the stairs and out of the palace.

Delia walked at a swift pace through the streets toward the Tower of London. She just had to get there before they closed the gate. A few men looked askance at her as she passed them in the street. Some looks lingered longer than others. But she held her head high and pretended not to be afraid of them. She had somewhere to go, something to do, someone to meet, and she did her best to convey that in her attitude and posture.

Just as she was nearing the open area that led up to the Tower, a man called out to her. "You there! Where are you bound?"

Delia ignored him and did her best to walk faster. *God, please don't let him come after me.* She wasn't sure she could make it to the Tower before he caught up with her if he chose to chase her.

There was the gate. *Thank You, God, it's still open.* The guards were visible in front and they had spotted her.

She entered and moved toward Wardroab Tower. When she got there, she did not see Sir Elliot standing guard, and she felt her spirits sink. It would have been reassuring to hear him say again that he would help her brothers. She might have even invited him up to her brothers' room to discuss ways to escape and places for them to hide.

The guard was new, but she told him she was there to see her brothers. He let her inside and accompanied her to the top of the stairs. They encountered the guard who had been stationed outside her brothers' room, and he unlocked the door to let her inside.

Her brothers looked surprised to see her.

"Are you well?" Edwin asked.

"I am. But is something wrong?" Her heart stuttered at the way Edwin tensed his jaw and pressed his lips together, and her other brothers seemed quite subdued.

"We were visited by Sir Geoffrey this evening."

By Edwin's expression, Sir Geoffrey must have had bad news.

Just then the door opened and Sir Geoffrey walked in. "Forgive me for intruding," he said. "I was across the Tower Green and saw Lady Delia making her way here." He was breathing hard, as if he'd run all the way.

"I was just about to tell her what happened when you spoke to the king," Edwin said.

"Yes, I wanted to tell you myself." Sir Geoffrey's face was as tense as Edwin's.

"You spoke to the king, then?" Delia's heart was in her throat.

"I did. But he was with his advisors. I could not find any other way to get to speak to him." He looked so remorseful, Delia wished she could hide her own devastation at knowing he must have failed to secure a pardon.

"And what were you able to tell him?"

"I told him your brothers were innocent and asked if he would pardon them. I pointed out that several of them were too young to have done the things they were accused of and told him your brothers were at your father's funeral when the crimes were committed, but he said he could not pardon them without evidence of their innocence."

The room was so quiet, Roland's sniff sounded loud.

"I am afraid the king's fear of displeasing his councilors may have been preventing him from granting my request."

"And your uncle? He is one of the king's councilors, is he not?" Delia couldn't help asking.

"He is. But how did you . . . ?"

"Sir Elliot told me."

Sir Geoffrey's mouth twisted in a grim frown. "Yes, my uncle was the one who vocally opposed me. It makes me wonder if he is being paid to make sure your brothers are executed."

"Who is your uncle?" Edwin asked.

"He is Baldric, the Earl of Yelverton. And I have no love for him. He maligned my father, falsely accusing him of murder and disloyalty to the king. Soon after, my father died under suspicious circumstances. Then his title and lands were stripped, and my sister and I . . ."

"You lost your inheritance," Edwin said, a statement rather than a question.

"And my uncle was granted the land that had been taken from my father. He is a greedy man, capable of every level of malice."

Again, the room fell silent. Roland and David looked pale, their eyes wide. If only she could protect them from this dreadful conversation, from the truth of the direness of their situation. Sympathy for her brothers, as well as for Sir Geoffrey, who had been so wronged by his own relative, nearly overwhelmed her. But there was no time for indulging in that kind of emotion. They had to discuss their next step with wisdom and prudence.

"It is our stepmother and her infant son who will profit from my brothers' deaths," Delia said, steeling herself as she spoke that last word, steeling her voice to ward off emotion. "This false accusation has been thrust on them by her, no doubt."

"The only hope," Sir Geoffrey said, "is to find evidence that will prove your innocence." He looked away from Delia to glance around at her brothers.

"But how?" she asked.

"We need to find someone who will discredit the witnesses. Do you know those men who spoke against you at the trial?"

"I've never seen either of them in my life," Edwin said.

"Perhaps they can be persuaded to recant their statements." Sir Geoffrey's expression hardened. "But it will take a combination of physical coercion and money. Do you have any?"

"Money? No." A muscle in Edwin's jaw twitched. "Any coin

or other valuables my father had disappeared after he married our stepmother."

"I have only a few farthings," Delia said. "My stepmother will have paid those men a lot more."

Sir Geoffrey frowned. "Perhaps coercion will work. But I will need more time to track down those two men."

Edwin shook his head sadly. "Among the seven of us, we can't even remember the given and surnames of both men."

"I made note of the names. John Albright of Bedfordshire and Andrew Goddard of Hertfordshire." Sir Geoffrey's face looked older somehow. "The problem is that we only have three days before the execution. There is not enough time to find those men. But if you can escape, that would buy us some time."

Delia and her brothers looked at each other.

"We are ready to escape," Merek said. "We have plans."

"We need a few things, however," Edwin said.

"At least a couple of swords, something to bind wrists together, gags," Gerard said.

"And a place to hide," Berenger added.

Her brothers and Sir Geoffrey spent the next while discussing their escape plans.

"I can get the swords and the rope," Sir Geoffrey said. "And I will try to find a place for you to hide."

"Perhaps Sir Elliot will know of a place," Delia said. "He promised to help."

One of Sir Geoffrey's brows quirked up as one corner of his mouth twisted down. "I would hope Sir Elliot would honor his promise, but we cannot count on his help."

"He said almost the same thing about you," Delia said, watching Sir Geoffrey's reaction.

"Yes, I can well believe it." He gazed into Delia's eyes. "If he does help, that is good, but if he doesn't, we will not need his help. I only say this to reassure you."

Truly, there was something so steady in his gaze. She nodded.

"I will make sure I am guarding the door to the tower that night," Sir Geoffrey said.

"No." Edwin lowered his brows. "You should not be anywhere near. If suspicion falls on you, they will torture you and kill you."

"But you will need me at the door."

"We will knock the guard unconscious and tie him up, just like the guards outside our cell door."

"You could knock me unconscious. Then no suspicion will fall on me."

"No!" Delia stared hard at Sir Geoffrey. Was he so willing to sacrifice his own well-being?

"Why not?" he asked.

"What if they hit you too hard and killed you?"

"Very well. I will say you hit me and knocked me unconscious, and you can just tie me up instead."

"Perhaps Sir Geoffrey is right," Gerard said. "It might look less suspicious if he is tied up. We can smear some blood in his hair so that it looks like we attacked him. If he is found tied up with the other guards . . ."

"Exactly," Berenger said. "After all, someone might remember that he spent all this time here tonight in our room and be suspicious."

Everyone was quiet as they mulled over this thought.

After they talked over more ideas, Sir Geoffrey left. Then they all, even Delia, settled down to sleep.

Delia glanced at her brothers, lying on the floor around her. Somehow they would survive. Somehow they would escape and they would live and not die, certainly not die because of Parnella's schemes. They would grow up and marry and have children, and live to glorify God.

TWELVE

DELIA LEFT EARLY THE NEXT MORNING, AS SOON AS THE gate was opened, to buy food from the market. When she arrived back at Wardroab Tower where her brothers were still sleeping, Sir Elliot was guarding the door. The sun was barely up and the thick clouds kept the light mostly hidden.

"Lady Delia. I am so sorry."

"Why? What has happened?"

"I was worried because there are only two more days . . . I am distraught." He stared hard at her. Was he trying to look compassionate? There was a shrewdness in the way he narrowed his eyes. But perhaps she imagined it.

"Do you know a place where my brothers can hide?"

"Are they escaping?"

Her mouth fell open. Why was he acting as though this was unknown to him? "You said you would help them escape."

Sir Elliot wasn't looking her in the eye. He took a deep breath and let it out, then reached for her hand. "I'm sorry, but I think it's impossible. But I want you to know, when the worst comes, I am here for you."

"What do you mean?" Just the thought that he had accepted that her brothers would be dead in two days made her chest tighten and her throat close up.

"I know. You are frightened. But I will be here to comfort you." He put a hand on her waist and tried to pull her to him.

Delia pushed him away. "I thought you believed my brothers were innocent. You said you wanted to help me, that you would help them escape." Her chest tightened even more. She had truly trusted him. Why was he no longer offering to help?

Sir Elliot stared down at her, unblinking. He opened his mouth as if to speak, then closed it and frowned. "Of course I believe your brothers are innocent," he said softly, touching the end of her braid, which lay on her shoulder. It was a strangely intimate gesture, and she had a sudden urge to slap his hand away.

"They are going to escape," Delia whispered. "We have a plan and will be leaving tomorrow. Will you help us? We just need a place to hide and—"

"Your brothers will try to escape tomorrow?" His eyes went wide and his mouth opened as he leaned toward her, taking hold of her arm.

"You knew if we couldn't get a pardon that we would try to escape." Delia felt the panic rising inside her again. She glanced around to make sure no one was listening.

"Did Sir Geoffrey say he tried to get a pardon from the king?" Sir Elliot shook his head, looking sorrowful. "I told you his uncle was one of the king's councilors who condemned your brothers."

He was changing the subject.

"Yes, Sir Geoffrey spoke to the king, but the king refused." She must not tell him anything else. What if he planned to betray them? He already knew too much. Her stomach clenched in fear.

"You don't believe he actually spoke to the king and tried to secure a pardon, do you?"

Delia simply stared back at him.

"It would be so easy for him to lie and say he did."

"Why are you saying these things?"

"I'm just trying to protect you, Lady Delia." He raised his brows and looked at her sadly. "It is impossible for your brothers to escape. Did Sir Geoffrey say he would help your brothers get out of the tower? You don't believe him, do you?"

"Yes, I believe him, just as I believed you would help us, as you said you would."

"I was only trying to give you hope. But now I fear you must accept the inevitable. I am very sorry to say it, but now is the time to say fare well to your brothers, to invite the priest to give them last rites, and—"

"Stop it. Stop saying these things."

"I care for you, Lady Delia. I do not want to see you friendless. I want you to know I am here for you."

"Take me to see my brothers." Delia turned away from Sir Elliot and faced the door, waiting for him to open it. If she looked at him now, he would know from her glare how angry she was. And it seemed wise, for the moment, to play along with him and let him think she still trusted him, until she could sort out her confused and furious thoughts.

"You are not upset with me, are you?"

"I just want to see my brothers. Will you open the door?"

"Of course." Sir Elliot unlocked the door and led her up the stairs. He stopped outside her brothers' door. Two men stood guard.

Sir Elliot said, "I will walk you back to the palace when you're ready."

"Do not trouble yourself. I am spending the night here with my brothers."

He put his hand on her shoulder. "You will need a friend, Lady Delia, and I am willing to be that friend."

She shrugged his hand off her shoulder. "Open the door."

He seemed to sense her hostility and quickly unlocked the door. Delia pushed past him and closed the door behind her.

Geoffrey secured rope from the supplies in the stable for the escape on the following day. He had a harder time procuring swords. He went into the weapons room next to the barracks. Knights kept their swords with them, but occasionally a new man-at-arms whose training had not included sword fighting would be given a sword so that he could receive instruction. Therefore a small store of swords was kept locked inside the weapons closet. He finally managed to procure the key and take two swords.

He carried the swords and rope wrapped inside a blanket tucked under his arm. He took them up Wardroab Tower to the boys' room and bid them hide them until they were needed.

Next, he went into the city in search of a good hiding place for eight people.

As he wandered the streets of London, searching the less traveled byways and alleys, he thought of all he was risking to help this young woman and her seven brothers, people he had only known a few weeks, people he did not know well now. He could easily lose his position as a captain in the king's guard, a knight of the realm. He'd already lost his inheritance. He'd have nothing if he could no longer serve the king as a soldier.

More importantly, he could be killed during this endeavor, or publicly executed if it failed. And then where would his sister be? Alone, with no one to care for her.

Was he doing this for Lady Delia? Had he lost his head over a pretty face and innocent-looking eyes?

He did feel something for Lady Delia, and certainly she played a big part in the reason for his actions. But he was doing this because it was right. It would be wrong, ignoble, and in violation of his vow to fight evil if he did nothing to save these young men. For he was now convinced that not only her younger brothers were innocent, but all of them were. From all that he had observed of them and of how they treated Lady Delia, they were good men with unselfish hearts, which were not easy to find, especially among peers—and he could not bear the injustice of it if they were executed. He had to help them. His conscience, his sense of duty, would not allow him to do otherwise. Besides, he could sympathize with their situation. He had seen his own future snatched from him and there had been no one to stand up on his and his father's behalf.

He had to help them because, though he might be betraying his king's wishes, God was his ultimate authority. He recalled the Scripture: "I tell you, My friends, do not be afraid of those who kill the body and after that can do no more. But I will show you whom you should fear: Fear him who, after your body has been killed, has authority to throw you into hell."

He rode his horse near the docks and followed the river. He peeked into a few warehouses that seemed empty but saw they were indeed being used. Eventually he came to a street where the houses were old, the shutters broken and poorly mended. A rat ran down the cobblestones, then darted into a hole in the wall. One house in particular looked dark and abandoned.

Geoffrey dismounted and knocked. There was no answer. He tried the door and it opened. He stepped inside.

The windows were closed, but a bit of light came in through the cracks in the shutters. Everything was covered in dust and cobwebs, and there was very little inside besides a fireplace at one end of the room and a couple of stools. A few odds and ends were scattered over the floor. There was a second story, so he went up the rickety steps and found two straw mattresses, a cot, a chair, a woolen cloak, and another fireplace. He walked over to the nearest mattress and ran his fingers over it. It was covered in dust.

His heart lifted. Had God shown him to this house, intended for him to find it? Obviously no one was living here from the level of dust covering everything.

Geoffrey went down to the door and looked outside. This house was at the end of the street, with only a large warehouse—the last one along the Thames—behind it. The street was quiet.

He watched for several minutes but no one came by, nor did he hear so much as a baby crying.

He stepped out, remounted his horse, and rode back to the Tower of London so that he could fetch Delia and show her the hiding place he had found.

Just as the sun was going down, there was a knock on Delia's brothers' door. A key grated in the lock, and Sir Geoffrey asked if he could come in.

Delia had been talking with her brothers about how Sir Elliot had gone back on his word and refused to help them and how dependent they now were on Sir Geoffrey.

"I found a place," Sir Geoffrey said as her brothers gathered around him.

The relief that flooded her at his words, at the look of confident assurance on his face, made tears sting her eyes. She turned her back on them while she struggled to control herself.

"Lady Delia," Sir Geoffrey said. "Come with me now so I can show you the place I found. Then you will be able to lead the boys there."

Delia desperately wiped at her eyes. She nodded and said, "I'll be right there."

She took a deep breath and blew it out. She deliberately forced her thoughts away from Sir Geoffrey and tried to think of her brothers, of their plan for the following day. But that also brought up strong feelings.

"Lady Delia?"

Sir Geoffrey's voice was so near, it made her jump. He stood just behind her shoulder.

"Forgive me for startling you."

"I'm not startled." Delia continued to take deep breaths and exhale through her mouth, trying to regain her composure.

"All will be well," Sir Geoffrey said, his voice still low and gentle, reminding her of how he'd comforted her just after her brothers' trial, when he'd found her sobbing. How humiliating for him to find her crying again.

Roland said in a loud whisper, "She's worried about us. That's why she's crying."

"I am not crying." Delia shook her head, turned, and faced Sir Geoffrey and her brothers. She was relieved that he'd found a place for them to hide, so she turned all that relief into the brightest smile she could muster.

Sir Geoffrey didn't say anything, but he was also smiling, a soft expression in his clear blue eyes.

"I am ready to go if you are." She held her head and shoulders high but couldn't quite hold his gaze. Looking into his eyes might invite more tears to flow if her thoughts again went to how grateful she was for all he was doing for her brothers.

"Let us go, then," Sir Geoffrey said.

They made their way down the stairs and to the door. When they knocked to be let out, she was startled to see Sir Elliot standing there.

"I was told you were here. Shall I escort you—" Sir Elliot's gaze rested on Sir Geoffrey.

"Sir Geoffrey is escorting me." Delia was filled with regret for telling Sir Elliot that Sir Geoffrey was helping her and her brothers to escape. She no longer trusted Sir Elliot, and no doubt Sir Geoffrey would not appreciate her giving Sir Elliot the information that her brothers were escaping tomorrow.

Sir Elliot and Sir Geoffrey were standing eye to eye. Then Sir Elliot said, without shifting his gaze from Sir Geoffrey, "Lady Delia, you should not trust this man."

"Why should I not?" she said, but her words were drowned out by Sir Geoffrey's reply.

"Should she trust you? What are your intentions toward Lady Delia?"

"My intentions? What are yours?"

Sir Elliot and Sir Geoffrey glared at each other, now standing so close their noses were almost touching.

Delia's stomach tightened. Would the two men come to blows?

Thirteen

"Hearken to me," Delia said in her sternest voice. "Do not draw attention to yourselves and thus endanger my brothers with this feuding. Excuse me while I do what I can to help my brothers."

Delia hurried past them. She could find a place for her brothers to hide, could she not? She didn't need either of the knights.

But how would she buy a cart and donkey to move her brothers, to keep them from being seen? She didn't have enough money. She might have to steal a cart. Or perhaps they could make it to Rosings Abbey without getting caught. If God helped them, they could do anything. If God was for them, who could be against them? God's purposes would be accomplished, whether by many or by few, whether by man or by woman.

The blood was pumping through her veins as she passed alone through the gate that led into town. She was walking along the lane when she heard footsteps behind her. She looked over her shoulder as Sir Geoffrey caught up with her.

"What has Sir Elliot been telling you?" Sir Geoffrey asked abruptly.

"He had said that he would help my brothers escape, but now he says he will not. He is not true to his word, and he says it is inevitable that they will be executed. He only wants to help me after they are dead." Her voice rose and she realized she was quite angry. How dare Sir Elliot say he would help them escape and then, when the time came to help, pretend he'd never meant what he said?

Sir Geoffrey stared straight ahead. His mouth was set in a grim line. "What did you tell him?" He turned to look at her while they walked. "Did you tell him our plans?"

What *had* she told him? "I didn't tell him any details, but I did tell him we were escaping."

Sir Geoffrey continued to stare straight ahead. Her stomach sank to her toes at the angry look on his face. "I'm sorry. I realize what a terrible mistake I made by trusting him. I shouldn't have told him anything."

"It will be all right. I do not blame you, I blame Sir Elliot. And he would have guessed as much anyway."

"Do you think he will tell someone?"

"I'll make sure he doesn't."

"But if he's questioned after we get away . . ."

"He'll have to say that he doesn't know where you are, because he will not. If he tries to accuse me, I'll say he's lying and he was the one who was offering to help you escape."

Delia's head was beginning to ache, like a hammer was pounding in her forehead. Sir Geoffrey turned down a street that followed close to the river. He was walking fast, but she matched his pace and kept up.

They were passing an alehouse along the wharf. Men were standing outside, some leaning against the doorpost, others against the outside wall.

"You there!" one of the men called.

"Caught a pretty young miss, have you, soldier?" someone else called out. They all guffawed as Delia and Sir Geoffrey walked past.

"They won't harm you," Sir Geoffrey said. But he nudged her gently with his arm.

Delia took the proffered arm, slipping her hand inside the crook of his elbow.

"Remember how we got here?" he asked.

"Yes. We are following the river."

"Pay attention because you will have to know where to go, how to show the boys the way."

Delia nodded. They followed that street a little farther, then turned left, then right, down two more streets. She went over the directions in her head, memorizing them. Then they came to the end of the street they were on.

"This is it." Sir Geoffrey's voice was soft and quiet as he stopped in front of a house, the last one on the street. He helped her up the steps and inside as if he owned the place, then closed the door behind them.

It was completely dark inside. She clutched his arm. But then she was able to make out shapes and tiny cracks of light coming into the dingy room.

"Do you think we can stay here?"

"No one seems to be living here or taking care of the property."

"What about these things?" Delia pointed to a pile of candles and matches stacked against the wall next to some firewood.

"I brought those earlier today. Upstairs you will find blankets and pillows and a small cot. There are two mattresses, but they are rather dusty, and I cannot attest to whether they are laden with bedbugs or lice. I did strew some lavender and pennyroyal on the mattresses and the floor, as our old nursemaid used them to keep away lice and other pests."

"That is very thoughtful. I thank you." Indeed, it was very kind of him to take so much trouble for them.

"Are you all right?" He was staring at her, and she realized she'd been rubbing her temple.

"Just a headache. I am well enough."

He bent to bring his eyes level with hers. "Perhaps a few sips of wine would help."

"No, I am well. And I am very glad you have found this—"

Delia jumped as a shout sounded from out on the street, then another and another.

Sir Geoffrey strode to the window and looked out through a crack in the shutter.

"Can you see anything?"

"Only some drunken seamen headed back to the docks."

The voices grew distant as the men must have moved off.

Delia shook her head and put her hands to her cheeks. "Forgive me. I had a sudden image of soldiers coming in and arresting us. Very silly." She smiled, but inside she was still quaking.

"Not silly at all, not after all you and your brothers have experienced in the last few weeks."

Her mind shifted to when he had comforted her while she was crying. She wished he was standing closer. She never would have been brave enough to lay her head against his chest, but she imagined how nice it would be if she did. The way he was looking at her, the way his eyes met hers, made her want to look away from the intimacy of it but also created a strange longing inside to get closer.

"I know how it feels to have everything in your life change in a moment."

"You do?"

"It happened when my uncle falsely accused my father of disloyalty to the king, of wanting to give the throne to someone else. My inheritance was taken. One moment I was destined to be a duke, and the next my father was dead and I was nearly destitute, nothing but a soldier, with a younger sister to look after who suddenly had no inducement for anyone to marry her."

"That is a grievous injustice." How it must have hurt him to see his family name falsely maligned, to lose everything to an evil relative's selfish gain. Yes, Delia understood how that must have felt.

"I used to think God would not allow terrible injustices to stand, that He would protect the innocent, right the wrongs, pay back those who had mistreated my father, my sister, and me. Every wrong, every lie, would be brought to light and made right.

But now I realize that even though God is good and just and He will eventually make all things right, sometimes wrongs are not made right in this life."

She wanted to argue with him, to tell him he was taking a gloomy view of things, that all would be made right in due time. But she did not know that. Indeed, she was afraid he was right.

Certainly it was unfair for her brothers to be falsely accused and imprisoned, to have to sleep on a cold, hard floor and run for their lives. Certainly there were others who had been falsely accused and even beheaded by this king and his advisors, and by previous rulers. And no doubt it would happen again.

"Where is your sister now?" Delia asked.

"Amicia is in a convent on the Continent. We have no other relatives who could take her in, none that I trusted. But she is safe where she is, though I think rather unhappy and lonely." A look of pain flashed across Sir Geoffrey's eyes, but he seemed to quickly suppress it.

"Forgive me. I've made you sad with my wretched tale of woe." He smiled, as if to make light of his troubles, then he frowned and took a step toward her.

"Not at all. I'm very sorry about what happened to you. It was wrong, and you did not deserve that, and I am sure your sister did not either."

He was standing very close now. She still longed to lean into him, but even more, she longed to press her hand to his cheek, to comfort him.

She imagined what it would be like to kiss his lips.

Could he read her thoughts? The way he was looking at her,

she couldn't help but wonder, because he was also looking from her eyes to her lips and back again.

Delia took a few steps back, putting some distance between them, as she pressed her hands against her warm cheeks. "I suppose we will need to be quiet in here, until we know if the owner lives nearby."

"I asked a neighbor when I brought the candles. They said the owner died a year ago and no one knows who owns it now. They think the man had a son, but the son has not been seen in several years. You shouldn't be here long, but you will have to be careful not to draw attention to yourselves. Only build small fires, and don't let any burning candles be seen near the windows."

Delia nodded.

"I'm sorry it isn't more comfortable and doesn't have more furniture."

"It is much better than I expected. I anticipated an old barn, bedding down with mice and cows and horses. No, you have found a very good place. I am sure my brothers will be very grateful. As I am." Truly, her heart was full as she gazed back at him. He was risking his life to help them, and she could never repay him.

"I could not do otherwise. I feel as if God pressed you on my heart, directing me to help you."

He had an expression of openness and humble sincerity on his face. When had she ever seen such a look on a man? On one or two of her brothers' faces, perhaps.

"I am very grateful to God and to you. I don't know how

I could have made the arrangements for their escape without you. And I don't know how I could live if . . . if I didn't have my brothers."

"Well, tomorrow is the big day. We have not succeeded yet, but if God is willing, we shall."

"My brothers are very confident they can overpower the two guards outside their door with the weapons you were able to bring them."

"If I am able, I shall arrange to be one of those guards."

"No, that is not a good idea." Delia shook her head. "You will implicate yourself, or at the very least, you will bring suspicion on yourself. No, you must stay far away."

"I might be able to help, in case something goes wrong."

Her stomach twisted at the thought.

He opened his mouth. Then closed it. He sighed and said, "The truth is, any number of things could go wrong."

Of course she knew the guards could very easily injure or kill one of her brothers.

"But if I'm one of the guards, I won't be able to help you once you are out of the tower. So perhaps it will be better if I'm on the outside." He seemed lost in thought. Then he said, "Either way, we decided you should attack the guards right when the sun goes down, just after the guards change, so that it will be twelve hours before the new guards come on duty and find you missing."

Delia nodded. "We will."

And without another word, they both started walking toward the stairs to leave.

Delia held on to Sir Geoffrey's arm all the way back to the

Tower of London. When they arrived at her brothers' prison tower, Sir Elliot was gone and another guard was there in his place. Sir Geoffrey greeted him as if he knew him, then unlocked the door himself. He escorted Delia up the stairs, nodded to the guards at the top, then said fare well as she went inside.

She looked back at him, and he met her eyes. She felt a sudden impulse to throw herself in his arms, but the guard closed the door on her and locked it.

Delia slept fitfully on the floor of her brothers' cell. She awoke with a start, clutching at her own throat. She'd been dreaming their escape had gone awry, that they'd been swarmed with guards and one had started choking Delia while the others attacked her brothers.

She squeezed her eyes closed and lay back on the floor, pillowing her head on her arm. *God, please help us*, she prayed for at least the hundredth time. *Don't let us be overcome, and don't let us seriously injure anyone.* After all, the guards were only doing their duty. Still, her brothers were worth fighting for, and if she had to save one of her brothers by killing a guard, she would do it.

Not that her brothers would allow her to fight. They would keep her behind them while they used the swords and knives that Sir Geoffrey had managed to smuggle to them.

Finally, after Delia had lain awake for what seemed like several hours, the sun arose.

The day progressed very slowly. She and her brothers spoke

in low voices, jumped at every noise, and looked at the sky through their one tiny window.

As the afternoon wore on, her brothers stopped going through their plans, how they would attack and fight. Edwin paced with a brooding but tense expression on his face. Roland and David told stories about climbing trees at home, games they used to play, and memories involving various servants and stable workers. Delia sat against the wall and knitted. Already she had finished four sweaters—for Roland, David, Charles, and Merek—and was nearly done with the fifth, Berenger's. She had figured out a way to strap her bag of yarn and knitting supplies over her shoulder under her warm cloak, which she would wear as they left the Tower of London.

It was quite cold, and the clouds looming overhead made it look as if snow was imminent.

Gerard went to stand next to Edwin. "What do you think?" Gerard asked.

"If it snows, it could be bad for us. We'll be easy to track." Edwin's voice was low and gruff.

"Or it could be good," Gerard said. "The snow could cover our tracks, if we're not discovered missing for some time."

Edwin nodded, but it seemed more of a nod of acknowledgment than of agreement.

"All will be well," Gerard said. "God will not allow us to be executed."

"You don't know that," Edwin said.

"God hates injustice."

"But He allows it."

Delia knew that was true, but why did He allow it? Was He not sovereign and all-powerful? God omniscient and omnipotent, the highest and holiest, as her priest had said many times? She would rather believe what Gerard had said, that God would not allow this injustice to come to fruition and harm her brothers.

Charles came over and started making jests with Edwin and Gerard, as he never liked to see anyone gloomy and would do or say any silly thing to cheer his sister and brothers.

Delia knitted and prayed, prayed and knitted. But she felt very little peace, her hands shaking and her needles clicking together.

Finally, the sun began to dip. Delia put away her knitting, strapping her bag over her shoulder and letting it hang under her opposite arm against her side. In case one of her brothers suffered a cut, or even if one of the guards did, she put the roll of bandages that Mistress Wattlesbrook had given her at the top of her bag where she could easily grab it.

Edwin and Gerard took out the swords, getting a feel for them, accustoming themselves to the weight of the blades, mentally preparing themselves for the fight ahead. Berenger and Merek wielded the daggers. The four older brothers did not talk as the sun moved closer and closer to setting, while the three youngest—Charles, David, and Roland—talked quietly, strangely subdued.

Delia's nerves under the skin in her arms seemed to jump and shiver to get out. She flexed her jaw, which had been clenching against her will.

"It's time." Edwin looked at his brothers. "Is everyone ready?"

"Ready," they all chimed as her older brothers drew near to the door, their weapons raised and at the ready.

Roland, David, and Charles hung back but kept their bodies between Delia and the door. Knowing they needed to feel at least that much power, Delia allowed them to protect her.

As they had planned, Gerard and Edwin stood at the door waiting for it to open. They both held their swords at the ready. Gerard raised his hand, looking back once more at his brothers. Then he used his knuckles to knock on the door.

Delia heard the familiar metallic sound of the key scraping inside the lock and her heart began to pound. This was the moment. *O God, help us.*

FOURTEEN

GEOFFREY HAD NOT BEEN ABLE TO GET STATIONED AT Wardroab Tower without inviting suspicion and was instead on general patrol around the grounds of the White Tower. As it was, there was nothing he could do beyond watching and waiting. Though what good that would do, he did not know. Undue commotion would draw several other guards, and then he could not help them. He couldn't fight so many. Even if he could, he'd be seen and eventually caught and executed for the worst of crimes—attacking his fellow guards, not to mention treason against his king and country.

He saw Sir Robert coming toward him and nodded in greeting. After a minute or two of conversation, Sir Robert grew more sober as he stared into the distance.

"A sad business, this execution that's happening tomorrow, beheading children." He spat on the ground and shook his head. "I heard they have a young sister, very fair of face, who is staying with them in their prison cell."

"Yes, I heard that too." Geoffrey was pleased he wasn't the only one who thought it dishonorable to execute children. But it was unfortunate that they knew about Delia.

"I might have thought the king would have granted them the stay of execution you asked him for."

So that was known as well. Would he be accused of helping them when they escaped? He wanted to ask Sir Robert how he knew about Geoffrey's request to the king and whether that was widespread knowledge. But although he trusted Sir Robert as much as anyone, he didn't trust him enough to ask those questions.

"I just wanted to at least try to get them pardoned. After all, as you say, some of them are only children and obviously the victims of some plot to take their inheritance, I would imagine."

Sir Robert grunted and nodded. "A dishonorable business."

"Indeed."

"But we can do naught but follow orders, as is our duty."

"Of course."

"I even heard they stationed an extra guard at the boys' cell door."

"Yes, two guards at their door and one at the lowest level."

"No, they added a third guard at their door, as if those poor boys were a threat."

Geoffrey's stomach sank to his toes. "Three guards, you say? Outside the door?"

"Ridiculous, is it not?"

Geoffrey looked toward the west. At that very moment, the sun was sinking out of sight. Could the brothers defeat three trained guards with swords? When they were only expecting to have to fight two?

His heart pounded. He had to go and help them if he could. But what could he do without getting caught and attracting the attention of more guards?

Sir Robert was now going on about some of his soldiers he'd caught drinking and carousing when they were supposed to have been on duty. Geoffrey took a deep breath. He couldn't show distress to Sir Robert. But he had to help them. He couldn't live with the guilt and dishonor of allowing them to be killed.

"I think I will go check on my guards at the gate."

"Shall I go with you?"

"No, no, I will just check on them, make sure they are at their posts."

Sir Robert nodded and Geoffrey hurried off toward Wardroab Tower at a brisk walk.

His heart was in his throat by the time he reached the tower. He greeted the guard at the lowest level.

"Everything quiet?" Geoffrey asked.

"All's well."

"I believe I will go up and check on the prisoners."

The guard opened the door and went inside with Geoffrey. When he did, Geoffrey heard, from somewhere above them, the loud clanging of steel on steel.

Geoffrey drew his sword.

"I'll get help," the soldier said. But as soon as he turned to leave, Geoffrey raised his sword hilt and slammed it down on the back of the man's head. He crumpled to the floor and lay still.

Geoffrey raced up the stairs. When he was halfway up, he heard a woman's scream. The high-pitched sound seemed to pierce his soul, and he said a quick, silent prayer as he took the stairs two at a time.

The door opened and a soldier appeared.

Edwin slammed his fisted hand, which held the hilt of his sword, into the guard's temple. The guard reeled, but unfortunately, he did not fall. He drew his sword, but Edwin beat him back.

The second guard burst through the door. Gerard leapt at him, and they began to cross blades. But then another guard pushed his way into the room.

Delia's heart seized inside her. They were not expecting a third guard.

The third guard raised his sword and struck at Berenger, who wielded only a dagger, the blade of which was not even half as long as the soldier's sword.

Merek, who was also armed only with a dagger, approached the third guard from behind and slashed at his sword hand. The guard snatched his hand back just in time and struck out at Merek. He raised his dagger and blocked the blow.

The soldier fighting Gerard was beating him back. Arms thrashed. Swords swung in short and wide arcs. They took up so much room, Delia and her younger brothers were forced to press themselves against the wall to stay out of their way.

She couldn't see Edwin, but she could hear him in the hall fighting.

She needed to help Gerard, but how? His opponent held him against the wall, their sword blades pressed together.

Suddenly Roland jumped on that guard's back and started choking him.

Delia leapt forward as Roland screamed, "Yield!"

Charles and David had no weapons either, but they grabbed the soldier's legs and, striking the backs of his knees, forced him to topple over backward. Roland landed on his feet and snatched away the soldier's sword. Gerard held his sword point to the man's throat. David went to get the rope to bind the man's hands together.

The guard who was engaging Berenger and Merek with their daggers had them pinned against the wall. He leapt back and was just bringing his sword down when little Roland blocked the blow with the sword he'd stolen from the downed guard. But when the guard's sword hit Roland's, he knocked it to the floor with a loud clatter, disarming her brave little brother.

The guard's face was red, and he roared as he turned on Roland and swung his sword. Roland stared at the descending blade, eyes wide with fear.

God, help!

Edwin advanced toward them, crossing the room in two strides, leaping the last few feet to dive in front of the sword that was coming straight for Roland's head. He did not get his sword up and at the right angle before the guard's blow landed on his upper arm, near his shoulder joint.

Blood spurted from Edwin's arm onto Gerard's face.

Delia screamed.

Gerard pounced on the guard and quickly disarmed him. Merek and Berenger wrestled him to the floor, pounding his face with their fists.

Delia cried out again, but this time she covered her mouth to stifle the sound.

Edwin said calmly, "Tie them up, quickly." He was holding on to his injured arm with his good hand, bending it at the elbow and holding it against his stomach. Blood poured from the wound, soaking his sleeve. His face was pale but he remained upright.

Delia hurried toward him with her roll of bandages. "O God," she breathed. *Please be merciful.*

Her brother's arm looked as if it was nearly completely severed from his shoulder.

Delia's vision began to blacken and her forehead burned. This must be how it felt to faint. But she couldn't faint. Edwin needed her to get the bleeding stopped.

She went to get more bandages. When she turned to go back to Edwin, Sir Geoffrey was in the doorway.

After a quick glance at the guards subdued on the floor, Sir Geoffrey said, "Thank God." But when he saw the blood soaking Edwin's sleeve and the gaping wound, his expression fell. Delia was already applying pressure to the wound with one hand and wrapping it with the bandages with her other hand.

Sir Geoffrey turned away and knelt on the floor, tying up Gerard's defeated foe.

Delia wrapped Edwin's arm as tightly as she could. Then she held his left hand, which he still pressed against his stomach, while she took the second roll of cloth and wrapped it around his wrist and then up to his shoulder, around his neck and back, and around the wrist again. She repeated the action two more times, then tied the ends of the bandage together, making a sling.

The blood had already soaked through the cloth. She went back to applying pressure to get the bleeding to stop. Thank God Mistress Wattlesbrook had taught Delia much about using healing herbs and caring for wounds.

Meanwhile, her brothers were quickly tying up the other guards and putting blindfolds over their eyes, and Sir Geoffrey was nowhere in sight. She'd been so consumed with Edwin and his injury she had blocked out everything else.

"Where is Sir—" She stopped herself before she said his name, lest the defeated guards hear her. But had they not already seen Sir Geoffrey's face? If they were able to identify him, not only could he never serve as a knight again, but he would be executed.

"He went to tie up the guard downstairs." Edwin was even paler, but he still looked calm and alert.

Roland, who stood staring at Edwin's arm, suddenly burst into sobs.

"All's well, Roland." Edwin's voice was gruff but steady. "Be brave. We still have to get out of here."

Roland's sobs ceased and he inhaled a big sniff, then wiped his face with his sleeve. Delia wanted to comfort her youngest brother, but she didn't dare cease her efforts to staunch Edwin's blood flow.

"We need to go, now." Merek was always quick to take charge.

Delia looked up at Edwin's face. *O God, surely You won't let my brother die.* He'd never done a bad thing in his life, never hurt anyone or put his own needs before someone else's.

But his arm was so badly injured. The thought of him losing it made her feel sick. But she wouldn't think about that. As long as he was alive, she would be grateful for that.

"Come, Delia. We must go." Edwin looked so brave. She went before him toward the door. Gerard also hung back, making sure all the guards were secured, allowing all of his brothers and Delia to go before him out of the small cell where they had spent weeks imprisoned together.

Once they were out in the hall, they descended the stairs, with no sound except their footsteps.

Delia heard Sir Geoffrey's voice, soft and low, at the bottom of the stairs. He must have been talking with Berenger, who was leading their group. Edwin was just behind Delia, and his breathing sounded labored. He had to be in tremendous pain.

Another wave of sickness washed over her. But she would not be overcome by it. She'd be mortified to draw attention to herself when Edwin was so severely injured.

Berenger was saying, "You can't let yourself be seen with us. Let us tie you up. It's the only way to keep suspicion off you."

Berenger was right. Sir Geoffrey must not be caught helping them.

"We have to get Edwin to a surgeon," she heard Sir Geoffrey saying as they got closer. "I know a good one." He held out a hand to Berenger. "Let me check and make sure no one's around."

Delia's heart seemed to get stuck in her throat. If Sir Geoffrey was seen coming out of this tower, he'd surely be arrested later, once it had been discovered that they had escaped. But he had already gone out the door, and it shut behind him.

She turned to Edwin. "Are you all right?"

"Well enough."

Her stomach churned and her chest ached. She'd never seen her oldest brother as anything but strong and brave and undefeatable. To see him in so much pain, severely injured and suffering . . . but she couldn't dwell on that. She had to think about how to help him, how to help all her brothers get to their safe house that Sir Geoffrey had found for them. Besides, he was alive, and that was what mattered.

Sir Geoffrey came back in. When he did, a gust of cold air and a flurry of snow accompanied him. It was snowing. Was that good or bad?

"Go, three of you," Sir Geoffrey said. "Walk past the guards at the gatehouse. Go toward East Smith Field and on the left you'll see a side street called Alewife's Alley. Wait there for me. I don't want anyone to see more than three of you together in one place."

Berenger took David and Roland and left quickly. A flash of whiteness met her eyes before the door closed.

Sir Geoffrey's eyes came to rest on Delia in the dim light of the corridor.

"Let the boys tie you up," Delia said. "You can tell them we hit you in the head and knocked you out."

"Don't worry about me. We have to get Edwin to a surgeon."

"Just tell me where to go and I'll take him. You can't be seen leaving with us."

Sir Geoffrey didn't answer right away. Finally, he said, "I think you should go with the rest of your brothers. I'll take Edwin to the surgeon, then bring him to you. You need to show them where the safe house is."

"But they will suspect you are helping us."

"I will be careful. Besides, none of the guards saw my face. Two of them were unconscious. Another was facing the wall and didn't see me, and Edwin dispatched his foe."

Dispatched him? Did that mean he'd killed him? Delia felt bile rising in her throat.

A man was lying on the floor at her feet. He was tied up, his eyes blindfolded, and some kind of cloth had been stuffed in his ears.

At least Sir Geoffrey was taking precautions.

She continued in a hushed tone. "You should get away while no one is looking. No one will know you were here. If you go through the gate with us, the guards at the gatehouse will see you."

Her four brothers were completely quiet, then Edwin coughed softly, weakly. Was he losing too much blood?

"Very well. Take Edwin to the surgeon, then find the others in Alewife's Alley and lead them to the safe house. Now, let Edwin lean on you. Keep your hood pulled low over your face and go straight through the gate without looking in any direction. Once you're out, turn toward London Bridge. The surgeon's house is the one with the red rooster sign. Ask for Brewster. Don't give him your names. Choose some false name if you have to. I will be there soon. Wait for me there, and if I am detained, leave Edwin at the surgeon's and make your way to the safe house. But Edwin must have his arm tended by a surgeon who knows what he's doing."

"If you are detained?"

"Don't worry. I'll be there." Then he added quietly, "If the Lord is willing."

O Lord, please be willing.

"Let us go," Edwin said.

Delia flipped Edwin's hood over his head, then pulled up her own. Holding on to Edwin's good arm, she opened the door of the tower and stepped outside.

FIFTEEN

GEOFFREY WATCHED DELIA WALK OUT WITH EDWIN. THE snow would show their footsteps, but if it continued snowing and didn't stop, it would also conceal them, as long as no one knew they had escaped right away. That was the key, was it not? That their escape go unnoticed for a while.

Poor Edwin. He was injured very badly. It was highly doubtful his arm could be saved. And Geoffrey only trusted an excellent surgeon to save his life.

He turned to the last three brothers, who waited quietly beside him. Any minute the guard at their feet could awaken and start trying to get free from his bonds. Though the door was thick, he might yell loud enough to be heard.

"Go and meet your brothers in the alley. Lady Delia will come soon to show you the safe house. Do you remember the way I told you to go?"

"We remember," they said.

They went out into the snow. Geoffrey stood praying for only half a minute before he took a deep breath, pulled the hood of his cloak over his head, and stepped out into the snow.

No one seemed to be about. After all, Wardroab Tower was on the east side of the Tower of London complex of buildings, and its entrance was near the wall and therefore more out of the way and hidden from the men-at-arms who guarded it.

As Geoffrey strode toward the gate, he saw bright-red spots of blood on the snow, a drip here, a drop there, all the way to the gate. Would the guards notice Edwin's bloody arm? They would certainly take note of the bright-red blood in the snow. They would stop him and question him.

Geoffrey's heart was thumping hard against his chest. The tiny flakes of snow were fewer and less thick than before.

He forced himself to walk slower as he neared the gate. Two men-at-arms stood guard. Geoffrey tried to look as if he had no cares and nowhere to be. The men stared at him but did not speak to him. Geoffrey knew who they were, but they were not in his company. He walked on.

Once out of sight of the guards, he quickened his pace. He saw the trail of blood in the snow and deliberately trod on the drops, hoping to hide them, but when he looked back, he could still see the blood, bright red against the compacted snow.

He was nearly to Brewster's when he spotted Lady Delia and Lord Edwin in a crowd of people on the street ahead of him.

Geoffrey did not know if he could trust Brewster to keep their visit a secret, especially if the king's guards questioned him.

He might figure out who Edwin and Delia were and report them. But Geoffrey knew him to be a very skilled surgeon.

Edwin's need was so great, they would just have to take that chance.

Delia was alarmed at the amount of blood dripping from Edwin's elbow. But she could see the red-and-white barber pole ahead, signifying that it was a surgeon's home, and the sign of a rooster, indicating this was Brewster's. She was relieved, as her greatest fear was that Edwin would lose all his lifeblood and die. Mistress Wattlesbrook once said, "When a person bleeds overmuch, he fades away and his spirit leaves him."

Would the surgeon be able to staunch the flow of blood? Delia knew yarrow root was good for stopping the bleeding, but would the surgeon know this also?

Delia couldn't stop thinking about Sir Geoffrey. His life was in as much danger as theirs, and she couldn't bear the thought that he might be killed while helping them. But she was so grateful for his help at the same time.

Edwin's breathing sounded more and more labored, and he was so weak he could barely walk, his face so pale as to be devoid of color. Was this what Mistress Wattlesbrook meant about fading away?

Sir Geoffrey was suddenly by her side. He leaned so close she could feel his breath on her cheek. "Can you find your way back to the alley where your brothers are hiding?"

"I think so."

He repeated the name of the alley and the street it was adjacent to.

"Yes, I'll find it."

"Very good. I'll stay with Edwin and bring him to you later tonight. I might have to borrow a cart, but I will get him there."

"I cannot possibly thank you enough," Delia said, allowing Sir Geoffrey to take her place next to Edwin and prop him up. "I am so very grateful."

"Just keep praying."

"Of course."

Sir Geoffrey put an arm around Edwin and pulled him forward, guiding him toward the sign with the red rooster. He opened the door and they disappeared inside the dark half-timbered building.

Delia had no choice but to turn and go to the rest of her brothers. She trusted Sir Geoffrey to take great care of Edwin.

Had anyone at the Tower discovered they were missing? Would the guards have been found tied up? Would they know Sir Geoffrey had helped them? Surely he would be missed from his duties and they would deduce that he had helped them escape.

Delia's thoughts twisted and tangled themselves around all the terrible things that might happen. What would she do if her brothers were caught? How could she bear it if Edwin died? Sir Geoffrey could very well be executed for helping them escape. How could Delia live with herself if she caused that man's death?

But she should be looking for Alewife's Alley. Had she passed it? The swirling snow was heavier now, changing the look of everything. She glanced all around. Where was she?

The snow was good in one sense. It would cover their tracks and Edwin's blood. *O God, help me find that alley. Help me find my brothers.*

Finally, she recognized some buildings and was more certain where she was. When she saw the sign for Alewife's Alley, her heart lifted.

From underneath her hood she scanned the people milling about. She was afraid to turn her head, afraid of looking suspicious in case someone was watching. But she saw no guards, so she proceeded down the alley.

Her brothers were huddled together at the other end, barely visible in the dark, narrow street. But when they saw Delia, they hurried toward her. She threw her arms around Roland and David.

Gerard said quietly, "We will follow you to the house, but not all together. We will stay several feet behind each other. Roland can walk with you. Then David and Berenger will walk together, just behind you, then the rest of us." Her usually calm brother spoke quickly, his tone tense.

"I will walk slowly, then."

"Not too slowly. We will keep up. Just walk at a normal pace."

Delia nodded. "Let us go."

"If anyone loses sight of the person in front of them," Gerard said, "stay where you are and we'll come back and find you."

Everyone agreed, so Delia and Roland set out, leading the way.

Delia kept her arm around her little brother as they walked.

It was cold, and though he wore the sweater she had knitted for him, he was shivering. She thought of what would happen to him if they were caught . . . *Slowly*, she reminded herself. *Don't walk too quickly.*

They moved through the street. A few people hurried past them to get where they were going in the dark, as the sun had now completely set and the snow clouds had blocked out any light that might have been visible. As she walked around one corner and then another, the temptation to glance over her shoulder became a physical ache across her back. But she resisted and kept a steady pace, one foot in front of the other. But what if she couldn't find the safe house?

Suddenly she realized nothing around her looked familiar. Had she gone too far? Had she missed the street? She'd never lived in London, was unfamiliar with it, and she'd only been to this house once. Would she have to turn back?

Her heart pounded against her chest. After all they had done, would Delia fail them and be the cause of their demise? She began to sweat under her arms and around her neck underneath her cloak.

O God, don't let me fail my brothers! Help me, God.

Then she recognized a building with tiny panes of glass in the uppermost window. She held her breath, searching for something else that looked familiar. When she saw the sign for the street she was looking for, the breath went out of her in a rush. She pulled Roland along and soon found the house. She opened the door slowly, so that the boys behind her would be sure to see where she had gone. She and Roland went inside.

Delia moved through the darkness to where she knew the candles were. She lit one and smiled at Roland. They stood waiting and watching the door. Soon Berenger and David entered, then Merek and Charles, then Gerard came in last, closing the door behind him and shaking the snow from his head and shoulders.

The tightness in her chest lessened now that they were in the house. Gerard and Merek lit another candle and went upstairs to make sure they were alone.

"Do you think we can risk starting a fire?" Berenger leaned toward the fireplace, then used his foot to nudge the half-burned log still lying on the grate.

"I think it will be all right. But Sir Geoffrey said we should only build a small fire and not let any light be visible through the windows."

The windows held glass panes, but not all were covered, as some of the shutters were broken.

"Let's see if we can find something to cover the windows." Gerard went looking for some cloth while Berenger set about making a fire.

Delia found a slightly damaged but serviceable broom to sweep the dusty floor.

Her brothers moved about the borrowed hideout, gathering the things they could use.

"I've thought of a way to prove we're innocent." Merek was walking by, carrying an armload of broken furniture toward the fireplace.

"What is your plan?" David asked eagerly.

"We hunt down those false witnesses and torture them until they tell the truth in court."

Several of the boys added their ideas for ways of torturing those men. They spoke of how to track them down and what they would say to them.

Would her brothers truly do these things? She knew they were fierce and brave, but would they be capable of torture? But worst of all, they were speaking of leaving this safe place and going out into London and beyond. Such a thing was much too dangerous. If they were caught, they would be put to death.

When there was nothing left to do, Delia sat down against the wall and pulled out her yarn and knitting needles. She had become accustomed to always having her knitting in her lap, and she needed something to keep her hands busy. She was working on Berenger's sweater now, and she prayed silently for Edwin and his horribly injured arm.

Her hands shook, but still she knitted, the needles flying into and around the yarn. She tried not to listen to her brothers and their ideas about how to prove their innocence, as each one was wilder and more foolhardy than the one before. Instead, she prayed to God to keep her brothers safe and to bring Edwin back to them.

Please don't let him die, she prayed over and over. *God, You are a God of justice, a God of compassion. And You know all, and therefore You know that Edwin is a good man who does not deserve to lose his arm or his life. He loves and protects his brothers and me. He loves You, God, and he always tries to do what is right. Please, God, in Your infinite mercy, don't let anything bad happen to him.*

God had allowed them to escape with their lives, and she needed to be thankful for that. Surely He would continue to watch over them and help them prove their innocence. The Holy Writ declared that God hated injustice. She had read it herself from the English-language version her mother had brought with her when she married Delia's father. God was all-powerful and all-knowing. God would not allow them to be so greatly wronged.

She thought of the story Sir Geoffrey had told her, about his uncle falsely accusing his father and stripping Sir Geoffrey of his title and inheritance. She didn't like to think about it, but evil did happen.

Her mother had not been an evil person, and neither were Delia or her brothers, who had suffered the loss of her.

God, I beg You not to take my brothers from me.

The night wore on. With each passing hour, Delia prayed and imagined all manner of terrible things as she waited for Sir Geoffrey and Edwin to come to them. Had they been caught? Were they being tortured at this very moment? Or had Edwin died at the hand of the surgeon and Sir Geoffrey was too distraught to come and tell them? Or perhaps it was too unsafe for him to come to them just now. Were guards swarming the area? If they knew one of them had been injured, they'd surely search the barbers' shops.

Edwin must have been captured.

Her breathing shallowed. Delia's chest tightened and her vision grew dim as her head seemed to spin around and around. She sat up straighter, leaning her aching back against the wall.

She concentrated on breathing until the dizziness went away. She had eaten very little in the last two days.

Roland, David, and Charles lay on the floor near the fireplace, asleep and looking quite peaceful, though they'd gone to sleep without any supper or any promise of anything with which to break their fast in the morning.

Suddenly she heard someone at the door. Was it the king's men-at-arms come to drag them back to the Tower?

Her brothers rushed on quiet feet to the door, watching as it opened.

Sir Geoffrey stuck his head in. "I need the two strongest men."

Gerard and Berenger rushed ahead of the others, but Merek also followed them out.

Delia got up off the floor and hurried to the door, looking out.

The snow had stopped falling. A pale moon shone overhead, offering only the barest bit of light. But Delia could make out a cart. Her brothers and Sir Geoffrey pulled at the blanket and revealed Edwin lying on his side, motionless. Her brothers supported his head and shoulders, then the rest of him as Sir Geoffrey helped lift him off the cart.

Delia held the door open as they brought Edwin in. They lay him on the small cot they had found upstairs. His eyes did not open and he did not move.

"Father God in heaven, please be merciful," Delia breathed, her last word getting choked off on a sob.

"He is all right. He lives," Sir Geoffrey said quickly.

"Thank You, God," Delia breathed. But Edwin was lying

on his right side and his left arm was . . . gone. Her stomach churned. But she quickly pushed away the sick feeling and asked, "What did the surgeon say for us to do for him? I'll fetch him another blanket."

Delia grabbed her blanket off the floor and spread it over Edwin's still body. She laid her hand on his cheek, then his forehead. He didn't feel feverish, and he seemed to be sleeping peacefully.

Berenger mumbled something unintelligible and put his hand over his eyes. Gerard groaned, a mournful sound, and turned away. Merek balled his hands into fists and said, "Someone will pay for this."

"But he's alive," Delia said. "We must be thankful to God for that." She did her best to look cheerful.

Her poor brother, always the strongest and bravest and noblest of her brothers, older and wiser and ever the good example to the rest of them. He may have lost his arm, but at least he was alive. How could she have borne it if he had died?

"Are you sure he's all right?" Delia looked to Sir Geoffrey.

"He is resting. The surgeon gave him some herbs and strong spirits to help him sleep, but he should heal." Sir Geoffrey swiped a hand across his face as he stared down at Edwin. "He's been through an ordeal. The more he can sleep, the better."

She suddenly noticed the dark patches underneath Sir Geoffrey's eyes and the way his shoulders were bowed. He was exhausted.

"Won't you stay here for the night?"

"I cannot. I have duty in a few hours."

Delia felt sick. "Will the other guards be suspicious that you helped my brothers escape?"

"I don't know. I went back to the Tower while the surgeon was tending to Edwin. No one seemed to know yet that you had escaped."

Her brothers were gathered around him, listening.

"I made sure to be seen by several of my fellow guards. With God's help and mercy, I won't be suspected."

God's help and mercy? A traitorous thought rose up, and she did her best to repress it. Wasn't there something in the Holy Scriptures about evil befalling good people?

She remembered reading about a man named Job who encountered many troubles. He'd lost everything he had, even his children. But God took care of Job and blessed him in the end. She knew Edwin and Sir Geoffrey, and they were both good. Perhaps God would bless them greatly in the end as well.

Roland had been awakened when they brought Edwin in, and he was staring down at his brother with an expression of abject misery. "No," he said, his voice a strangled cry. He looked up at Delia, his eyes wide, his mouth open. He shook his head and his lip started to tremble.

Delia enveloped him in a hug, but he didn't allow the embrace for long. He pulled away, wiped his face, and went to the fireplace. He sat and stared into the fire.

Someone was tucking a cloth into her hand. It was Sir Geoffrey.

"Thank you," she whispered and used the handkerchief to wipe her eyes. She had to be strong for her brothers' sakes. She couldn't be crying and indulging her own fears and doubts. Her younger brothers needed her.

"Edwin will be all right," Sir Geoffrey said softly to Delia. "And Roland will be too."

"I know. And I know Edwin is a better, stronger man with one arm than almost anyone else is with two."

"I am sure you are right. Edwin will not let this keep him from doing anything he wishes to do."

Delia nodded. They both watched as Roland stood, wiping his eyes, and went over to Edwin. He laid a gentle hand on Edwin's leg for a moment, then lay down again beside David. He curled his body into a ball, his head touching David's back.

"We will get those who falsely accused us. They will be punished for this." Merek's voice was low and gruff as he stared down at Edwin.

Berenger rubbed his face, then the back of his neck, while Gerard stared unmoving at his older brother's still, sleeping body, the stump of his left arm wrapped with a thick layer of bandages.

If only Delia could have done something to help. She should have found a weapon somewhere, anywhere. If they'd had one more weapon, this might not have happened.

"This is my fault," Gerard said. "I should have been quicker. I should have gotten between that guard and Roland."

"So that you could be lying there instead of Edwin?" Berenger shook his head. "This is not your fault. We all did the best we could."

"I should have been there." Sir Geoffrey's voice was gruff and strained. "I should have come sooner."

Her brothers shook their heads. "No, no."

"If not for you," Berenger said, "we'd all be executed tomorrow."

"We never could have escaped without the weapons you brought for us," Gerard said.

"Yes, we appreciate your help so very much," Delia said.

"I wish I could have done more."

No one spoke. The only sound was the crackling of the fire in the fireplace. Finally, Gerard cleared his throat.

"You may stay and get some sleep."

Sir Geoffrey heaved a heavy sigh. "I would like to stay, to be here and help you in the morning—you will need someone to go out and buy food—but as I said, if I'm not accounted for in the morning, many questions will be asked. I must go back to the barracks."

"Of course," Gerard said, placing a hand on his shoulder.

Sir Geoffrey turned to Delia. He pressed some coins in her hand. "Be careful and try to keep your face covered when you go out. If you think someone is following, don't come straight back here. Try to lose them in a crowded place first."

Delia nodded. She opened her mouth to tell him not to give her his money, to insist he take it back. But instead, she swallowed and said, "Thank you."

"Also, be wary of Sir Elliot. I know you consider him a friend, but I pray you, should you encounter him, do not tell him anything. I fear he is not to be trusted."

"I fear you are right." Delia remembered her last encounter with Sir Elliot. "I would not take the chance that he might bring harm to you, Sir Geoffrey."

He gave a quick nod and turned to leave.

"Sir Geoffrey?"

He turned around. "Yes?"

His eyes met hers with such intensity it made her heart flutter. She imagined walking to him and slipping her arms around him.

Instead, she said, "Be watchful."

"I will." He flipped his hood over his head and went out the door, closing it quickly behind him.

Sixteen

Delia slept near Edwin. Or, rather, she lay near him, for she slept very little, and she checked on him frequently to make sure he was still breathing and sleeping peacefully. When the cracks around the window shutters began to lighten, Delia arose and did her best to disguise herself. She tied up her hair, covered it with a plain white wimple, and put on a clean dress. Over everything she put on her cloak, pulling the hood down low over her forehead.

Her brothers were still lying on the floor. They decided not to build a fire upstairs, so they had brought the mattresses down the stairs and slept all in one room near the downstairs fire. None of them moved while she got ready. Even Edwin still slept, although he had groaned in his sleep a few times during the night. Her heart had squeezed in pity. She'd tried to think of what she could do to help ease his pain, but decided it was best to let him sleep.

Delia opened the door and stepped out into the early morning light.

The sun still had not risen, but she hurried toward the marketplace where she might be able to at least buy bread, hoping a few vendors would be out already.

As she neared the market, a soldier stood ahead of her. He stopped a woman and appeared to be asking her a question.

"I'm just a servant girl," Delia whispered to herself, trying to feign the accent of a rustic, the type who worked as a house servant. "I work on the other side of town. I'm here to buy food for my family who live nearby, as it is my off day."

She kept walking to blend into the crowd and moved as far away from the soldier as possible. But as she rounded the corner of the square where the vendors would be set up, more men-at-arms were milling about, stopping people and asking questions.

They were certainly looking for Delia and her brothers.

Her heart thumped fast and hard against her chest. Should she turn around and go back to the house? Or would that look suspicious? She kept walking, focusing on a booth where a vendor was selling bread. She kept her eyes straight ahead, refusing to look at any of the brightly uniformed soldiers. Finally, she reached the booth.

"May I buy four loaves of barley bread? And do you have anything else?"

"Bread is all I have. Perhaps you'd like a few loaves of this fine white wheat bread?"

Delia shook her head. She paid the man and placed the four barley loaves in her bag that was slung around her shoulder. She would love to buy cheese and apples, perhaps some dried fruit and nuts, but there were so many soldiers about, she needed to go straight home and pray she didn't get halted by one.

She turned to go back the way she had come, but right in front of her stood a knight, complete with quilted gambeson and sword. It was Sir Elliot, talking to someone only ten feet away.

She sucked in a breath and turned quickly on her heel. If only there were somewhere to hide. But in this open-air market-place, there was nothing but cobblestone street and booths. And it would attract too much attention to try to hide behind a booth.

Delia walked toward a cheese vendor. The plump woman saw her coming and greeted her. She began telling her about her various cheeses.

"This is a round of the most delicious cheese you've ever tasted. It is mild but flavorful. Will you have a taste?"

Delia's knees were shaking, her mind on Sir Elliot. Had he seen her? Was he right behind her? Would he follow her? How could she get past him without being seen?

"How much is it?" Delia asked.

"You haven't even tasted it. Here." She cut a tiny piece off an open wedge and passed the knife to Delia, who carefully used her teeth to extract the bit of cheese from the blade. She chewed and nodded.

"Very good. How much?"

The woman gave her prices for various amounts of the cheese. Delia's anxiety rose. The longer she stood there, the longer Sir Elliot had to recognize her. But perhaps Sir Elliot would walk away, or become so occupied with questioning someone that he wouldn't notice her leave.

"I'll take a fourth," Delia said.

The woman happily took Delia's money and handed her the hefty wedge of cheese, which Delia placed in her bag with the loaves of bread. There was nothing left to do but turn around and go home. *God, please let Sir Elliot be gone.*

She kept her head low but peeked up from underneath her hood. She headed toward the street, walking at a brisk pace as she steered herself through the crowd.

Someone grabbed her shoulder. Delia jumped, stifling a scream. Sir Elliot's face was just beside hers.

"You startled me." Delia pressed a hand over her heart. A hysterical laugh bubbled up in her throat, but she let out a burst of breath instead, forcing herself to smile at Sir Elliot.

"I am so very glad to see you."

Sir Elliot leaned so close, Delia jerked away, an instinctual reaction.

"It is good to see you too." Delia's voice sounded quite breathless. She needed to slow her breathing.

"Where are your brothers?" At least he asked the question quietly, but still Delia's heart raced in fear that someone had overheard him.

"You know as well as I do they're at the Tower of London." She did her best to let tears well up in her eyes—not difficult to do in her terrified state—and her lip started to tremble.

"They are not." He looked closely at her face, watching her. "What do you mean?"

"You know they have escaped. You must know. You helped them. Tell me where they are and I shall help you."

"They have escaped? I hope they are safe. Were any of them hurt?" She pressed a hand to her neck.

"We suspect at least one of them was injured in the fight. Tell me, Delia. Tell me, and I will help you." His eyes looked cold, his light-green eyes almost gray.

"I am glad they have escaped, but I know nothing." She shook her head.

"You are lying. If you do not tell me, I shall reveal who you are to all these soldiers here." He glanced around the marketplace.

Delia dared to glance around too. Soldiers were everywhere. She had not known there were so many.

"Why are you being so cruel?" Delia kept her voice soft and low.

"Come with me, sweet Delia," he hissed in her ear, squeezing her shoulder. "Come with me, or I will tell everyone that Sir Geoffrey was involved. He will be executed unless you come with me now."

"Come with you where?" Her heart lurched. What would he do to her? But she could not bear to see Sir Geoffrey killed if she could prevent it. Defying Sir Elliot now could mean death for Sir Geoffrey.

Sir Elliot's smile was wolfish. How had she ever thought him handsome? He was hideous, his eyes as colorless as his skin.

She let him pull her out of the marketplace, still holding tightly to her shoulder. He went down one street, then another. Delia paid close attention to her surroundings so she would know her way out. Somehow she had to get free of this man.

They walked down a narrow street until they came to an inn. Sir Elliot pulled her inside.

Her thoughts raced as she realized why he had brought her here. She had to get away. She couldn't let him trap her inside this inn. Should she scream and hope a bystander would help her? But he was a knight, a powerful man. He could just have Sir Geoffrey arrested. She wasn't sure what to do, but she felt a strange peace come over her, even as her mind stayed clear and alert.

Sir Elliot kept hold of Delia's arm, pulling her along behind him while he sought out the proprietor, spoke quietly to the man, then gave him some coins. The man gave Sir Elliot a key.

Sir Elliot gripped her arm and headed toward the stairs. Delia's heart beat hard. She had to get away from him.

She remembered how brave her brothers had been, how they had fought, how Sir Geoffrey had risked his life to come to their rescue and take out the guard at the bottom of the steps. And she would fight too. She would not allow Sir Elliot to harm her. She would do whatever she had to do to get away from this odious man and get back so she could help her brothers escape.

God, help me, I pray. Come and save me.

She walked slowly up the steps behind Sir Elliot, his hand still holding on to her forearm. When he reached a door at the top of the stairs, he opened it with the key and pulled her inside, then locked it. Delia watched him place the key in his pocket.

"You were always meant to be mine," he said with that wolfish grin. His top teeth on either side were even pointed like a wolf's.

Delia glanced around the room. There was a stool against the wall, a bed, and a ceramic pitcher of water and a small metal cup on a table. Nothing else. But she would find something to help her escape.

Her brothers and all the female servants had spoken about men like Sir Elliot. They had warned her. She knew what he wanted from her. But how would she get away from him? He had locked the door and the key was in his pocket.

Somehow she had to get that key.

Sir Elliot grabbed her other arm and pulled her closer. His lips suddenly came at her.

Delia turned her head and her gaze locked on the pitcher of water.

"I'm not ready." There was desperation in her voice. Did he hear it? "I need a drink of water."

He let her go. He must have been confident she could not get away. His eyes followed her as she walked around him to the pitcher of water. She lifted it. Why did her hand start to shake now, when she needed her strength? *God, help me.*

"You are all mine now," he said, coming up behind her.

She could do this. She would do it.

Delia spun around and slammed the pitcher into Sir Elliot's head. It shattered, sending water all over both of them, but he did not fall to the floor. He bent forward, yelling and holding his head and cursing her.

What was she to do now?

Delia ran to the stool and picked it up. Sir Elliot was drawing his sword and stumbling to one side. She raised the stool over her head and swung it at Sir Elliot's head. It connected with his forehead with a loud crack, and he fell over, hitting the floor with a thud.

Delia screamed. Then she laughed. Her hands were shaking so hard, her breath coming so fast, she bent forward, propping her hands on her bent knees, and tried to slow her breathing and calm herself. But she never took her eyes off Sir Elliot. Would he jump up and kill her with his sword? Any moment he might open his eyes.

She had to get out of there, get back to her brothers.

She stood over his still body. *O God, forgive me if I've killed him. But please don't let him wake up yet.*

Her hands shook as she reached into his outer garment, a wool cloak, fearing every moment that he would open his eyes and grab her wrist. She watched his face as she slipped her hand into a pocket. Her fingers touched something metal and she pulled out the key.

Her hands were shaking so much she couldn't even get the key into the keyhole. It was taking too long. She looked over her shoulder. He still had not moved. Finally, she got the key inside and turned it. The lock clicked and the door opened.

Suddenly she remembered she needed the bag of food for her brothers. She turned and faced the room again. Her bag was in the middle of the floor. Should she go back inside for it? Her heart pounding, she ran in and grabbed it, then ran out of the room.

She could leave the door ajar so someone would find Sir Elliot and prevent him from dying alone in the room from his injuries. But she couldn't have him following her either. Her stomach felt sick at the thought of him waking up and running after her or finding her brothers. If she'd eaten anything, she probably would have vomited. She closed the door, locked it, and took the key with her as she ran downstairs.

Forcing herself to slow to a walk, she moved through the dining guests on the ground level of the inn, her eyes focused on the door. She flipped her hood up and over her head and stepped out into the street.

"Left at the sign of the wild boar, right at the apothecary shop, and left through the marketplace." She repeated the directions over and over, though she kept getting interrupted by memories of her terror, the horror of what he'd been planning to do to her, and the horrible thing she had just done.

That wasn't my fault, God. I had to defend myself.

Sir Elliot had tried to take advantage of her in the vilest way, just when she needed help the most. Men like him were the devil's tools. She did not have to feel bad about what she'd done. She did what she had to do and she wasn't sorry.

She turned left at the sign with the boar.

How could he have treated her that way? Threatening to get Sir Geoffrey killed for helping them, threatening to turn her over to the authorities, willing to let her and her brothers be executed.

Her heart staggered inside her. How terrifying to have made yet another enemy in Sir Elliot—if he was alive. What would he do to them when he awakened? Would he try to get Sir Geoffrey in trouble? Would he chase after her?

She looked over her shoulder. No one was following her, but

a soldier was nearby. He was turning his head in her direction, so she shifted her eyes forward again and kept walking, clutching her bag of food to her chest.

Ahead was the apothecary shop. She turned right. The marketplace was not far away. Her stomach churned as she remembered all the king's soldiers who had been milling around there with Sir Elliot, asking questions. Delia pulled her hood lower over her face and kept her head down, walking straight ahead. Perhaps if she walked with quickness and purpose, no one would stop her or ask any questions.

She turned right and plunged into the rows of vendors and the crowd of people.

Seventeen

More people shuffled around the market now, as the sun had risen above the horizon. Delia saw flashes of the king's colors, letting her know soldiers were about. Why had she not gone a different way, around the marketplace instead of directly through it? She hadn't been thinking clearly. Her mind was so jumbled.

What if she had hit Sir Elliot so hard he never woke up? What would the soldiers do if they knew she had killed one of their brothers-in-arms? No doubt they would treat her very roughly. They'd beat her and drag her back to the Tower of London and lock her away. They'd try her in court and have her executed.

Her heart thumped and her stomach threatened to heave. When she was finally at the other end of the marketplace, she turned left toward the safe house.

When she arrived, her brothers were kneeling beside Edwin's bed. His eyes were open, but his cheeks were red and he looked feverish.

Roland moved toward Delia. "Berenger and Gerard are giving Edwin some of the herbs the surgeon sent with Sir Geoffrey."

"Good. Has he been talking?" Delia threw off her hood and set down the bag of food and went to Edwin's bedside.

"A little."

"I brought some food." She smiled at Roland and pointed to the bag. "Edwin? I'm so glad you're awake."

Edwin grunted. "I am not so glad."

"Are you in much pain?"

"One might think an arm that was no longer there could not hurt, but one would be wrong. I can still feel it."

Delia swallowed. "I brought some bread and cheese. Do you think you can eat something?"

"I don't know."

She took a loaf of bread and broke off a good-size hunk. Edwin held it in his right hand and took a bite. He chewed slowly and finally swallowed. "Thank you, Delia."

Her brothers all stood around, as quiet as if they were standing in church during the Holy Eucharist.

"You were gone a long time," Gerard said. "Did you have any trouble?"

She could suddenly see Sir Elliot's lips coming toward her, feel his hand gripping her shoulder.

"Do you know if they've discovered we escaped?" Berenger said.

Delia glanced at her three youngest brothers. They were staring up at her.

"We should eat now. We can talk later." Delia felt the

tears starting to prick her eyes. No, no, no, she wouldn't think about what happened. She mustn't frighten her brothers. All turned out well. She escaped, and she didn't want to make much ado over nothing. She'd been frightened, but nothing bad had taken place. But the tears continued to gather behind her eyes.

She turned away from her brothers' questioning gazes. "Let us break our fast, shall we? Some bread and cheese will make us feel better." She handed out the loaves. David gave her his knife so that she could slice the cheese and give a portion to each of them.

They ate the bread and cheese quietly, casting many glances Delia's way. She tried to eat as well, but the food kept getting stuck in her throat.

Charles passed her a cup of water. She drank, but water went down the wrong way and she started coughing. Tears squeezed from her eyes, but she could blame it on the coughing fit.

"Delia?" Gerard raised his brows at her. "What happened this morning?"

Delia took another drink of water. But she couldn't put them off any longer. "They know you have escaped. I saw several guards on the streets, mostly in the marketplace, and they were asking people about us."

Suddenly she wanted to tell her brothers everything, even wished Sir Geoffrey was there so he could hear as well. But that was foolish. Still, she needed to tell her brothers.

"Something did happen. I was recognized by Sir Elliot, the knight I thought was our friend. He is not our friend, as it turns out. He tried to get me to tell him where you are, but when I refused, he threatened to tell the other soldiers who I was, and also to tell them that Sir Geoffrey helped us escape."

"That dirty— I'll show him who to threaten." Merek's face was hard and set.

"What happened?" Gerard asked, leaning toward her.

Delia's hands started shaking as badly as before. Should she tell them everything? She'd already alarmed them. She might as well reveal all of it.

"He said if I didn't go with him he would turn Sir Geoffrey in. So I went. He took me to an inn . . . but I escaped." The horror, fury, and dismay on her brothers' faces made her question whether she should have told them.

Merek called him a bad name.

"How did you get away?" Roland stared at her with big, round, innocent eyes.

"I broke the water pitcher over his head." Her voice was starting to shake. "And when he didn't fall down, I hit him in the head with a stool."

Delia started to laugh, as she had done when she knocked Sir Elliot unconscious. Had she gone mad? She was just so horrified and relieved at the same time. But then she remembered the way the stool had felt and sounded as it connected with Sir Elliot's head, and her laughter turned to sobs. He had squeezed her arm so hard it hurt. The feelings washed over her and her shoulders shook. She covered her face with her hands.

"Are you all right? Is he dead?" Gerard's voice rose over her other brothers'. But poor Edwin. He didn't need to hear this.

"He didn't hurt me, and I don't know." She shook her head, pushing back the sobs with a deep inhale.

"I will kill him!" Merek and Berenger said at the same time.

Edwin said something that Delia couldn't make out.

"Let Delia speak," Gerard said.

"I only know he didn't get up or open his eyes. But I got away. He didn't hurt me, and he didn't follow me. No one knows where we are."

The thought of killing a man, of Sir Elliot lying dead from her blows to his head, sent a cold, hollow feeling all through her. But if he was dead, at least he couldn't hurt her or cast suspicion on Sir Geoffrey.

God, forgive me if that is a sinful thought. I never meant to kill him.

Her brothers gathered around her, putting a hand or an arm around her. But she didn't want to take their attention away from Edwin.

"I am not hurt. Only frightened." A sob rose into her throat, but she managed to suppress it. She took a deep breath, calming herself again. "I am well." She wiped her face with her hands and even managed to smile.

"We should be asking Edwin what he needs. Edwin?" She moved closer to her brother's bedside. "Is there anything we can do for you?"

"No," he said quietly. "I am only glad you were not harmed today. And I am sorry we weren't there to defend you." His voice was so solemn and sad, it wrenched Delia's heart.

"Do not worry, Edwin," Delia said, gently touching her brother's forearm. She could still feel her hand shaking, but at least the tremor wasn't visible. "Once we are able to prove your innocence to the king, things will get better."

"Do you think we will be able to?" Roland was looking up at her with wide eyes. Charles and David were watching her as well.

"Of course, Roland. We need to have faith that all will work out as it is supposed to, in our favor."

But even as she said the words, she wasn't sure she had that kind of faith. In fact, her doubts seemed to gain strength every day. She only had to look around her to see the pain that injustice had caused her beloved brothers, the only people in the world she loved—the only people in the world who loved her. Why would God allow that? What possible purpose could it serve?

But her attitude was not right. Her thoughts were rebellious, yet she could not unthink them or stop feeling what she felt.

And what was happening to Sir Geoffrey? Would he be executed for helping them? It seemed more likely than ever.

"We have to find those two witnesses," Merek said, balling up his fist and striking the palm of his other hand. "We'll force them to tell us who paid them to lie."

"Yes," Berenger said. "We'll drag them to the king and make them confess."

"Why would they confess?" Gerard shook his head. "We have to find them and make friends with them, see if they will tell us in confidence who is behind all this."

"We know it is our stepmother," Delia said.

"Yes, but we must have proof." Edwin's voice sounded weak, but he was thinking clearly, at least.

"Perhaps we need to go back to Bedfordshire and find out who actually set the fires and vandalized the property we're accused of destroying and who killed the coroner." Gerard glanced around at his brothers.

"You boys are so reckless, talking of going here and there when you must not be seen," Delia said. "You must stay hidden. There is no way for you to survive if you don't."

Merek stared sullenly at the floor and Gerard at the wall. Berenger pressed a hand to the back of his neck and looked thoughtful.

"We must get the information that will clear us of wrong-doing," Gerard said. "Yes, it is a risk to go out, but we must take that chance, for we cannot prove our innocence while hiding away."

"Let me go. I can do it." Delia held out her hand, pleading.

"No." Gerard looked kind but firm.

"I am sorry to say it," Berenger said, "but it is even more of a risk for you, Delia. Consider what happened today when you only went out to get food."

"That was because I encountered Sir Elliot." Delia could feel the heat rising inside her. "I can avoid him in the future, if he's even alive." The thought that he might be dead, might never be able to harm them again, caused a flood of relief to crash over her.

"There are other guards who would recognize you." Edwin spoke up from his bed.

"How would you travel to Bedfordshire? How will you befriend John Albright and Andrew Goddard?" Gerard shook his head again. "It is not safe for a woman."

"I can disguise myself as a man." The desperation was welling up inside her. "I can do it. I know I can."

Her brothers were all shaking their heads at her. "We can't let you put yourself in such peril." Berenger touched her arm, as if to comfort her, but Delia pulled away from him.

"I am not a child." She almost said, *"And I hate being a woman."* She turned her back on her brothers, bringing her hand up to her eyes.

She'd always embraced being a woman, but after what had happened with Sir Elliot . . . Being a woman made her vulnerable, made her not powerful enough to do what she needed to do to take care of her brothers.

O God, why did You make me a woman? So that men could try to take advantage of me? I am no good to my brothers when they need me the most. Am I only useful for making them sweaters?

The pain inside wrapped around her heart.

An arm came around her shoulders. Her hands were over her face as she struggled to calm her breathing. Finally, she took a deep breath, stilled her trembling lip, and removed her hands from her face. She was surprised to see Gerard was the one embracing and comforting her. Berenger was her most affectionate brother, but Gerard's gaze was also full of compassion.

"You have had a hard day and night. Why don't you lie down and get some sleep."

If she'd been a man, he would not have thought she needed to lie down. But the other part of her was grateful that he seemed to understand she felt shaken.

"I fought him," Delia said, quiet but emphatic. "I didn't let him hurt me."

"I am very proud of you," Gerard said.

"Great work, Delia," Berenger said.

"You have earned a rest," Gerard went on. "Besides, there is nothing to do at the moment."

"What about Edwin?" she whispered.

"We'll take care of him. Go on and lie down."

"This mattress is the softest," David said, motioning her closer to the fireplace.

Should she do what they were asking? Should she allow them to take care of her? She was supposed to be taking care of them. But she was so very weary.

"You will not do anything daft, will you? You won't go out and try to find those men?"

"We need a plan first," Merek said.

"No going out of here at all." Delia pointed a finger at each of them in turn.

"We won't," Berenger and Gerard both said. They were placating her, but she was so exhausted and tears were flooding her eyes. Perhaps all of this terrible injustice that had happened to her family was God's way of humbling her.

If that was true, then it had worked. She felt quite humble at the moment—barely any food, very little money, hiding from dangerous men, her brothers all in grave danger, her oldest brother crippled, and no way of knowing what had happened to Sir Geoffrey.

She lay down and closed her eyes, and as she felt herself drifting, she prayed . . . *God, please don't let anyone hurt Sir Geoffrey.*

Eighteen

Geoffrey awakened to someone yelling, "Escaped prisoners!"

He sat up and quickly strapped on his sword belt like the rest of his fellow captains, knights, and soldiers. He said yet another prayer that somehow he wouldn't be implicated. He'd shown his face to the guard at the entrance to Wardroab Tower just before he knocked him unconscious when his back was turned. Surely he remembered Geoffrey was there, even if he wasn't sure if Geoffrey had been the one to hit him.

Geoffrey was anxious to find out if any of the guards had been seriously wounded. He was fairly certain the one Edwin had fought had been killed. But any of the others might have expired as well.

How his fellow guards would hate him, would consider him the worst of traitors, if they knew he had anything to do with the escape.

It was still dark, the sun not yet above the horizon, as Geoffrey ordered his men to meet by Wardroab Tower. The ones who were ready followed him as he strode the short way across the green.

Geoffrey had no experience with lying. When he was in on a secret, such as when he had played games as a child, he was never good at deceiving the other players. But this was no game. He had to pretend to know nothing of this escape. Delia's and her brothers' lives were at stake. Not to mention his own.

Soldiers were already milling around outside Wardroab Tower.

As he drew near, he noticed the guard whom he had hit on the head. He was sitting on the ground, obviously telling his story.

Would the man recognize Geoffrey? He was new and hopefully didn't know Geoffrey yet, but it would be better not to take the chance.

Geoffrey slipped past him without being seen and went up the stairs. Several other guards were there. They were helping to remove a dead soldier's body. So Edwin had killed him. The other injured guards must have been taken away already.

He stayed inside, pretending to examine the evidence, but in actuality, he was waiting for the guard outside to leave so as not to risk being identified by him.

One of the guards came into the brothers' cell.

"Does anyone know what happened here?" Geoffrey asked.

"I heard they took the guards' swords and attacked them. How the guards let that happen, I don't know. They got away during the night."

"Was anyone else killed?"

"No."

Another guard walked in, and the two began discussing what happened.

"They must have had weapons of their own," the second guard said. "Our men still had their swords."

"How would they have acquired weapons?" Geoffrey asked.

"Someone must have smuggled them in," the second guard said. "They had a sister, I heard one of the injured guards say. She must have done it."

Geoffrey's heart clenched at the thought of these men finding Delia. He should go warn her not to go out. "Does anyone know what the sister looks like?"

The guard frowned. "Some of the men saw her."

"Were the others badly hurt?"

The first guard shrugged. "One appeared to have a flesh wound. The other one just looked embarrassed. They had been tied up and blindfolded. The prisoners are long gone by now."

"I suppose they could have killed all the guards. Would have been safer for them." Geoffrey hoped to create at least a bit of favorability in his fellow soldiers toward Delia and her brothers. And it was true. They hadn't wanted to kill anyone, only to escape. They'd taken extra care not to kill them.

The second guard grunted. Then the two soldiers headed toward the stairs, as if to leave. There was nothing for Geoffrey to do but walk with them.

At the bottom of the stairs, someone opened the door. It was Sir Robert.

The light coming in must have shone on Geoffrey's face, for Sir Robert said, "There you are, Sir Geoffrey. I've been sent to fetch you. Come with me."

Geoffrey's heart raced. Was he caught? Did they know? But he had no choice. He followed Sir Robert as he started toward St. Thomas's Tower. Fortunately, the guard Geoffrey had knocked unconscious was gone.

"Is anything amiss?" Geoffrey was thankful his voice at least sounded calm.

"I only know a Westminster Palace guard just came and charged me with finding you and escorting you to the Chapel Royal in St. Thomas's Tower."

It was a short walk to the tower that housed the king's personal apartments at the Tower of London. Geoffrey had never been inside. His hands were sweating, and he had to concentrate on keeping his face expressionless and his voice calm.

Sir Robert led him into a chapel decorated in bright colors, with a stained glass window overlooking the River Thames. Waiting inside was his uncle, Baldric.

"My nephew, Geoffrey." Baldric gave him a semblance of a smile. "How good to see you again so soon."

"You wished to speak to me?"

"Yes. I am concerned about you."

"Concerned about me?"

"Yes. You have perhaps heard that the Lords Dericott have escaped their imprisonment. They were to be executed for treason today."

"Yes, I have heard."

"I am worried that suspicion might fall on you, since you advocated for them to be pardoned by the king."

"Suspicion?"

"Suspicion that you helped them escape. Of course, I know you would never do anything so dishonorable as that."

Geoffrey's gut twisted. *He's baiting you*, said a voice inside his head. Of course. Geoffrey had to be cautious and consider his words carefully.

"I'm glad you realize I would never do anything so dishonorable." He wanted to let his voice linger on that last word, to convey the irony of his uncle speaking of dishonorable behavior. But he restrained himself.

"It is strange that they were able to procure weapons." His uncle eyed him. "I cannot imagine where they could have obtained swords. Can you?"

Geoffrey shrugged and shook his head, as if the matter hardly concerned him. "I have duties," he said, "and I do not believe my commanding officer knows where I am. I should go."

"Yes, you should go, but, Geoffrey?"

"Yes, Uncle?"

"Take care not to say the wrong thing to anyone. These are dangerous times. If you know where the escaped prisoners are hiding, you would get into the king's good graces if you told us. Who knows? He might even restore your father's title to you."

Why did he want them caught? "These brothers are that dangerous? So valuable to the king that he would grant such a favor to me?"

Uncle Baldric's expression hardened, his jaw clenching. "They were declared guilty of treason against the king. They must be found and executed."

"Of course." Geoffrey's eye was caught by the crucifix on the wall, of Jesus hanging on the cross, His head bowed. What kind of humility did it take to allow oneself to be nailed to a cross, hanging in agony until dead? The contrast between the humble Lord Jesus and his lying, conniving uncle standing in front of him was so stark it took Geoffrey's breath away. He suddenly sank to one knee, bowed his head, and crossed himself.

God, help me.

"Go with God, my son. Godspeed to you," his uncle said.

But when Geoffrey looked up, Baldric had such a cold look of hatred in his dark eyes, he felt a shiver run down his spine. He crossed himself again.

Geoffrey nodded and turned to go.

Why would his uncle take such an interest in the Earl of Dericott and his brothers? He remembered how he'd spoken against them when Geoffrey tried to talk the king into pardoning them. Was there a connection between Baldric and their stepmother?

Geoffrey could almost feel his uncle's hard stare. He would need to watch his back.

During the long night, he had thought of a good place for Delia and her brothers to hide, somewhere away from London, which would be safer. There was a small house on his family's property, hidden in the forest, where no one was living. However, it would be better for Edwin if they waited until he was stronger and more healed from the trauma of losing his arm before moving.

Geoffrey went to his duty station, but his commander ordered him to guard the gate, as most of the guards had been sent to search for the escaped prisoners.

The grizzled older man shook his head. "All this commotion over prisoners who were mostly children. If they had not killed one of their guards . . . But it would not have mattered. Killing the guard only makes it worse for them. But I don't suppose they felt their situation could get any worse, eh?" The man chuckled.

"No, since they would have been executed today." Geoffrey said no more. He could not show any favorability toward them.

Only one other guard stood with him at the gate, and the fellow eyed him until Geoffrey tried to start a conversation. "I have not seen you at the Tower of London before."

"My normal duties are at the palace. I was sent here as reinforcement." He stared at him a moment longer, then said, "Are you not the guard who tried to get the king to pardon those same prisoners?"

Geoffrey did not speak for a moment. But he might as well admit the truth.

"Yes, I was the captain of the company of guards who arrested the Earl of Dericott and his brothers. I wondered if I might be able to convince the king to release them. Several of them were so young." He shrugged, hoping the guard would not persist in questioning him about it.

The guard continued to narrow his gaze at Geoffrey, but he said nothing.

Geoffrey stood at the gate most of the day watching everyone who came and went from the Tower of London fortress of castle keeps, walls, gates, and towers. Late in the afternoon another captain came through and stopped when he saw Geoffrey.

"You knew those escaped prisoners. I saw you bring them to the Tower." The tall, thin man pointed at Geoffrey. "You should be out looking for them."

"I would gladly go and search for them, but I was sent here. The gate needed more men."

Another guard came up and said in a lowered voice, "Perhaps he knows where they are . . . but does not want to say."

The first guard then turned toward Geoffrey. "Are you willing to allow him to accuse you of such a thing?"

"If he did help them, let him confess it," his accuser went on, bowing his back and narrowing his eyes at Geoffrey. "The guard who was killed was from my company. Someone should be hanged for such a thing. Justice is justice."

Geoffrey glared at the man and put his hand on his sword hilt. He would defend himself, but he would not attack. It was dishonorable to attack a fellow soldier, especially when he spoke the truth.

The other guard looked him over, from his feet to his head, then relaxed his scowl. "I just hope the one who killed him will face justice for it." He walked on, as if he'd never accused Geoffrey.

It was only a matter of time before his uncle, or someone else, found evidence—or a witness—to prove Geoffrey had helped Delia and her brothers.

As the sun went down, new guards came to relieve him from his post. He walked back to the soldiers' barracks.

Should he even go to bed tonight? If he did, would he be arrested before morning?

"Everybody up!"

Geoffrey sat up. The commander was speaking. It was still dark, but he had no idea how long he'd been asleep. He and his fellow soldiers started readying themselves, getting out of bed and putting on their clothes.

"We have reason to believe," the commander went on, "the escaped prisoners are hiding somewhere in the vicinity of Smithfield Market. They have already killed one of our men, and now we have discovered they attacked Sir Elliot and wounded him severely. Be ready to kill these dangerous men on sight, if necessary."

Geoffrey's heart thumped hard as he pulled on his boots. He had to get to Delia and her brothers and warn them.

But his uncle was probably having him followed. Could he risk helping them get away when he might inadvertently lead the soldiers to them?

He hurried to be the first one out the door, strapping his sword belt on as he walked, and headed for the gate. A soldier was already unlocking it to let him out. But other men-at-arms were right behind him. He glanced over his shoulder. Only two or three men had made it out of the barracks, and even they looked a bit sleepy-eyed and slow. Had one or more of them been assigned to follow him?

He quickened his pace, and instead of heading for town, he headed for the stable to get his horse. They would need his steed if the brothers and Delia had to travel, especially with Edwin so gravely injured.

A groom helped Geoffrey saddle his horse. He hurriedly mounted and rode toward the house where Delia and her brothers were staying, but he took the long way to try to avoid any soldiers, and none of the rest were on horseback, having chosen to walk instead of ride.

When he was near the house, he dismounted and led his horse to the back, where he found a small mew. The pen looked as if it had once held chickens, but the birds were all gone now. He tied his horse there, then knocked on the back door.

NINETEEN

DELIA HEARD A DISTINCT KNOCK COMING FROM THE BACK of the house—three strong raps. Her heart seemed to stop, then lurch into beating double time.

Gerard stood and held up a hand. Edwin sat up, propping himself with his right hand. Gerard and Berenger took the two swords and went to the back door. Delia followed.

Her brothers looked out the back windows, one on either side of the door. Then they both said in quiet voices, "Sir Geoffrey."

Delia's heart lurched again, but this time with a lighter, fluttery feeling.

Gerard opened the door and Sir Geoffrey slipped in quickly, shutting the door behind him.

"You need to leave as quickly as possible." Sir Geoffrey's eyes were wide and bright, his whole body seemingly on edge.

"Leave?"

"Why?"

"What is happening?"

Her brothers were as curious as she was, but seeing Sir Geoffrey's face again caused her heart to lift, and she suddenly felt no fear at all, only peace and something akin to joy.

Sir Geoffrey's hair was damp from the early morning dew and mist. His eyes met hers.

"Are you well?" he asked.

"We are well," Gerard said, "but I don't know if Edwin can walk."

"I am well enough to walk."

Delia turned to Edwin, who stood just behind her. He looked weak, his face pale, and his shoulders slightly bowed, but her joy rose at seeing him standing and walking again.

"I have a horse for you," Sir Geoffrey said.

How thoughtful of him. Her brother could not possibly travel without a horse. *Thank You, God.*

"You all need to get out of London as quickly as possible," Sir Geoffrey was saying, "before the gates are closed against us."

"Why?" Merek asked.

"Are they closing the gates?" Gerard asked.

"Are we not safe hidden here?" Berenger still held his sword.

"They know you're in this vicinity and they've sent guards to search the area for you. They'll station guards at the gates who can recognize you. We have to get you out before they can do that."

"Thank you so much, Sir Geoffrey." Delia reached out to touch his arm, but he caught her hand in his and gently squeezed it.

"I am pleased I can help. And I must ask for your help as well, that you will allow me to come with you."

"Won't that be dangerous for you?" Gerard asked as the brothers gathered around Sir Geoffrey.

"Are you sure?" Delia asked. "They will assume you are guilty of helping us if you disappear."

"I am already under suspicion. It is possible my uncle is having me followed, but I made sure no one followed me here. Still, it is inevitable that they will find you if you stay."

Delia's cheeks tingled as if the blood were draining from her face. She put a hand up to her cheek. "Did Sir Elliot accuse you?"

"Sir Elliot? Possibly. I believe he is the one who alerted the guards that you were hiding in the vicinity of the Smithfield Market. They will be swarming this area, searching every house for you. We have to go. Now."

Delia and her brothers scrambled to gather up the most important things, though there wasn't much, and stuff them into cloth bags they could carry around their shoulders. She took the extra hooded cloak they'd found on the topmost floor of the old house and gave it to Sir Geoffrey to cover his soldier's uniform, the king's colors. They gathered their meager amount of belongings and supplies and soon they were ready to go.

Sir Geoffrey led them out the back way, then he and Gerard helped Edwin mount the horse. They took the road that led away from Smithfield Market toward the east, their hoods pulled over their heads. They put a hundred feet between their small groups so that it didn't look like they were all together.

Delia found herself walking with Sir Geoffrey and alongside Edwin's horse. She knew her older brothers would look after the younger ones.

She cast a glance at Sir Geoffrey. He was looking at her. Her heart skipped a beat. Had he thought about her as much as she'd thought about him the last two days? The sight of him coming to help them was burned in her memory, the way he had smuggled in swords and fought valiantly to help them escape, the way he took charge of Edwin and brought him back to them from the surgeon, all at great risk to himself. Her heart swelled. She didn't want to say too much about the depth of her feelings, but she did want him to know . . .

"I'm sorry you are having to flee London with us, that you are losing so much." Her chest ached. He was losing his knighthood, all that he'd worked for, his very way of life, for them.

"I chose this. I could not bear to live with the dishonor of having played a part in your innocent brothers' execution. When all is done, I must answer only to God, and I chose the better path."

He looked into her eyes. He meant what he was saying. He was not sorry.

"Thank you."

He was no ordinary man. Sir Geoffrey was a true knight, a man of integrity and honor.

She had despised him the first time she saw him. And later she had resented his handsome appearance. But now, the way his hair fell across his forehead, the thick, dark brows, the eyes that were clear and kind—his outward features seemed to fit his good character.

"So what happened with Sir Elliot? Did he encounter your brothers in the market?"

Delia took a deep breath and let it out. She was not

comfortable talking about that. It was still so fresh in her mind. How could she explain? Would Sir Geoffrey blame her and think she had done something wrong? She didn't think he would. How she wanted him to understand, to even be proud of her for fighting back and escaping.

She longed to be in his arms again, the way he had comforted her after her brothers' trial.

Did he feel as much for her as she felt for him? Or was he only being kind to her as any friend would comfort a friend? What would he do if he knew how she felt about him? She might make a fool of herself, but Sir Geoffrey would never try to take advantage of her the way Sir Elliot had.

Her stomach roiled at the memory of Sir Elliot and the thought of what might have happened. Sir Geoffrey never would have treated her so dishonorably. She was certain of that. He was gentle and noble, not like Sir Elliot at all. But he might not be thinking of her as tenderly as she was thinking of him.

He was staring, waiting for her to answer his question. She knew she could trust him, so she decided to tell him what Sir Elliot had done. The wind was blowing and Edwin and the others were far enough away that she didn't think anyone could hear her.

"No, my brothers did not encounter Sir Elliot. I did."

"You?" Sir Geoffrey's brows drew together. "What happened? Tell me. Did . . ." Sir Geoffrey seemed to stop and swallow, his eyes fixed on her face. "Did he hurt you?"

"He would have. I got away from him before he could." Delia felt the tremble in her stomach, the fear and loathing causing bile to rise into her throat. But she pushed it down. She didn't want to embarrass herself in front of Sir Geoffrey. She wouldn't allow herself to feel the full measure of the fear, or it might overwhelm her again.

"Tell me everything that happened. That is, if you do not mind speaking of it."

Could she tell him everything without too much emotion? She had not even told her brothers all that had happened, but she felt safe opening up to Sir Geoffrey. Even if she became emotional, she didn't think he would be embarrassed.

She told him how Sir Elliot had so aggressively made his demands on her, the way he had grabbed her shoulder and squeezed it, threatening her and taking her to the inn.

"He brought me into a room in the inn and locked the door." She was almost afraid to look Sir Geoffrey in the eye. But when she glanced up, he was staring down at her so intently, with such a look of protection and anger, she felt tears prick her eyes.

Why did his concern make her want to cry? It also made her trust him even more, and gave her courage to continue to reveal everything to him.

"If I'd been there I would have killed him." Sir Geoffrey's voice was gruff and raspy.

Her heart skipped a beat at the mental image of him coming to her defense.

"I was afraid, but before he could truly hurt me, I told him I needed some water. I picked up the pitcher and hit him over the head with it."

His lips parted, his eyes even more intent on hers. "I wish I could have seen that."

"That blow did not knock him out, which frightened me very much. He started to draw his sword, so I picked up a stool, and just before he got his sword unsheathed, I hit him with the stool. That knocked him unconscious, thanks be to God." She paused her narrative for a heavy sigh, hiding her hands, which had started shaking, in the folds of her cloak.

"You were very brave." Sir Geoffrey touched her shoulder, and Delia flinched away from him.

She hadn't meant to react that way. But when he touched her shoulder, it was as if Sir Elliot were there again. Memories of how he had grabbed her, of her desperation to escape his grasp, sent a wave of fear crashing over her.

"Forgive me," he said, pulling his hand away.

"No, it's not your fault." And it wasn't, but her heart was thumping hard. "I suppose I'm still a bit shaken from what happened." She reached out and touched his arm, unsure how to explain her feelings. Though she knew Sir Geoffrey would never abuse her or take advantage of her, at his touch all the fear of that moment had come rushing back.

"I'm sorry for being forward," he said, placing his hand over his chest. "I would never harm you. Upon my honor, I would not."

"I know you wouldn't. I reacted strangely, I know, but I am well now."

"Go on, then," he said gently. "What did you do next?"

She took a breath and continued.

"He was lying on the floor, not moving. I had to get the key out of his pocket. I didn't want to touch him." Delia swallowed, remembering again the fear of having to reach into his pocket and retrieve the key, of being that close to him, fearing any moment he would open his eyes and grab her.

"But you got the key?"

Delia nodded. "I unlocked the door and ran out. I had to walk back through the marketplace, where all the guards were walking around asking questions. I tried not to look at anyone. No one stopped me, thankfully."

"I wish I had been there. But I'm proud of you for defending yourself, for being resourceful. You were very courageous."

His praise poured over her like warm sunshine. She loved that he was proud of her for fighting for herself. And the thought of him wishing he could have saved her from Sir Elliot, the picture in her mind of him stepping between her and Sir Elliot, telling him he was never to lay a hand on her again, gave her an intensely satisfying feeling.

Delia couldn't meet his eye. "Thank you." But it bothered her that she had flinched when he touched her. Would she react that way again, should he ever try to touch her or put his arms around her, as he had done after her brothers' trial?

They walked through the back streets until they reached the wall of the city. Sir Geoffrey kept his head down as they passed through the gate. Had the guards here not been warned yet that the seven escaped brothers and their sister might be passing through? They surely knew about their escape, as it had been discovered twenty-four hours ago. But perhaps Sir Geoffrey had reached them before this new search had been undertaken. And thankfully Edwin's cloak covered him so that no one could see his bandages or that he was missing an arm.

The very thought, the very words *Edwin is missing an arm*, made Delia feel sick. How would he bear up under the weight of this misfortune? She could not imagine her loving oldest brother not looking perfectly whole and healthy, strong and stalwart, standing tall and facing the world as the Earl of Dericott, the brave and strong protector, landlord, and fighter. Instead, now he would be called a cripple.

Forgive me, God. I am so very grateful he's alive. Thank You, thank You, for not letting him die. Please help him bear this bravely.

As they went through the gate, the guards did not seem to notice them or look their way. They were standing languidly, conversing quietly with each other as they went by. She squelched the now-familiar urge to look over her shoulder to see if her brothers were getting through safely. They had a plan to meet a little way down the road, so she would find out soon.

Sir Geoffrey was looking over at Edwin. "How are you holding up?" he asked.

"I am well enough." Edwin's eyes still looked feverish with a dull sheen, his cheeks flushed, though she had plied him with feverfew tea twice today. Was the fever from the shock of the dreadful wound? Or was it infected with disease? Sir Geoffrey had said the surgeon warned them to keep the wound clean and to watch out for putridity, that a fever from the latter was more serious.

"How long do you think you can ride without stopping to rest?" Sir Geoffrey asked softly.

"I am well, for now. I don't want to slow us down. You can leave me somewhere along the way and I should be well enough until you can come back for me."

Sir Geoffrey said, "Absolutely not. We will all rest together. Your comfort shall be our guide. When you're tired, we shall rest."

Delia had given Edwin some herbs that morning, along with the feverfew, that were supposed to dull his pain. He'd drunk the last of the liquid just before Sir Geoffrey had arrived. She knew the herbs made Edwin sleepy, so she marveled that he wasn't nodding forward in the saddle.

Had all her brothers made it through the gate? She imagined guards swarming them before the last of her brothers could get through. Her heart beat fast. She had to calm herself and stop imagining trouble.

"Do you know who is bringing up the rear?"

"Gerard, Charles, and Merek."

She could see his gaze on her out of the corner of her eye.

"You can take my arm," he said quietly. He added, "If you get tired."

"Thank you." She wasn't tired, but she did want to take his arm.

The whole incident with Sir Elliot had shaken her. Would she react the same way every time a man touched her, even innocently? Would she always be haunted by what Sir Elliot had done? She didn't want to let that dishonorable knave cause her to lose all faith in men.

After all, she had her brothers, and she knew them to be good men. And Sir Geoffrey had selflessly given up his livelihood, and possibly even his life, to help them. He was nothing like Sir Elliot.

The thought leapt into her mind that if Sir Geoffrey wished

to, he could lead them into a trap to hand them over for some kind of reward.

She shuddered at the thought of him betraying them. But she was only imagining the worst again, for she would never think Sir Geoffrey capable of treachery. She had not become so world-weary and cynical that she would suspect him of such a thing.

Sir Geoffrey had never made her feel afraid or uncomfortable, but Sir Elliot had, and she'd ignored her own instincts about him. She'd wanted to think well of him, even though there had been signs that he was not as genuine as he claimed to be. She had ignored them in her desperation to save her brothers. His promises to help them escape had given her hope. And if she was honest, she'd been flattered by his attention and assertions of ardor and love for her. She'd ignored the times when he'd made her feel uncomfortable, choosing instead to believe he was good.

And in the end the uncomfortable moments, the little niggling doubts, had been correct. He had been not a friend but a very demon intent on hurting her and her brothers. She never should have trusted him. And Sir Geoffrey had warned her. She should have listened to him.

"Do you see that little bridge?" Sir Geoffrey asked, nodding in the direction they were heading.

She focused on the crossroads ahead, the boundary stone, and the trees just off the road. "Yes."

"It spans a small spring. We will take the horse down to the stream and water him and fill up our water flask."

His manner was so gentle, respectful, and attentive. He made her feel safe and protected.

"Why are you doing this?" The words were out of her mouth before she took the time to think them through.

He looked at her with a glint of inquisitiveness, then sadness, in his eyes. He sighed. "Do you not believe I could be a good man who just wanted to help you?"

"You didn't know me or my brothers."

"But I quickly discovered that you were good people. I was the one who arrested your brothers, and I did not want that on my conscience. The dishonor of it haunted me at night. But there was another reason." He looked away from her.

They were approaching the little stream. Sir Geoffrey led Edwin and the horse straight up to the water, and the horse began to drink.

Sir Geoffrey still did not go on, so Delia said, "You had another reason? For helping us?"

"Can you not guess it?" There was a tiny frown on his lips and one brow went up. "I would think it is obvious."

"What do you mean?" Her heart fluttered up to her throat.

He motioned for her to move farther away from Edwin. Her brother was sitting as tall as before atop his horse, his head bent and eyes closed. He did not seem in danger of falling, so Delia followed Sir Geoffrey a few feet downstream.

Sir Geoffrey frowned, then pressed his lips together. Finally, he said, "Perhaps it is not the right time to speak of it, but . . . I did it for you, Lady Delia. More than any other reason, I did it for you."

TWENTY

DELIA FELT HERSELF BLUSHING. DID HE MEAN HE . . . could be falling in love . . . with her? He did not say that, exactly. But she was afraid to ask him what he meant.

"I don't want to make you uncomfortable, but I . . ."

"Yes?"

Sir Geoffrey was looking past her. "Your brothers."

She turned to see Berenger, Roland, and David coming toward them, mingling with a few other travelers with packs on their backs—a man with a donkey loaded with multiple sacks, and a man with a horse and cart.

She turned back to Sir Geoffrey. She wanted so desperately to know what he was about to say. As she drew closer to him, his gaze softened. Was it her imagination? Or was there a look of longing, almost pain, in his eyes?

"I should not tell you the other reason, as I am no longer even a lowly knight, with no inheritance or wealth, but I . . ." He lifted his hand, holding it out as if making a request. Then he let it drop. "I wanted to help you, Delia. As much as I wanted to help your brothers, I believe my desire to help them was equally for your sake. You didn't deserve to lose your brothers."

It was not the boldest declaration. Why was he holding back, not saying what he had started to say? But perhaps she was imagining things again. He said he had helped her brothers for her sake as much as for theirs. That meant he had at least some feelings for her. But the fear that she cared more for him than he did for her kept her from being too buoyed by his words.

"I thank you again for your kindness to me and my brothers." Truly, it was selfless and good of him to help them, and noble and honorable. So why did she want to demand he say more, to demand he tell her exactly what he was thinking and how he felt about her?

Her gaze lingered on his face. How handsome he was. His nose was straight and just the right size. His hair was dark and thick, his blue eyes clear and bright. His jawline and cheekbones were masculine and firm. In truth, she had never seen a more handsome man. He did not have the wide shoulders her older brothers possessed, but he was tall and lean and looked just as strong. She knew he'd trained long and hard and had earned his place as a knight. But more than training, Sir Geoffrey had character. His heart was noble, and therefore his actions and words were noble.

She imagined reaching out and touching his face, standing on her toes to reach his lips with hers and kissing him.

Her cheeks started to burn and she turned away as her

brothers approached. She tried to make her mind stop running away with stray thoughts of kissing this man.

Berenger, Roland, and David joined them at the stream. They spoke with Edwin to see how he was feeling, then described their trek through the city, having seen several soldiers, but none of the soldiers even looked at them. The horse finished drinking, then they all took a sip from the water flasks Sir Geoffrey had in his saddlebags. They would refill them at the next village well. They talked quietly and watched the road for Gerard, Merek, and Charles.

Delia searched every face as soon as it came into view. Had her brothers been stopped at the gate? She was beginning to imagine all manner of terrifying possibilities when three figures, one much shorter than the other two, came into view.

They were all safely out of London and all together. She took in a deep breath and let it out slowly. *Thank You, God.*

They still had a long way to go. And as long as her brothers' names were not cleared of wrongdoing, they would be outcasts and fugitives, running and hiding to stay alive. They had to find something, or someone, to help prove they were innocent.

Geoffrey spotted the last of the brothers and let out the breath he'd been holding.

Delia went to stand beside Edwin and his horse. "How are you feeling?" She turned to Gerard. "Help me up so I can feel his forehead."

Her brother lifted her up and she laid her hand on Edwin's face.

"How is he?" Roland asked.

"He doesn't feel as warm as he did earlier this morning." She smiled, but Geoffrey thought he detected worry in her eyes.

Edwin was still looking pale and haggard, but they could not tarry any longer. They had to keep moving. There was no way to know when the guards would leave the city and begin scouring the countryside for them. But the sky was not lightening as it should this time of the morning. The clouds were thick and portended more snow. However, they could not risk spending the night in an inn. Too many people would see them.

An hour later, Delia whispered to Geoffrey that they needed to let Edwin rest. They all seemed to be looking to him to lead them, so he suggested they move off the road to a stand of trees. They helped Edwin off his horse and let him lie on the grass. He closed his eyes and appeared to fall asleep instantly.

The rest of them moved away a bit to talk without disturbing Edwin.

"Do we have a plan as to where we're going?" Merek asked.

Delia looked at Geoffrey. "Even though we talked over several options, we left so quickly; we hadn't made any definite plans."

"Earlier I had thought to take you to a small house on my mother's land in Hertfordshire, but once they realize I am gone as well, that may be the first place they look for us."

"We can't go home," Berenger said.

"Our stepmother would hand us over to the king's men."

Merek's eyes narrowed. "She'd probably kill us herself if she could get away with it."

"What about Rosings Abbey?" Delia said. "Surely our aunt would protect us."

"There's no safer place than an abbey," Berenger said.

"But can you trust your aunt and the other nuns at the abbey not to betray us if the king's guards were to come asking for us, demanding they give us up?"

Delia's smile faded and she chewed her lip. "I don't know."

They could not be certain about who might betray them, but they had to go somewhere.

"Rosings Abbey seems a better choice than anywhere else I can think of," Geoffrey said. "What do you all think?"

The others agreed, so after an hour's rest they set out, this time with Gerard walking up front with David and Roland, as Gerard knew where the abbey was located. Delia seemed eager to stay with Edwin and watch over him, and Geoffrey stayed by her side, while Berenger, Merek, and Charles traveled together at the rear. He was relieved they had a plan and would hopefully find refuge at the abbey, although Delia said she didn't think they would be able to reach it before nightfall walking at this pace.

They had no food but hopefully would be able to buy some at the next village. Thankfully he had some money, but it would run out before too long. Since his uncle took everything from his family, Geoffrey had to live off his wages as a knight in the king's service. He had been hoping to visit his sister, Amicia, soon, but now he wasn't sure when that might happen.

He wondered how he or Amicia would ever marry and have

a family. He had no dowry to give her, and he was only a guard. He had no land or means of owning a house. He'd once been the only son of one of the wealthiest dukes in England. He'd grown up thinking he would be able to marry anyone he wished. Instead, he was nearly destitute, without the honor of his father's good name, which had been sullied by his uncle's accusations. But most troubling of all, he was his sister's only guardian. A guardian who could provide very little to her. A guardian who would now be hunted by the king and his men.

His conscience pricked him again, as it had many times in the last few days, when he thought of Amicia. What would become of her if something happened to him?

A little after midday they came to a small market town. Geoffrey went alone to buy food while the rest of them stayed hidden in a copse of trees. He also procured a couple of linen tunics so that he could stop wearing his soldier's garb and not be easily identified.

Then they all sat together to eat near a clear flowing spring.

Delia set about making sure Edwin was comfortable as she helped him prop his back against a tree. She put his food within easy reach and gave him feverfew to try to stave off the fever that was making his cheeks flushed again. But after Edwin ate a little bit of bread, he lay down on the grass and fell asleep.

"I asked if there was any news," Geoffrey said. "But no one seemed concerned about anything that might have happened in London."

"So the soldiers haven't been here looking for us?" Charles asked.

Geoffrey shook his head. "It would seem not."

Delia looked satisfied that Edwin was asleep and all her other brothers had what they needed. She sat down near Geoffrey, then lay back on the cold ground.

It would be entirely too cold to sleep outside tonight, especially since there weren't enough warm cloaks to go around. Some of the brothers had the sweaters Delia made for them, but there weren't enough blankets either, as they'd left so much behind in their escape. Somehow he'd have to find shelter for them. And what if it snowed again? They'd be cold *and* wet.

Delia was very lovely at all times, but now, as she lay with her eyes closed and her face at rest, she was even more beautiful.

Her brothers were all gathered together, talking and resting. Only Delia and Geoffrey and Edwin were outside their circle.

"Have you forgiven me?" Geoffrey asked.

Delia opened her eyes and stared at him as if she wasn't sure she'd heard him correctly. "Forgiven you?"

"For my part in imprisoning your brothers." He leaned toward her. "You hated me at first." It felt bold to state what he was thinking, to ask the question that was on his heart. But now was the time to be bold. They could be captured at any moment, or they could be scattered and forced to run for their lives. Anything could happen. And he needed to know how she felt about him.

"I know you weren't to blame, but you were the one who took my brothers away, and it was difficult for me not to associate you with that day."

Why had he brought that up?

"I did not intend to bring you pain by speaking of a memory so distressing."

"I forgave you." Her eyes were wide and guileless. She sat up enough to prop herself on her elbow.

"I believe I forgave you when you brought me the yarn to make sweaters." She smiled, heartening him even more.

But what right did he have to encourage her feelings for him, or his own for her? He had nothing to give her. She had been an earl's daughter, and if her brothers could prove their innocence, if they could get pardoned and restored to their rightful place, she'd be too far above him to marry him. But those were very big ifs.

What could it hurt to try to discover if she felt anything for him?

"But I am so very sorry you are in so much trouble because of helping my brothers and me." She blinked rapidly, her eyes shiny. "And I'm so sorry for what your uncle did to you."

She was on the verge of tears at the thought of his trouble, of the consequences he might suffer for helping them, and for what he had lost. After all that she'd been through, all the suffering that lay ahead for her and her brothers, could she be so selfless as to shed a tear for him?

They sat in silence for some moments. He struggled to hide his feelings, but his heart expanded in his chest and threatened to lift him off the ground.

"Your uncle greatly wronged you," she said, gazing at him, but only for a moment before looking back down at her hands. "I don't understand why so many unjust things happen. I know I should accept it as part of life in a fallen world. But it's so wrong—what happened to you and what has happened to my brothers, to Edwin." She took a breath. "God is just and good. So why did He allow these terrible things?"

When Geoffrey didn't immediately reply, Delia went on. "My brothers' freedom was taken away, their good name tarnished, and they were thrown into prison and sentenced to death for something they did not do. And Edwin . . ." She pressed her fingers to her lips and did not go on.

His heart ached to see her pain. He imagined being able to exact revenge on those who had hurt her, those two witnesses and the judges who had sentenced her brothers to death. Anger welled up inside him, but anger was not what Delia needed from him.

"I don't understand either, but there are evil people in this world and . . ."

She knew all this. What could he say to make her feel better? How could he comfort her? He longed to pull her into his arms and hold her, or at least put a hand on her shoulder. But she had flinched away from him the last time. Besides, her brothers were only a few feet away, and he was not sure how they—or she— would react to his being so familiar toward her.

She shook her head and scrunched her face. "I hate the injustice of it, the injustice of what has happened to you, of evil people getting away with stealing and wrongly accusing innocent people."

"Bearing false witness against one's neighbor is a violation of the Ten Commandments. God will serve His justice to them in the end." But she knew that too. All he was doing was stating obvious facts. He felt so powerless to help her.

She shivered and sat up, hugging her arms. He remembered the blanket he had in his saddlebag.

He jumped up and retrieved the rolled-up blanket and brought it back to her. "It's clean." He shook it out and draped it around her shoulders.

She grabbed the ends of the blanket. Her hands brushed against his, sending a shiver up his arm.

"Thank you." She gazed into his eyes.

"What are you two talking about?"

Geoffrey turned around to see Merek eyeing him.

Delia answered, "We were just talking about how God's justice will be served to those who break His commandment not to bear false witness."

Merek looked back and forth between them. Though he was younger than Delia, he was doing his best to stare Geoffrey down. Geoffrey would do the same if he saw a man talking quietly with his sister and then wrapping a blanket around her shoulders.

Delia glanced at Merek, then gave Geoffrey a crooked smile.

His heart did a strange flip inside his chest. He sat back down next to Delia. Merek kept a wary eye on him, but nothing could take away this feeling. He'd nearly confessed it that morning to Delia. But it was best if he kept it to himself, at least while they were running for their lives.

TWENTY-ONE

DELIA WAS RELIEVED TO SEE ROSINGS ABBEY COME INTO view. It had taken less time to reach it than they had all thought. They arrived on the lane to Rosings just as the sun retreated below the horizon.

Edwin was slumped so far forward he looked as if he might fall off the horse at any moment. She'd forced him to drink water, to take the feverfew, and to eat a bit of bread and cheese a couple of times, and he had stayed on his horse almost all day so that they could make better time. Her stomach was tied in knots at seeing him so exhausted. She longed to get him safely to the abbey where he could rest.

Beside the road to the abbey was a pond with ducks and swans. Delia thought of the eight swans she'd seen on the bank of the Thames that had made her think of herself and her brothers. It had almost seemed like a harbinger of something to come. But here there were only two swans. Again, their heads were down and they looked a bit forlorn.

At the abbey they were met by a couple of servants, with two guards standing nearby.

Sir Geoffrey was the first to approach Edwin, and Gerard and Berenger helped him get Edwin down off the horse. They carried him into the abbey, and Delia and the servants followed close behind.

A nun was quickly apprised of the situation. She took over and led them into a chamber in the main building.

Delia prayed, *God, please give Edwin a good healer, someone who will help him.*

They laid Edwin on a bed and a woman, old and wrinkled, her back bent, with a hump all the way across where her shoulder blades should have been, stepped out of a back room.

Sir Geoffrey explained, "He was injured and his arm was removed by a surgeon, but he is weak and feverish. Can you help him?"

"If God is willing." The old woman approached Edwin without so much as looking at the rest of them. "You may all go. I will send for you if his condition changes."

She was touching his face and starting to take off his clothes. She turned and gave orders to a young boy who stood behind her, apparently an assistant or servant.

"Come," the nun said. "I will show you to your rooms where you may rest from your travels."

Delia spoke up. "We need to see the abbess."

The nun fixed her eyes on Delia. "I remember you. You are Abbess Beatrice's niece."

Delia nodded. They had agreed not to tell anyone they encountered on the road who they were, but she had imagined she might be recognized at the abbey. "May I speak to her?"

"Of course."

"And may these men come and speak to her as well?"

"If you wish it." The nun glanced at her brothers and Sir Geoffrey.

"Yes, thank you."

"Follow me."

They walked behind the nun on the same circuitous route that Delia remembered from before. Had it only been a few weeks since she'd first come here to speak to her aunt? So much had happened. She felt much older.

The nun stopped at a door. "Wait here." She went inside. A few moments later, she reemerged.

"I am sorry, but Abbess Beatrice will only speak to Lady Delia." She motioned to Delia, who followed her inside.

Her aunt stood in the same place in the same room where Delia had met her before. Delia went to her, bowed, and knelt to kiss her proffered hand.

"What has happened?" her aunt said with uncharacteristic haste and interest. "I was informed that your brothers were condemned to die by beheading."

"Did you not get the letter my brother Edwin sent?"

The abbess stared a moment. "No, I did not get a letter."

Had someone, like Sir Geoffrey's uncle, intercepted Edwin's letter? It didn't matter now.

"They were condemned to die by beheading. But we—they— have escaped from the Tower of London, and we've come here seeking asylum."

The abbess stared with wide eyes for a moment. She inhaled, her chest expanding, then slowly exhaled. She pressed her lips together as she seemed to be deep in thought.

"I am not sure if it is fortuitous or disastrous, but I have just learned this morning that Anne of Bohemia, King Richard's soon-to-be queen, has landed secretly at Dover. She will be visiting the abbey before traveling on to London to wed the king."

"This abbey?" Delia's heart thrummed and leapt. "She is coming here?"

"Indeed. It seems she is eager to establish herself as a friend of the Church. She shall stay here a few days before going on to spend Christmas at Leeds Castle. She arrives on the morrow. We are all anxious to accommodate her properly. But with you and your brothers here . . ."

"It could bring people here who might recognize us and seize us."

Aunt Beatrice gave an almost imperceptible nod.

"But it could also be the opportunity we need, if I could speak to Lady Anne, and if she would be willing to speak to King Richard on our behalf, to ask him to pardon my brothers."

"And how would a pardon be helpful?" her aunt asked.

"I . . . I am not sure what you mean. It would be helpful for saving their lives."

"But if they are accused of treason and murder, they can never be titled men. They will never be rid of the disgrace of being murderers and traitors, can never take their rightful place among the peers of England."

The abbess had such a frustrating way of stating things Delia did not wish to hear. But she looked her aunt in the eye and refused to be unsettled. "Which is why we were traveling this way," Delia said.

"I thought you came to seek asylum."

"Yes, but we also wish to clear my brothers of wrongdoing. We are seeking your protection while we search for the truth about who killed the man my brothers are accused of murdering."

"And do you have a plan for finding this person and this evidence?"

Her aunt's blunt way of speaking caused Delia to concentrate on answering in as calm a manner as possible, to truly think before she spoke. Was she trying to force Delia to consider the complications of her intentions?

"We have the names of the witnesses who spoke out against my brothers."

The abbess shook her head, a small movement. "Those witnesses have probably been sent away, to the Continent I would assume, by whoever paid them to lie to the court. If you were hoping to force them into a confession . . . you will not find them."

A pain stabbed Delia's heart. She'd been counting on Sir Geoffrey and her brothers finding those men and convincing them to confess to the truth.

"But you can tell your brothers that I have been looking into this matter and I just got word . . . I still don't know who killed the coroner, but I know that your father did not die a natural death from being thrown from his horse. He was murdered as well."

Delia suddenly felt a bit dizzy. But this was good news! Her brothers would be vindicated, their good names restored.

"Sit down before you fall. You are not prone to fainting, I should hope."

"No, I have never fainted and I am not about to faint now." The thought of her aunt's disdain if she did made her more determined not to. "Who killed Father?"

"Do you know the Earl of Yelverton?"

"Yes, he was at my brothers' trial. He is an advisor of the king." And he was also Sir Geoffrey's uncle.

"He is one of the king's councilors, yes. He certainly would have spoken against your brothers to the judges, because he is connected to your stepmother. She has met with him on multiple occasions. I do not know what it is that binds them, but she was seen at his estate when he was known to be in residence, and his close servant, Rostand, was seen coming out of the stables on the day your father went riding and was thrown."

"The strange man who was seen that day! Mistress Wattlesbrook mentioned that. She thought it very suspicious. But how did you—"

"And your stepmother was visiting Lord Baldric's estate when his brother, the Duke of Strachleigh, was killed. He died in a similar riding accident. Did you know that?"

"No." Poor Sir Geoffrey! How would he react to learning his father might have been murdered? But perhaps he already suspected it.

"How did you discover all of this?" Delia was shocked that her aunt had been seeking out the truth and trying to help her brothers, especially after she'd seemed so reluctant to help before.

"I am the abbess, and what good is power if one cannot use it to help free those who have been wrongly accused? I knew your brothers—my nephews—were not guilty of murder or treason. Why should I not send out my servants to ask questions, to discover the truth, and perchance to correct an injustice? I only received this information today, and I had thought my efforts would be fruitless, since they were supposed to have been executed today. Besides that, I do not have any evidence that proves what I have just told you."

"But I am so very grateful to you for discovering all this. Thank you so much. I am sure my brothers will be able to find who is responsible for the murders."

"Even if they do, it may not help you. Lord Yelverton is very influential with the king and the other councilors. To some people, the truth is irrelevant."

Delia's heart sank. Then she had a happy thought. "But Lady Anne is coming here." She drew in a deep breath. "Perhaps she will help us."

"She will be much more likely to help if you have facts to lay before her. And I no longer have the luxury of time to help you. I must prepare for the lady's visit. There is still much that needs to be done, and I shall be occupied with making the abbey ready to accommodate the future queen. Much food must be bought and prepared for the queen and her entire retinue."

"But if the future queen is here, I can speak with her, convince her—"

"You must have evidence. We have none as yet. Murder is a serious crime, especially murder of the king's coroner. The law demands that the murderer be executed. Besides that, Anne of Bohemia will stay for only a short visit, to rest, before going on to Leeds Castle and then to London for her marriage and coronation. You must hurry and find the evidence to present to her."

There was too little time. "How should I go about finding this evidence? Will you help me?"

"I have given you all the information I was able to obtain. My sources would not give me any names other than the ones I've told you. Now it is up to you. My advice is to go to Wycrofton. Meanwhile, I have a duty and responsibility as the leader of this abbey, and a duty and responsibility to my king and his future queen. Anne of Bohemia and her retinue will be arriving soon, and my time has been appropriated by this important event. You and your brothers must work out your own salvation, as it were."

Delia could feel her throat constricting. But as always, she knew showing fear would not gain her anything. She could do this. She could find the people responsible for her brothers' imprisonment—the false witnesses who had accused them of murder and treason. She had to. And now she wasn't alone.

After leaving her aunt, she went to Sir Geoffrey and her brothers and told them all the information her aunt had just given her. They made a plan to head out first thing the next morning.

She thought she had lost her chance to speak to the future queen when her brothers were so quickly tried and sentenced to death, when they'd been forced to escape their prison and leave London. But perhaps all hope was not lost.

Delia opened her eyes to someone pounding on her door. The only light was from a few glowing embers in the fireplace. Where was she?

She sat up as it came to her. She was at Rosings Abbey with her brothers and Sir Geoffrey. She had been placed in a room with another woman who was traveling to London. The tiny bit of gray light around the window shutters revealed it must be dawn.

The knock came again, very insistent. The other woman did not rise, or even move, that Delia could see.

Delia wore only her underdress, but it covered her from head to toe. Nevertheless, she drew on her cloak before hurrying to the door and using the key to unlock it. Sir Geoffrey stood there, his face barely visible in the dark corridor. Men were not allowed in this part of the convent.

"What is it?"

"Your brothers are gone."

Delia's heart stopped. "What do you mean?"

"They were taken during the night." He motioned for her to follow him. She stepped out and closed the door behind her. *O God, don't let anything happen to them.*

"I was sleeping in the healer's chamber with Edwin when a servant came and said soldiers had stormed into the abbey and seized your brothers—all except Edwin."

She could hardly breathe. "But surely this couldn't happen. Aunt Beatrice . . ." She struggled to draw in enough breath to speak. "She would not allow soldiers . . . Perhaps my brothers left to go find evidence."

But she knew from the grim look on Sir Geoffrey's face . . .

"No, no, no, no, no." Delia bent forward, the most excruciating pain sinking down on her, on her shoulders, inside her chest. *God, why did You not save them?*

Sir Geoffrey took her arm, as if to hold her up.

"We can go after them." Delia grabbed hold of Sir Geoffrey's shirt. "We can save them, rescue them when they stop for water or to rest their horses."

"There will be too many of them," Sir Geoffrey said gently. "We need to find witnesses, or even evidence of their innocence. That is the best thing we can do for them."

"They did not take Edwin?"

"No. Your brothers told them Edwin had died from a putrid wound. The soldiers seemed eager to leave the abbey—one of the men mumbled there would be a curse on them for entering the abbey and removing someone who had taken refuge in a house of God—and they left quickly."

"Does my aunt know?"

"Yes. She sent a servant boy to tell me."

Was there no one to help them? Delia's heart seemed to break in two.

"I am surprised they did not look for you or me as well, as they must know by now that you and I played a part in their escape, but there may have been some miscommunication. Or their fear, or the abbey guards, forced them to leave before they could search for us."

O God, O God. Delia could not even pray, could not form words, could only cry out silently.

"Get dressed if you wish to come with me." Sir Geoffrey was standing quite close, still holding tightly to her arm, as if to keep her attention. "Or do you want to stay here?"

"I am coming with you." Delia opened the door behind her and stumbled inside, then shut it.

She was breathing hard as she found her dress and pulled it on over her head, put on her shoes. She was too horrified, too frozen inside, to cry. *My brothers, God. My brothers.* They would be in prison again and in the clutches of the Earl of Yelverton and Parnella. *Please help them, God, please.*

She clasped her belt around her waist, her small money pouch attached. Then she hurried out the door to where Sir Geoffrey was waiting for her. So stalwart and faithful. So kind.

"At least they didn't arrest you." As soon as she said the words, she threw her arms around him and let her forehead rest on his chest.

His arms immediately went around her, and he pulled her closer. Why did his embrace feel so comforting? And why did she feel as if she were completely alone in the world except for this man? He was her only friend now.

His arms gave her strength. She would stand up straight and tall. She would not give in to frailty or give up on saving her brothers.

"Forgive me. I don't want to slow us down," Delia said, lifting her head.

Sir Geoffrey's face was very near hers, his eyes so close, a brilliant blue. When she tilted her head ever so slightly, all she could see were his lips and his stubbly chin. She wanted to touch his face. With her fingers. And her lips.

She pulled away and Sir Geoffrey let her go. But she felt stronger, as if his strength was flowing through her. They headed toward the front door.

Delia walked quickly to the stables. "How is Edwin? Does he still have a fever?"

"I believe it was much better this morning."

"Do you think he will be all right without us?"

"The healer will take good care of him. She said her assistant can stay with him until he is well enough to be left alone."

She was so thankful he had not been arrested with the rest of her brothers. Poor Roland and David. They must be so afraid. And Charles would be afraid as well, but he would never show it. Were the soldiers who arrested them treating them well? Or were they cruel?

How could this be happening again? How long would they let them live before they executed them? *God, please. Help. We need You.*

Sir Geoffrey was quick at saddling his horse, and the stable boy helped her saddle a gentle mare, assuring her it was fast and strong. They were soon mounted and headed toward Wycrofton, the village where the coroner, Sir John Stanley, had been murdered.

About midday they stopped to rest the horses near a bubbling spring. They sat down and ate some bread and cheese Sir Geoffrey had procured from the abbey kitchen.

"It seems terrible to be traveling away from London instead of toward it." And her brothers. "My home—or my old home—is not far to the west of here."

Sir Geoffrey looked quizzically at her. "My old home—my father's estate before it was taken and given to my uncle—is not far to the east of here." He squinted at the ground. "I find it interesting that your stepmother and my uncle are situated so near each other. And interesting that they both seem to want land and titles that aren't rightfully their own. And they also both seem to want your brothers to be executed and out of the way."

"What could that mean?" A chill snaked across Delia's shoulders.

"Who was your stepmother before she married your father?"

"Parnella is the daughter of the Baron Delaford—"

"Baron Delaford? Your stepmother is the daughter of the Baron Delaford? She had a . . . something . . . with my uncle, even though she's young enough to be his daughter. My aunt was furious. As I recall, this woman—your stepmother—married your father shortly thereafter, and then my aunt fell ill and died."

"My father was thrown from his horse and died just a few months after my half brother was born. My brothers were home for the funeral when you arrested them. Aunt Beatrice said your uncle's servant was there when he died, and that your father died in a similar fashion. Do you think these events are related—that all of this is connected in some way?"

"I think it likely that the two of them are conspiring to combine the two estates by getting rid of the rightful heirs and marrying each other. Either that or they are just helping each other. He helps her kill the people who are standing in her way of getting what she wants . . ."

"And she helps him kill the people who are standing in his way."

"Precisely."

"But that is so evil." Delia's breath left her for a moment. How could anyone be so diabolical? "I always knew my step-mother was not a kind person, and I knew she must have been the one who accused my brothers, but it's still so shocking that she would help your uncle . . ." *Kill your father.* "I'm so sorry."

"My father's death looked like an accident, and my uncle was far away when it happened."

"But it could have been done by my stepmother or one of her servants, just as this Rostand whom Aunt Beatrice mentioned must have been the one to cause Father's saddle girth to break. The groom believed it may have been cut. Afterward, the girth was inexplicably lost."

"The murderer made sure of that." Sir Geoffrey's face was grim, his jaw set and hard.

They both stood and strode to their horses. Sir Geoffrey helped her into her saddle, quickly placing her foot in the stirrup and grabbing her other foot and boosting her up, as if he had often helped ladies onto their horses.

His gaze arrested her. "We must tread lightly and not reveal who we are."

"Hearken and consider whether I am able to sound like a country rustic." Delia nearly laughed at her rough change of accent.

Sir Geoffrey gave her a crooked smile. "That is a good try, but no one who looks at you could ever think you anything other than a well-bred lady."

Delia stared back. "Truly? You could not imagine me as a servant, born to a poor mother in a wattle-and-daub house?"

Sir Geoffrey shook his head. "No."

"Are a country girl and a wealthy lady so easily distinguishable?"

"It's not only your unusual beauty," he said as they rode along at a trot, side by side on the road. "It's your mannerisms, the way you walk, the expression of your eyes. Rustics don't move so . . . daintily."

"I'm not sure I like being called dainty."

Sir Geoffrey turned toward her, a meek look on his face, his mouth slightly open.

"I'd rather be thought of as strong and resilient. Like a country rustic."

"You are strong and resilient."

"You don't have to flatter me." Delia laughed. "And I cry far too much to be thought of as strong."

"Not so. Showing your emotions does not make you weak. Just as not showing emotions does not make you strong. You don't allow your emotions to stop you from taking action, do you? But if one never shows emotion . . . that might mean that person is cold and unfeeling."

He was right. Showing emotion wasn't weakness. She may cry, but she would not shrink from doing whatever was needed to defend her brothers. She'd never seen her father show any emotion except occasional anger. And yet he'd seemed very weak in the face of her stepmother's badgering. He'd been controlled by her and had done whatever she wanted.

"You are wise beyond your years, Sir Geoffrey."

He smiled wryly, as if he thought she was teasing him.

They rode on in silence. Not long after, their destination, the village of Wycrofton, was in sight.

TWENTY-TWO

DELIA AND SIR GEOFFREY RODE INTO THE VILLAGE OF Wycrofton at a walk. The rutted main road passed shops and houses, and then on the right was a blackened site where a house had once been. Delia was well aware her brothers had precious little time, so she was grateful Sir Geoffrey stopped the first person he saw on the road.

"Is this where the coroner, Sir John Stanley, perished in his home?"

The woman looked at him with squinty eyes. "It is." She walked away quickly, as though afraid of him.

Delia, who had distanced herself from him while he questioned the woman, moved closer.

"Perhaps you should allow me to ask the questions. You scare people." She gave him a half smile and a grimace to soften her words.

"What do you mean, I scare people?"

"You're a man, you're tall, and you look like a soldier." She shrugged apologetically.

He could hardly help any of those things, and he looked as though he might tell her so.

"You look intimidating and intent on a particular purpose, whereas I can present myself as a timid woman, only curious, nothing more."

"Very well," he said. "If we find someone who might answer our questions, I shall try to stay silent, let you do all the talking." He frowned. "And I'll try not to appear intimidating or soldierly."

"Very good." She nodded, then proceeded down the short lane to the blackened ruins of the house where the coroner had died.

She wasn't sure what she hoped to find. There were only a few stones left, and charred wood timbers and mostly burned debris were all around. There certainly could be no evidence left here; everything of value surely had been burned up or taken by scavengers. And if there had been any evidence, the culprit who set the fire and killed the coroner would have had ample time to come back and take it, as it had been months since the uprising and the burning of the coroner.

God, I know You can do anything. Please help us find something that everyone else has missed. Help us find a bit of evidence to save my brothers.

She kicked a piece of wood out of the way. Perhaps something important could be underneath it. She kicked at the ashes, which were soft and mushy from the recent snow. But there was nothing there.

Sir Geoffrey was squatting by the fireplace and looking inside it.

"Do you see anything?"

"No." He stood up and moved on, all the while staring at the ground.

Delia continued in the opposite direction, looking at the ground. She overturned anything larger than her hand, kicked at the ashes. She moved slowly, but after a while, she came upon Sir Geoffrey, who had searched in a circle and had come back around to her.

"I don't see anything useful." Sir Geoffrey sighed.

Delia's heart squeezed painfully.

"Perhaps we should look again, move the stones over there."

"I will if you wish it." But Sir Geoffrey looked doubtful, pitying. It was obvious he did not believe anything was there.

"What will we do, then?" Delia was asking herself and God as much as she was asking Sir Geoffrey.

"We can talk to people, try to find the coroner's servants who may have survived the fire and ask them if they saw anything. But you know as well as I do, a servant's word means nothing when accusing your stepmother, who is the daughter of a baron, or my uncle, who is an earl."

"Of course. But if they knew something, knew where some bit of evidence was . . ." Fear welled up inside Delia. What if they couldn't find anything? She did not even know what she was looking for.

"Come." Sir Geoffrey bent slightly to look into her eyes. "We'll go to an inn and get something hot to eat. While we're there we're sure to find someone who wants to talk about what happened to the coroner."

Delia nodded, and they walked with their horses down the main road through the village. People greeted them, but there was suspicion in their eyes. The village was not a market town and was not on the main road to London, so they probably did not see a lot of strangers.

They found the only inn in the village and went inside. Sir Geoffrey ordered stew, and they sat down at a small table to eat. It was not as good as her cook's stew back at home, but it was the best she'd had in a long time. The bread was also good, not too coarse, and the innkeeper even provided a bit of butter.

Delia sighed and felt herself relaxing. But before she'd eaten the next bite, she remembered how dire her brothers' situation was. Were they being mistreated at this very moment? Would the soldiers beat them, knowing they'd had a part in killing one of their fellow guards? Or would they execute them quickly, since they'd escaped once before?

"What's the matter?" Sir Geoffrey leaned close. "Are you unwell?"

"I can't eat any more. You may have the rest of mine." She pushed her bowl toward Sir Geoffrey.

"You should eat it. You need your strength."

"No, no, it is more than I can eat. I've already eaten my bread."

"If you are certain . . ."

"I am."

Sir Geoffrey finished his bowl of stew, then ate what remained of hers while Delia scanned the people in the inn. Who might be willing to talk to her about the night the coroner was killed? There was an older man sitting alone. He had a frown on his face, his eyes tense. A group of men sat at another table talking loudly and occasionally slapping the table and laughing. There was not another woman in the entire place.

Perhaps she should try to engage the innkeeper in conversation. He must hear all the gossip in the village. But he looked far too busy to sit and talk.

Sir Geoffrey was also looking around the room. "Who do you fancy?" he said, leaning a bit closer to her. "I don't want to scare anyone off, so I'll just let you choose who you want to question."

He was teasing her now. Her stomach churned a bit as she realized she did not wish to approach any of these men and could not imagine any of them wishing to talk to a curious female asking about the death of their most prominent citizen during Wat Tyler's Rebellion months before.

"Perhaps you could ask someone," she whispered to Sir Geoffrey.

He looked at her, a smile twisting his lips. "If you are sure I will not scare anyone."

"You may make all the jests you want. But there are a lot of rough-looking men in here. I'd be more comfortable if you did the approaching and the asking."

"Very well. I will not tease you. Not now, anyway."

He started to get out of his chair when a man walked into the inn, looked around, and began walking toward her and Sir Geoffrey. He came right up to them.

"May I sit?" he asked, grabbing a chair from a nearby table.

"Of course." Sir Geoffrey motioned an invitation with his hand.

"Thank you." The man, gray-haired but looking only about forty years old, pulled the chair up close to Sir Geoffrey's and sat down.

Delia's heart was in her throat. This man wanted to talk to them. But who was he? And how did he know who they were?

"My mistress sent me to speak with you. She saw you looking around the burned-out home of our coroner. She wants to know why you were searching the rubble."

"Who is your mistress?" Sir Geoffrey leaned closer to the man. Delia also leaned in, scooting closer to Sir Geoffrey to better hear what they were saying.

"My mistress is from a prominent noble family. She is respected and is not accustomed to being gainsaid. And she wishes to know why you were searching the burned house."

"We are trying to discover who killed the coroner and why." Sir Geoffrey raised his brows at the man.

The man said nothing.

"We want the truth about who killed him." Delia made sure to stare into the man's eyes when she said the words.

"My mistress can help you." The man sat back. "Would you like to come with me and talk to her?"

Sir Geoffrey looked at Delia. They were taking a risk, of course, but Delia stood up. The man stood as well, and they followed him out of the inn.

The man waited for them to retrieve their horses, then he led them down the road past the community well, past a blacksmith shop, and past a bakery and a butcher shop, then turned down a narrow lane that led up to a large house made out of stone, two stories high.

Sir Geoffrey leaned close to her, so close his shoulder was pressed against hers. He whispered, "This is the Baron Delaford's house."

A chill went down Delia's spine. This was the house where her stepmother had lived most of her life. It was even possible that her stepmother was here now, visiting her mother and father.

"To whom are you taking us?" Delia demanded of the stranger.

The man looked over his shoulder, then stopped and turned toward her.

"You have no reason to fear. My mistress is Larissa, the unmarried daughter of the baron, and she wishes to offer you help in your search."

Delia remembered Parnella mentioning a sister, but she'd called her "my half-witted sister."

"Why does she wish to help us? Forgive me, but I am only being cautious." Delia smiled as pleasantly as she could while her heart was pounding and her hands were shaking.

"My mistress is on the side of truth and does not wish innocent boys and men to be executed for an act committed by someone else."

Delia turned her head slightly to glance at Sir Geoffrey. He was looking at her. He leaned close and whispered in her ear, "The two sisters are not on friendly terms. Larissa hates your stepmother."

The way Sir Geoffrey's warm breath caressed her ear made

her shiver, while the information sent the breath rushing back into her chest.

"Lead on," she said to the man.

They made their way up to the front door. The man held it open for them, then followed them inside.

"My lady is waiting for you." The man led the way down a long corridor, then up some stairs to a door, which he opened, waving them inside.

Delia had a strange impulse to grab Sir Geoffrey's hand. He glanced down at her at that moment and her heart fluttered. But she restrained herself.

The room was large and full of cushioned benches and chairs. A woman was sitting on a bench with a bundle of yarn in her lap, knitting with two large knitting needles. She was thin and delicate, with sharp cheekbones, and when she looked up at them, she raised her brows and gave a tiny smile.

Her small, pale eyes studied them, flitting back and forth between Delia and Sir Geoffrey.

"Jennings, who have you brought me?"

"Mistress, they did not tell me their names."

"Then let me guess."

The room fell silent as the lady continued to study their faces. Would she actually try to guess their names? Or did she somehow know who they were? She was such an odd little woman, with such frail shoulders and long, pale hair completely uncovered and unfettered. There was a slight resemblance to Delia's stepmother in the pale color of her hair and the shape of her face, but this woman was older.

"The only young woman I can imagine who would be out trying to find evidence of who killed our coroner, who is so beautiful that my vain sister would be jealous of her, is the daughter of the Earl of Dericott. I am guessing that you are Lady Delia."

Delia's heart skipped a beat. So Parnella's sister had heard about her. And Parnella was jealous. That explained why—or at least one reason why—she looked at Delia with so much hatred.

"And this handsome young man I have seen before, though he may not remember me. Sir Geoffrey, the son of the departed Duke of Strachleigh, may he rest in peace."

Sir Geoffrey gave her a small bow.

"Forgive me for my poor manners. Jennings, go and ask Cook for something fruity to drink and some sweet cakes and pasties for my guests and for me."

Jennings hurried away, leaving the three of them alone.

"It seems I forget to eat when I'm alone, but when guests come, they remind me how hungry I am. Won't you sit?" She indicated the bench to her left with a sweep of her hand.

Delia and Sir Geoffrey sat.

"I hope the fire is not too hot for you. I am rather prone to be cold."

"Not at all," Delia said, more to be polite than anything, for the temperature of the room had not entered her mind. "Larissa, do you know who killed the coroner, whom my brothers are accused of murdering?"

"I do. Of course."

Delia's heart leapt. And this woman was the daughter of a

baron. Her word would carry weight. Parnella was just being spiteful, calling her a half-wit. She was perfectly intelligent.

Larissa went on. "Before we talk about that . . . I was told your brothers escaped from the Tower of London. I hope that they are somewhere safe now."

"I am sorry to say that they were recaptured this morning before dawn."

"Oh. That is unfortunate. There is no time to lose, then. As soon as Jennings brings our small repast, I shall tell you how I can help you."

"Do you have evidence of who killed the coroner?" Delia held her breath, waiting for Larissa's answer.

"I do."

"Will you come with us to London to be a witness, to testify before the king?"

"I don't believe that will be necessary."

"It would certainly help to save the young lords who have been falsely accused." Sir Geoffrey leaned toward Larissa. The look on his face was so earnest. Who could ever say no to that face?

"I am not accustomed to leaving Wycrofton. In fact . . . I like to stay very close to home."

What did she mean? As concerned as she seemed, surely she would agree to provide her testimony to save Delia's brothers.

"We would possibly only need you to come to Rosings Abbey to tell Anne of Bohemia, the future queen, what you know."

Larissa pursed her lips. "No, I would not like to do that either. You see, it is a known fact that I . . . don't leave this house."

Parnella almost never mentioned her older sister, but Delia now recalled the cruel look on her stepmother's face one day as she ridiculed her sister for having "an imbecilic fear" of leaving her house and laughing at her reason for never marrying.

God, have we come this far only to fail because this woman won't leave her house and tell anyone what she knows?

Her heart sank all over again. But Larissa did say she had evidence.

Sir Geoffrey was perched on the edge of the bench beside her, his mouth open slightly, as if he wanted to say something but couldn't quite decide how to proceed.

They couldn't fail now.

Twenty-Three

Jennings came in the room carrying a pitcher. A servant woman came in behind him with a second tray holding fruit pasties and cakes. They set them on the low table in front of Larissa, then left without saying a word.

Larissa began pouring red liquid out of the large pitcher into three goblets. She gave one to Delia then one to Sir Geoffrey. Delia took a sip. It tasted of cherries, strawberries, and honey.

"So, you do have evidence? Of who killed the coroner?" Delia couldn't help prompting her. After all, her brothers were in danger. Did this woman not know that she could not just sit here and drink compote and talk in circles while her brothers' lives were in imminent danger?

Larissa picked up a plate and held it out to Delia. "These fruit pasties are very good. Please take one."

Delia took one and so did Sir Geoffrey.

Larissa took one also and immediately bit into it. "Mmm." She nodded while she chewed.

Delia and Sir Geoffrey also each took a bite, but Delia's frustration was mounting. Why must she pretend she was perfectly happy to eat pasties when the only thing she really wanted to do was get the evidence that would save her brothers and leave this place?

But she chewed the bit of apple pasty and silently begged, *Please hurry up and get the evidence. Please let this be what we need. Please, God.*

Larissa ate the pasty, which was smaller than the palm of her hand, in three bites, then closed her eyes. "My favorite."

The small woman stood up and walked to the opposite side of the room. She lifted an embroidered tapestry and uncovered a wooden chest. She reached inside and drew out a rectangular object about a foot long, half a foot wide, and half a foot deep, which she carried in her hands as if it was heavy. She sat back down on the bench and held the box, which looked to be made of a heavy metal, possibly iron, in her lap.

"I found this in the coroner's house."

"So you do leave your house? Sometimes?" Sir Geoffrey sounded tentative, as if afraid of offending her with his question.

"I go out at night . . . sometimes . . . with a servant."

Delia nodded, wanting her to go on.

"It appears to be Sir John's strongbox. He had some silver coins inside, which I gave to his heirs. But what I found most interesting were these two pieces of parchment."

Larissa drew out a roll of parchment, tied with a ribbon. She untied it and carefully passed the parchment to Delia.

Delia unrolled two similarly shaped sheets of parchment. Sir

Geoffrey pressed his shoulder to hers, his head very near, and they both studied the words on the first one, as well as the drawing of a man's figure, with four Xs on the back of the figure's head.

"It is a coroner's report," Larissa said.

Then Delia saw it. Her father's name.

Her stomach flipped queasily. She pulled out the second sheet of parchment. A similarly drawn figure and similar Xs and words filled that page as well. The name on it was George, Duke of Strachleigh. Sir Geoffrey's father.

Sir Geoffrey took that sheet from her hand and left her with the one bearing her father's name.

"I speculate that the coroner wrote two reports—the fake ones, which he gave to the king's officials in London, and the real ones, which you hold in your hands."

Delia clutched the parchment. It spoke of multiple violent blows to the head that were not consistent with a fall from a horse. The word *murder* jumped out at her.

"My stepmother did this." Delia's voice was harsh and barely above a whisper.

"If she did—and I also believe she did—then she would have paid the coroner, Sir John, not to speak of it."

"And my uncle would have paid him not to speak of my father's death." Sir Geoffrey put a hand to his face as he continued to stare at the document in his hand.

"Does that one show the same thing?" Delia asked.

"Murder. Multiple violent blows to the head." Sir Geoffrey's voice cracked on the last word.

Delia squeezed his arm. He was so close to her she didn't

even have to reach. If only they'd been alone, she would have put her arms around him and tried to comfort him. Her own heart hurt at the thought of her father being murdered, but Sir Geoffrey had been close to his father, knowing him to be a good man. It must have been terribly painful to learn that his father had died a violent death, had been so unjustly treated. And it had affected not only his innocent father but Sir Geoffrey and his sister as well.

She noticed Sir Geoffrey wiping his eyes. Her stomach twisted.

"That is the evidence you need, is it not?" Larissa said.

"This only proves that both our fathers were murdered. We also need you to tell where you found this evidence," Delia said.

"And this doesn't prove who killed the coroner, or even who killed our fathers. If we are to free Lady Delia's brothers, we need clear evidence of who committed these murders and who killed the coroner."

Larissa suddenly wouldn't look them in the eye. She fidgeted with her dress sleeve. She reached for her drink, took a sip, then put it down. She twirled her hair around her finger. She cleared her throat and shifted her weight on the bench, shuffling her feet and rearranging her skirt over her legs.

Delia stared hard at her. "Do you know who set fire to the coroner's house with him inside?"

Larissa took a deep breath and let it out. "Yes."

"Who was it?" Sir Geoffrey leaned forward.

"It was the two men who falsely accused your brothers, Lady Delia. It was John Albright and Andrew Goddard."

"You saw them?" Delia's heart was in her throat.

"I told you I sometimes go out at night. It is easier for me than in the daytime, I don't know why. Perhaps because I hardly ever encounter other people at night. And I saw those two men setting fire to the coroner's house."

Delia's heart soared, then sank again when she realized how difficult it would be to prove. However, the word of a baron's daughter would be quite significant, especially to Lady Anne, who had not been bribed to turn a blind eye to the truth.

"Please, Larissa. Will you come with us back to Rosings Abbey?"

"You only have to tell the future queen, Lady Anne," Sir Geoffrey said.

"You know, of course, that she would want me to testify at a new trial, at the king's court in London."

"Perhaps not." Delia moved to the edge of her seat, eager to convince her.

"I am terrified to go so far. I cannot."

"At the future queen's request, the king will not force us all to go through a second trial. Perhaps he will simply set things right," Sir Geoffrey said.

Larissa began taking deep breaths and blowing them out through her mouth.

"You can bring some servants with you—Jennings and anyone else you like." Delia had to convince her.

"Yes, of course. All will be well. We shall protect you." Sir Geoffrey seemed to deepen his voice as he said those last words.

Delia's nerves tingled, whether from the way he said they

would protect Larissa, or the way he looked so strong and fearless, or the way he was being so kind and gentle and didn't scoff at Larissa's fear of leaving her house. Perhaps it was just the fact that he was here, trying to save her brothers. He had not abandoned her.

Larissa's forehead wrinkled and her lips pursed. She squeezed her hands together, her knuckles white.

"I don't know if I can do it," she rasped.

"We can leave after it gets dark," Sir Geoffrey said. "We'll travel at night. Your father can send his men—he must have a few guards. That would make you feel more at ease, would it not?"

"No, none of my father's guards. And my father is not to know I am leaving. He might tell Parnella, or he might come after us himself." She set her jaw, then said, "I will do it."

"Oh, thank you, Larissa. You are saving my brothers' lives." Delia was so happy, she clasped her hands together and smiled with joy.

"I am glad I can save them. I am tired of innocent people being cruelly wronged by my sister and that evil man, Lord Yelverton."

"Thank you," Delia and Sir Geoffrey said at the same time.

"And now we must prepare." Larissa stood. "We shall leave as soon as it is dark."

Delia and Sir Geoffrey also stood, so close she could feel the back of his hand touching hers. She turned her hand over and he clasped it in his.

Delia lost her breath at the intimacy of holding his hand, the touch of his skin on hers, the way he intertwined his fingers with hers. His grasp was warm and solid.

Thank You, God, for this man.

The sky was dark as Geoffrey helped Lady Delia and Larissa onto their horses.

Larissa was so small and light, and her hands were shaking—he could feel it as he took her hand on the mounting step and helped her into the saddle. But at least she was going with them.

After making inquiries, he had discovered that her father, the baron, was not at home. Perhaps that made it easier for her to come with them. Geoffrey and Lady Delia had been shown to separate rooms where they could rest for a few hours until nightfall. They'd be riding most of the night to get back to the abbey.

Now as he helped Lady Delia onto her horse, she smiled down at him. He took the chance to squeeze her gloved hand. She squeezed back.

His heart swelled as he went to mount his own horse and they started out, the three of them with only Larissa's manservant, Jennings, to accompany them.

The night was cold, and Larissa had provided fur robes to keep them warm. But as they rode, the bitter cold wind made his eyes water, the tears stinging his skin.

They were over halfway there when Larissa slowed her horse and asked, "Is there an inn nearby where we could stop and get warm before continuing on?"

"I believe there is a village ahead, not very far from here."
Geoffrey did not want to stop, but it would be better for the
horses to rest for half an hour.

A quarter of an hour later, they did come upon a village with
an inn. They stopped their horses and took them to the stable
beside the inn, laying blankets on them to warm them and paying the stable boy to water them and give them each some hay
and oats. Geoffrey went inside the inn first to make sure none of
the king's guards were there.

Larissa's eyes kept darting all around. She walked so close to
Lady Delia and was so small that she almost looked like a child
holding on to her mother's cloak. Jennings was at Larissa's other
side, but Lady Delia was very attentive to Larissa, making sure
she didn't walk too fast or leave her behind. And since it was
the middle of the night, the only person inside the main room
of the inn was one young man.

"What can I get for you? A room? Two rooms?"

"We just need some warm drinks. What do you have?"

"We have spiced cider and spiced wine."

They all chose the cider. Geoffrey didn't want anything that
might make him sleepy. They still had hours to go before they
reached the abbey, and even when they arrived, they would hardly
have time to sleep before they would need to talk to the abbess.

They sat close to the large fireplace and sipped their cider.
Larissa was slumped down in her chair. She spoke only when he
or Lady Delia asked her a question.

Lady Delia was also rather quiet, and she looked a little tired.
When her eyes met his, she smiled.

What did that smile mean? Certainly she must be happy because they had a witness who could testify as to who killed the coroner. But would the future queen and the king believe Larissa, this daughter of a baron? Had the king been bribed—or intimidated—into going along with what Geoffrey's uncle Baldric wanted, which was for Lady Delia's brothers—and now Geoffrey—to be executed? The influence of his future bride might not be enough to sway him.

Geoffrey heard horses' hooves outside. Several of them. Who could it be, traveling in the middle of the night, besides the king's guards looking for them? He stood and motioned to Delia and Larissa to get up too.

"Is there somewhere we can hide?" he said to the young man who'd served them their cider.

The man just stared at them with his mouth open.

Geoffrey couldn't wait for his answer. He took the ladies' arms and steered them toward what he assumed was the door to the kitchen, with Jennings close behind. They slipped through the doorway just as he heard men's voices entering the inn.

He closed the door to the kitchen, but then pushed it open a crack and peeked through.

Soldiers, about five of them.

"Is anyone else here?" they asked the young man.

Geoffrey held his breath as he waited for the young man to answer.

He shrugged and glanced around. "No."

"No guests in your rooms?"

"There is a married couple. They are asleep."

The soldiers stomped their way to the stairs and started up. One lingered behind and asked him for the key.

Geoffrey motioned for Delia, Larissa, and Jennings to come with him, and he led the way to the door, which he hoped led outside.

He pushed the door open enough to put his head out. In the dark he could just make out several horses being led into the stable, but it was only the stable boy who had taken their horses. Had he told the soldiers they were there?

Geoffrey opened the door and the rest of them followed him outside. He hurried across the green and into the stable.

"We need our horses," he rasped as quietly as he could to the stable boy.

"Yes, sir. They are still saddled."

The four of them found their horses, and Lady Delia led hers out first. But as soon as she left the stable, he heard her make a strange noise.

Geoffrey hurried forward. Silhouetted in the doorway of the stable was Lady Delia and a man with his hand around her throat. Sir Elliot.

Twenty-Four

DELIA'S HEART POUNDED AS SIR ELLIOT PULLED HER BACK against his chest. She clawed at his hand, which was wrapped around her neck. Her whole body shuddered at his nearness, at his vile touch, at the memories that flooded her of the last time she'd been in his presence, terrified and at his mercy.

O God, save me.

"How dare you try to kill me?" Sir Elliot said, his voice sounding like a frog's croak.

"Let me go," Delia managed to choke out.

"You nearly killed me."

Suddenly Sir Elliot jerked away from the door, dragging her with him and holding her arms behind her back with one hand, his other hand still gripping her throat.

"Sir Geoffrey, my old friend," Sir Elliot snarled.

Sir Geoffrey stood in the doorway with his sword drawn. "Let her go."

"Why should I? She tried to kill me."

"She was defending herself."

"Traitor. You participated in killing one of your own, a fellow guard in the king's service. You are so hated, even your own father wouldn't defend you—if he were still alive. But I forgot. He wouldn't mind. He was also a traitor."

Sir Elliot squeezed her wrists behind her back, sending a jolt of pain up her arms. She cried out again, a strangled sound as she tried not to make any noise loud enough to bring any more soldiers out to assist Sir Elliot.

Sir Geoffrey lunged at Sir Elliot, who placed her between him and Sir Geoffrey's sword. Sir Geoffrey drew back.

Delia sputtered and coughed, hoping Sir Elliot would think he was choking her to death and loosen his grip. It must have worked because he did release most of the pressure on her throat, although his fingers still dug into the sides of her neck.

Delia rasped, "Don't worry about me, just kill him."

Sir Elliot jerked her arms back, making her shoulders burn. But she refused to cry out.

Sir Geoffrey threw down his sword and leapt at Sir Elliot, his hands slipping past Delia's face as they went for Sir Elliot's throat.

Sir Elliot let her go in order to defend himself.

Delia spun around as the two men fell to the ground, rolling and grappling at each other's throats.

She could not allow Sir Elliot to hurt Sir Geoffrey.

She picked up Sir Geoffrey's sword off the ground. Sir Elliot was on top of Sir Geoffrey, choking him. Delia drew back the sword and with both hands thrust the sword point straight into Sir Elliot's side, then she drew it back out.

The knight made a strange, guttural sound. He rose up, letting go of Sir Geoffrey's neck.

Sir Geoffrey kicked his enemy to the ground and scrambled to his feet.

Delia handed him the sword, unable to take her eyes off Sir Elliot as he lay on his back, clutching his side.

"We need to go." Sir Geoffrey's voice was urgent as he headed back toward the stable. Larissa and Jennings stood with the reins of all their horses. Jennings boosted Larissa into her saddle while Sir Geoffrey boosted Delia, then mounted his own horse. They were riding out onto the road and away from the inn where she may have just killed a man, the same man she thought she had killed before.

O God, I didn't want to kill him. But thank You that we got away and he didn't hurt Sir Geoffrey.

Her hands were shaking so badly she could barely hold the reins.

Sir Geoffrey was setting a fast pace, constantly glancing over his shoulder, no doubt to make sure she and Larissa and Jennings were keeping up and that they weren't being followed by the other guards.

Poor Larissa. Was she frightened nearly to death? Delia had not been able to see her face to gauge her reaction to the terrifying attack back at the inn. Would she make it to the abbey? If the soldiers caught up to them, would they be able to get their evidence to the king? But Larissa was still atop her horse, thankfully. She hadn't been too panicked to ride.

They rode fast and hard. Delia found herself straining to

listen, dreading to hear the soldiers coming after them. *God, please don't let the soldiers catch up to us. Let us make it to the abbey.*

She began to fear they would miss seeing the lane that led to the abbey. If they did, they would surely be overtaken by the soldiers. Perhaps they could find a place to hide so the soldiers would pass by them.

But the clouds parted and revealed the moon, allowing its light to shine on the road ahead of them. And still they rode, the pounding of her horse's hooves jarring every bone in Delia's body.

Then she saw it. Up ahead was the lane and beyond that was Rosings Abbey, its highest tower stretching tall into the night sky in the light of the moon.

Sir Geoffrey turned down the lane, looking over his shoulder to make sure they were following him. Delia turned after him, with Larissa and Jennings right beside her.

Abbey guards met them at the door and hurried all four of them inside.

"How is my brother?" Delia asked the guards. "Lord Dericott? Do you know if he is well?"

"He lives," said one guard. "That is all I know."

"I heard his fever left him," said another.

Air rushed into her lungs. *Thank You, God.*

As they were walking down the corridor, she could feel Sir Geoffrey's eyes on her. She turned to look at him in the faint torchlight.

"Are you all right?" he asked. He brushed the back of her hand with his. She turned over her hand and let him clasp her fingers in his gentle grip.

"I am well." Her throat was sore and she had some scratches on her wrists, but nothing that seemed worth mentioning. "Thank you for saving me from Sir Elliot."

"And thank you for saving me."

He drew quite close for a moment and she thought he might kiss her, but the guards stopped ahead of them.

"These are your rooms," one of the guards said. "You may rest until dawn, then Abbess Beatrice will see you."

Sir Geoffrey parted from her with another squeeze of her hand, then he and Jennings took one room while Delia and Larissa proceeded into the other.

Delia was still shaking a bit as she shed her riding clothes and turned to Larissa.

"I'm so sorry for everything that happened. I hope you weren't too frighten—"

"Do not worry about me. I am just glad you were not injured by that hateful soldier. I am happy you stabbed him."

Larissa's lips shook, as if she was trying to smile but her mouth did not quite have the strength.

"I need to lie down, I think." Larissa lay across her bed without even taking off her outer dress. She simply pulled the blankets up to her neck and was still, her eyes closed.

Delia took off everything except her underdress and lay down. "Thank You, God," she whispered. At least they'd made it to the abbey. And the guards outside their door made her feel safer. And even her shaking was starting to subside.

Sir Geoffrey. They'd hardly had a moment to speak or even for their eyes to meet after the dreadful encounter with Sir Elliot.

How she wanted to throw her arms around him when she thanked him for saving her. But the corridor had been crowded with guards, and she had been happy with just a squeeze of his hand.

Thinking about Sir Geoffrey in the room next to hers calmed her heart and slowed her breathing. Soon she was drifting into a blessedly dreamless sleep.

Delia awoke with a start to Jennings standing beside Larissa's bed saying, "Wake up. The guards are here to take you to the abbess."

Delia grabbed her bliaud and pulled it over her head as quickly as she could while sitting up in bed, even though Jennings was very deliberately not looking in her direction. In fact, once Larissa had assured him she was awake, he walked out and closed the door.

Delia darted out of bed and immediately felt sick, the lack of sleep over the last few days taking its toll. She poured herself a cup of water from the pitcher in their room and took a few tiny sips until the feeling subsided. She filled the cup again and handed it to Larissa, who took it and drank a sip.

"I am ready." Larissa's hands were clasped tightly in front of her, white knuckles and pursed lips showing her anxiety. But her expression was stoic and her eyes stared straight ahead.

Someone knocked on their door. Delia opened it.

"Are you ready?" Sir Geoffrey had a half smile on his face. He motioned for her to come into the hall with him.

"We are ready." Delia stepped out and closed the door behind her.

"I have been to see Edwin this morning," Sir Geoffrey said.

"Oh! How is he?"

"His fever is completely gone and he is sitting up and eating."

"Thanks be to God," Delia said, exhaling. She crossed herself.

How noble and courageous Sir Geoffrey was, always doing the right thing, always ready to help her, never wavering.

"Yes." Sir Geoffrey was staring so intently at her, his expression so strange, as if he was longing for something, for her to say something . . . Or was he just longing for her?

Her heart seemed to expand, threatening to come out of her chest, as if it longed for him too.

Delia whispered, "I do so admire you, Sir Geoffrey. Your kindness and your . . ."

He leaned down, his face near hers. He placed his hand very lightly against her cheek, his fingers sinking into her hair, brushing her ear. His gaze moved from her eyes to her mouth.

". . . courage," Delia rasped.

Would he kiss her? If he didn't, she might just stand on her toes and kiss him. Was that too bold? Too scandalous and forward?

Just then the door opened behind her and Jennings appeared beside them.

"We should go." Sir Geoffrey kissed her forehead, a quick peck, and straightened, then wrapped his hand around hers and squeezed.

Delia's heart dropped, then lifted again as she realized he probably would have kissed her if Larissa and Jennings had not been there. She would have kissed him in front of them! She *was* scandalous.

Two abbey guards soon appeared and walked them down the long corridor. Sir Geoffrey still held her hand. She peeked up at him. He looked down at her and winked. The gesture was probably meant to bolster her courage, but it made her heart flutter.

The guards stopped in front of a door. Sir Geoffrey let go of her hand as they were ushered into a small room with Abbess Beatrice. The guards shut the door, leaving Delia, Sir Geoffrey, Jennings, and Larissa with the abbess.

"Please allow me," Delia said, "to present Larissa, daughter of the Baron Delaford."

"Larissa," Aunt Beatrice greeted her. "I pray you are well."

"I am well, Your Grace."

"Will you tell me what you know of the crime Lady Delia's brothers are accused of? Do you know who killed the coroner, Sir John Stanley?"

"Yes, I saw the two men who set fire to the house, and I know their names and can identify them."

"Come with me, then. The future queen is an early riser." The abbess stood and went to a small door that led into a larger room.

Inside the room, sitting on the large chair that Delia was accustomed to seeing her aunt occupying, was a very small, very young woman. Reports were that the future queen was only fifteen years old.

Lady Anne of Bohemia turned her head to look at them as they entered.

Delia bowed down to the floor, as the rest of her little party were doing.

"Please rise," said a small, girlish voice.

They all arose. The future queen's facial features were dainty, her hands tiny, and her skin almost translucent.

"Lady Anne," the abbess said, "please allow me to present Lady Delia Raynsford, sister of the Earl of Dericott, Larissa, daughter of Baron Delaford, and Sir Geoffrey Grenefeld, former heir to the dukedom of Strachleigh. They have a request for you, my lady."

"I am ready to hear the details of it. Please don't be afraid to speak truth." Lady Anne smiled after uttering the quiet, sweetly intoned words.

Delia glanced at Larissa. Even out of the corner of her eye, she could see that the lady was shaking. Would she even be able to speak? She had seemed rather self-assured in her own home, but here . . . She was obviously struggling even to breathe and stay upright.

"My lady," Delia said, "I am most humbly grateful, on behalf of myself and my brothers, for your willingness to hear our story and possibly advocate for us."

It was strange to speak so formally to a woman three years younger than Delia and quite small for her age. But she was the future queen, set to marry their boy-king within a month. She sat regally without fidgeting, a benevolent look in her eyes that was far beyond her years.

"Go on," Lady Anne said.

"My brothers, all seven of them, were accused of murdering the king's coroner, Sir John Stanley of Wycrofton, Bedfordshire, by burning him in his home during Wat Tyler's Rebellion. Three of my brothers are still very young, younger than yourself, my lady. None of my brothers have ever been near this man, nor ever had a treasonous thought against our king. I would never dream of bothering you with this, but my brothers, even though they are innocent, were tried and found guilty by the court. They were set to be executed. They escaped but now have been recaptured and taken back to the Tower of London."

Delia tried to speak quickly so as not to seem inconsiderate of Lady Anne's time.

"Sir Geoffrey and I went to Wycrofton and found someone who was a witness to the coroner's murder, Larissa Lupton, the daughter of Baron Delaford. She saw who set fire to the house. She knows the persons who set the fire, and she saw that it was not my brothers."

"Larissa? Is this true?"

Delia prayed, *God, help Larissa.*

"Yes, my lady." Larissa's voice shook and her words were breathy. "I was out walking at night . . ." Larissa stopped to catch her breath and swallow. ". . . and I saw two men whom I knew from my village, who had both done work for my father. They were setting fire to Sir John's house. They each carried some wood . . . Forgive me." Larissa was so nervous, she kept pausing to take a breath.

"You are doing very well. No need to rush."

Thank You, God, that Lady Anne is so gracious. Please help Larissa, Lord.

"They each carried some wood and hay and a lantern and approached the coroner's house. I was suspicious of them, so Jennings and I stayed and watched. A few minutes later, the house was engulfed in flames. Had I known the coroner was still inside his house, we certainly would have done what we could to get him out."

"Did you see the Earl of Dericott or any of his brothers there that night?"

"No, my lady. They were not there." Larissa swayed to one side, then the other. Jennings rushed up behind her and steadied her.

"Let her sit down." Lady Anne motioned to a chair set against the wall. One of the guards who was standing as still as a statue suddenly went and brought the chair to Larissa as Jennings helped her sit.

Delia stepped toward Larissa and bent to ask, "Are you well?"

Larissa nodded but kept her head down. Delia squeezed her hand.

"Thank you for coming here and talking about this," Lady Anne said, nodding to Larissa. Then she turned her gaze on Delia.

"It is very troubling that your brothers have been wrongly accused, Lady Delia." Lady Anne's voice was quiet and calm. "What brought this about? Who accused them?"

"We do not know who the peer of the realm was that accused them, as their testimony was written down and kept secret. Only the king and his councilors and the judges were privy to it. But the two men who witnessed against them at the trial were the same two men Larissa saw setting fire to the house."

"And where are these men now?"

"I do not know, my lady. It is believed they may have left the country."

They all waited for Lady Anne to speak again. Her brows were lowered, the only indication she was feeling any emotion at all.

"I shall speak to the king and use what influence I have to save your brothers." She paused, then said, "It is my will that they be exonerated outright, but I am not the king. We must all bow to his will."

Delia bowed her head to indicate that she understood and she would also bow to the will of the king.

"It is perhaps fortuitous that I will be able to speak to the king very soon, even today."

Delia looked up.

"He has sent word that he is coming here to Rosings Abbey, today, to . . . meet with me."

Was it Delia's imagination, or was the future queen blushing? Her cheeks were a rosy hue. Her hands moved to her lap and twisted together, then she moved them back to rest on the chair arms.

So this would be the first meeting between the king and his bride-to-be. It was courageous of her to wish to advocate on their behalf with a future husband she had yet to meet. Though if their first meeting went badly, no doubt she would not even mention Delia's brothers' plight to him.

Delia turned to look at Sir Geoffrey just before he turned his eyes on her. Was he thinking the same thing? And should they mention the death reports they'd found in the dead coroner's strongbox? They might never get another opportunity to speak to the future queen. The time to do it was now.

Delia and Sir Geoffrey both opened their mouths to speak. Delia nodded, deferring to Sir Geoffrey.

"My lady, if I may . . ." Sir Geoffrey explained the two reports, signed by the coroner, that showed that both his father and Delia's had been murdered in similar fashion and their deaths had not been accidental, as had been previously assumed. He explained who had the most to gain from their deaths—Delia's stepmother and Sir Geoffrey's uncle, who had also accused his father, a duke, of treason and had been granted Sir Geoffrey's father's secondary title of earl.

"May I see those coroner reports?" she asked.

Delia and Sir Geoffrey handed the documents to a guard, who brought them to Lady Anne. She looked them over.

"I shall keep these reports, if you do not mind, to show to the king." Lady Anne was quiet for a moment, then said, "As his guards will accompany him here, I think it best if you stay out of sight, in your rooms."

"Of course." Delia was happy to comply with that request.

"I will strive to at least secure the king's promise to send word that your brothers, Lady Delia, not be mistreated in any way and that their sentence not be carried out until this matter has been presented to the king and he has made his decision. I believe I may promise you this much."

"Oh, thank you, my lady. I am most grateful to you."

Lady Anne nodded. "And now, you must be tired after riding most of the night. You may go."

Delia had not realized just how exhausted she was until she left the future queen's presence and was standing in the corridor with Larissa and Sir Geoffrey, waiting for the guards to escort them back to their rooms. A nun came out behind them and said, "Some food will be sent to your rooms."

"Thank you," Delia said.

Sir Geoffrey offered her his arm and she wrapped her arm through his. They walked close together all the way back.

"Rest well," he said softly as they parted and went into their separate rooms.

Delia looked closely at Larissa's face. "You did very well today, speaking to the future queen. You can't know how grateful I am to you for all your help. Is there anything I can get you? Anything you need?"

"I am very well. I am quite proud of myself, actually." Larissa covered her enormous smile with her hand.

"As well you should be." Delia smiled back. "You are very brave to speak to Anne of Bohemia on my brothers' behalf, when there was nothing to be gained for you."

"I did gain something," Larissa said, sitting down on the side of her bed.

"What is that?"

"My sister, Parnella, may finally get what she deserves. She has always lied and schemed and manipulated to get just what she desires—power and wealth and whatever man she fancies. But now she will see that she cannot destroy any more lives. Her schemes will finally be brought out into the open, and I have the satisfaction of knowing I had a part in that." Larissa lay on her bed and turned her face to the wall.

Delia would not judge Larissa. She could only imagine what

the woman had gone through by being the sister of someone as evil as Parnella. Though the Bible said, "It is mine to avenge; I will repay, says the Lord," judgment was also the Lord's, and Delia had no desire to take on that right or duty. But she had a deep desire, just as Larissa did, to see justice done. She wanted her stepmother and Sir Geoffrey's uncle to be revealed as the evil people they were. But most importantly, she wanted her brothers to be publicly vindicated and shown to be innocent of all accusations.

Soon food arrived. Delia gratefully ate, then lay down. She would rest for a bit, then go and see how Edwin was doing and find out what she could do for him.

As soon as her eyes were closed, she fell asleep.

TWENTY-FIVE

GEOFFREY WAS AWAKENED BY SOMEONE POUNDING ON THE door.

He leapt out of bed. He always slept wearing at least hose, in case he had to be ready for action, and this time he had left all his clothes on, since it was daytime when he lay down.

As he strode to the door, it burst open and three of the king's guards entered. They came straight at Geoffrey and one slammed his fist into his gut.

Geoffrey bent forward, an involuntary reaction, while another guard struck him in the side of his face.

"That is for killing a fellow guard while helping those brothers escape," a deep voice growled, just before another blow to the head knocked him to the floor.

They pummeled him in the back and kicked him in the stomach. Geoffrey tried to fight back, but there were too many of them.

He heard scrambling and footsteps and then a scream. Were

they hurting Lady Delia? He tried harder to get up, and as soon as he was able, he sprang to his feet.

The king's guards who had attacked him were leaving the room. Lady Delia was staring at him with an open mouth and horror in her eyes.

"What is happening?" Abbey guards entered the room moments after the king's guards had left.

"Those guards attacked Sir Geoffrey!" Lady Delia hurried toward him.

Geoffrey tasted blood in his mouth, and the pain in his head and stomach kept him from standing all the way upright. He sat down on his bed, leaning forward. They had truly worked their revenge on him by making him look weak in front of Lady Delia. Jennings was lying on the floor against the wall.

"Check on Jennings." He pointed at Larissa's manservant.

Lady Delia hurried over to him as his eyes fluttered open. He groaned and then sat up.

"I am well," he said, holding his head and looking at Geoffrey.

The abbey guards only stared, as if wondering what to do.

Lady Delia moved to Geoffrey's side while telling the guards, "Go find those men!"

She knelt beside where he was sitting on the low bed.

"You're hurt! I must take you to the healer."

"No, no, it is nothing." But he could hardly talk, the pain in his side and stomach was so sharp. His voice sounded strained even though he was trying to sound normal.

"You are bleeding." She looked as if she might cry as she examined his face.

"I am well enough."

"Why were those men trying to kill you?"

"They were only letting me know they didn't like what we did . . . when we escaped."

"Because Edwin killed that guard?"

Geoffrey nodded. He felt around his mouth with his tongue. At least he hadn't lost any teeth.

"Do you think they'll come back?"

"I suspect not."

"Where do you hurt the most?" She put her hands on his shoulders and peered into his face.

She was so pretty, so sweet.

Jennings left the room, letting them know he was going to check on Larissa.

"I need to clean these cuts."

Lady Delia's brows were drawn together in an expression of concern as her gaze flitted from his busted lip to the rest of his face, where he could only imagine he had cuts and bruises.

"What do you think is your worst injury? What hurts the most?"

"I am not seriously hurt. I imagine the worst thing is a few broken ribs."

"Oh no! Should you lie down?"

"I will be all right." He couldn't help smiling at how she was fussing over him, although the simple act of smiling brought pain to the cut on his lip. "The ribs will heal on their own. No need to lie down."

She got up and fetched a basin of water and a cloth. She

touched his eyebrow with the dampened cloth, very gently dabbing at it. The cloth came away red, but she kept dabbing until she looked satisfied and rinsed the cloth in the basin of water.

She seemed to purposely be avoiding looking him in the eye. But he didn't mind, as he could get his fill of staring at her pretty face, her large, upturned eyes, her plump lips, and her perfect chin. Her hair fell across her forehead in a pretty wave of dark curls, as if she had just rolled out of bed, which she undoubtedly had.

Next, she started dabbing at his cheekbone. It stung a bit, even though she was being very gentle. He didn't flinch, and she finally met his eyes, shaking her head.

"What?"

"You look as if you attacked those men with your face."

"That is unfair," he protested. "There were three of them and only one of me, and they ambushed me in my room while I was sleeping."

"I am only making a jest. Be still, please." She was smiling now as she moved on to his lip, touching it with the wet cloth.

Just the sight of her staring at his mouth made him stare at hers . . . and wish he could kiss it. But would she be repulsed at his bloody, broken lip? He hadn't even had a chance to rinse the blood from his mouth.

She moved even closer. "Your poor lip," she whispered.

Geoffrey's heart was in his throat at being alone with her. This was his chance to speak. Perhaps the king would see things as his guards saw them and would have Geoffrey and Lady Delia's brothers executed, but just in case they were to get out of this alive . . . he had to speak.

"Lady Delia," he said.

Her gaze flitted from his lips to his eyes. "Yes?"

"You must have noticed that I . . . I admire you very much."
Why was this so hard? If only he knew for certain that she felt
the same way about him. How did she feel?

She only stared at him for a moment and lowered the cloth
from his face, dropping it in the basin of water.

"No, I don't believe I . . . noticed that."

"You are honest and sincere and very brave." He leaned closer
to her. What was she thinking? But she said nothing. So he went
on. "And you are very beautiful. I wonder if you could ever think
of me . . ."

"Think of you? Of course." She sounded breathless.

He was being a coward. He needed to tell her what was truly
in his mind and heart. "I love you and I want to marry you, Lady
Delia. And if I can ever . . . That is, if things change . . ."

"Yes." She looked him in the eye.

"Yes?"

"Yes."

He caressed her cheek with his thumb, then leaned down
closer, so close his lips and hers were almost touching. When
she closed her eyes, his heart squeezed inside him. He brushed
his lips against hers.

She did a quick intake of breath, which made his stomach
flip over itself. He pressed his mouth against hers in earnest now.
She was unutterably sweet, her lips so soft and warm they made
his heart thump wildly. The slight pain in his lip did not deter
him at all. He slid his arms around her.

After a moment he pulled away. Anyone might come into the room and see them. They were in a convent, after all. Nuns went up and down the corridors at all hours, and the door was wide open. Not only that, but Jennings could return at any moment. But gazing down at her relaxed face, the way her eyes were slow to flutter open, made him want to forget everything and everyone else and just keep kissing her.

But that would not be right.

"Forgive me," he said, slowly letting her go as he pulled away even more. "If you and your brothers get your freedom and titles and land back, and if I am still just a lowly knight, I will not expect you to marry me."

"That isn't a very nice thing to say." Delia's brows drew down.

"What do you mean?"

"Either you are saying that I only want you if you have money, or that you wouldn't wish for your wife to have a higher place in society than you."

Her words stung. "That doesn't make me sound very honorable, does it?" The last thing he wanted was to be seen as dishonorable.

"No, and I want to marry you because you are a good man, the most honorable man I've ever known, and I don't intend to release you from marrying me no matter what happens. So no, I will not let you out of it. I consider it a binding betrothal."

His heart soared, his smile stretching wide.

She suddenly leaned forward and kissed him so gently on the lips, Geoffrey never wanted it to end, but it did, all too quickly. Delia stood to her feet.

"I shall bring you some water to drink." She had not taken more than a step when he heard heavy footsteps coming closer.

Delia heard someone coming down the corridor, the sound getting louder and nearer. She hurried to fetch the heavy clay pitcher full of water. If she had to use it to fend off the king's angry guards wanting to hurt Sir Geoffrey again, she would. It wouldn't be the first time she'd used a pitcher as a weapon.

The guards stopped in the doorway. Sir Geoffrey was standing up, his body in a defensive and tense posture. The guards did not enter the room, but the one in the lead spoke. "The king wishes to see Sir Geoffrey and Lady Delia and Mistress Larissa."

Delia put down the pitcher. She would get her chance to speak to the king! Her hand shook as she reached out to Sir Geoffrey and laid her hand on his arm. This was her chance, no doubt her last and only chance, to save her brothers.

Soon she and Sir Geoffrey and Larissa were walking down the corridor, surrounded by the guards.

Larissa walked close to Delia again, between her and Sir Geoffrey. But she was willing to forgo holding his hand to help Larissa feel more at ease. She was so grateful for Larissa's help that she would have done almost anything for her.

They reached the same room where they previously had an audience with Lady Anne. Delia barely caught a glimpse of the king and his future queen before bowing.

"Please rise," said the king.

The young couple was seated in two grand armchairs on a raised dais at one end of the room.

The king, who looked childlike with his thin face, yellow hair, and fine features, motioned to them with his hand.

"You may move closer." There was no hint of irony in his voice. He was straightforward but regal.

Delia, Larissa, and Sir Geoffrey walked toward him. Delia, having never been to court, followed Sir Geoffrey's lead. He moved all the way up to the dais before kneeling and bowing his head again. Larissa was so close to Delia that when Delia curtsied, Larissa followed suit almost in unison.

"Your Grace and my lady," Sir Geoffrey said in a very sober and respectful voice. "We thank you for granting us this audience."

"Sir Geoffrey of Strachleigh, I presume?"

"Yes, Your Grace."

"And Lady Delia of Dericott?"

"Yes, Your Grace." Delia curtsied again.

"And Mistress Larissa of Wycrofton?"

"Y-y-yes, Your Grace." Larissa's voice was so breathless, Delia wondered if the king could even hear her.

"I have seen the coroner's reports that you gave to my future queen, Lady Anne," King Richard said, glancing down at his lap where the sheets of parchment lay. "You may tell me now what you think happened and who the real murderers are in these three incidents."

Sir Geoffrey looked at Delia. She nodded to him, wanting him to speak first.

He took a deep breath and began telling the king about

arresting Delia's brothers and how they all believed that Delia's stepmother, Parnella, and Sir Geoffrey's uncle, Baldric, had conspired to rid themselves of anyone preventing them from inheriting what they wanted—namely, Delia's and Sir Geoffrey's inheritances. The coroner had been their pawn, and they'd murdered him to ensure his silence and pinned the murder on Delia's brothers, who were the last remaining people in their way.

"Forgive me, Your Grace," Sir Geoffrey said, "for I know my uncle is one of your councilors. I can understand why you'd be reluctant to trust what I say about him."

"On the contrary," King Richard said, "I am inclined to believe you. Your uncle, the Earl of Yelverton, nearly had an apoplectic fit when I told him I was coming here without any of my advisors so that I might meet my future bride in private. He said some rather insulting things about my youth and lack of wisdom. His reaction was suspicious. At the time I was unaware of you being here, but he would have known that your brothers, Lady Delia, were arrested from here and that your aunt was the abbess."

Delia's heart soared at hearing the king's response.

"Lady Delia, do you affirm Sir Geoffrey's account of things?"

"Yes, Your Grace. It is all correct and true, to the best of my knowledge and understanding."

"And you, Mistress Larissa? What say you?"

"Y-y—" Larissa stopped and swallowed. "It is all true. My sister, Parnella, Lady Dericott, is an evil woman. She has no conscience at all and would not scruple to murder anyone who was in her way."

Larissa's face turned red during her speech, her expression defiant. But now that she had finished, her lips were parted and she was breathing hard, her chest rising and falling rapidly.

"I have already sent word to London that the Lords Dericott should not be harmed. Their sentence shall not be carried out. I have also sent some of my men to apprehend Lady Dericott and Lord Yelverton and have them brought to the Tower of London until my return."

"Oh, thank you, Your Grace," Delia blurted out. "We are so grateful."

The king held up his hand as if to silence her. "It is my pleasure to right any injustices that I can. Also, I wish to reinstate your father's title, Sir Geoffrey. Henceforth you shall be the Duke of Strachleigh and shall take your rightful place among the peers. Any land that was taken from your father's estate and given to your uncle shall be restored to you forthwith."

Sir Geoffrey bowed. "I thank you most fervently."

"There is also the matter of the guard who was killed during your escape."

"We are heartily sorry, Your Grace," Sir Geoffrey said. "Deeply sorry. It was not our intention to greatly harm any of the guards in our escape, but given that the Lords Dericott were about to be wrongly executed and were thus fighting for their lives . . . We thought of it as self-defense."

"Your Grace," Delia said, "forgive me, but my brothers did not want to kill anyone. They took care to only bind the other three guards."

"Indeed," the king said. "Which makes me inclined to accept

the plea of self-defense. And as for this Sir Elliot, who my guards have told me has twice been attacked and wounded by Lady Delia . . . Can you explain why you assaulted him?"

"Yes, Your Grace." She gave a brief explanation of what had happened in both incidences, ending with, "I stabbed him to save Sir Geoffrey's life."

"Very well. He shall be dismissed for his harassment of a woman and will not be allowed to guard my palace, the Tower of London, nor any other of my holdings."

Through all of this discourse, Lady Anne sat demurely quiet and still beside her future husband. But obviously she had spoken to him on their behalf. Perhaps they had even bonded over this story.

How must Lady Anne be feeling, knowing she was to marry this man whom she had just met?

Delia had known Sir Geoffrey for only a few weeks, but she knew in her heart, by the way this man had proven himself kind and just and brave, noble and upright, that she wanted to marry him and love him for the rest of her life. He wasn't boastful or arrogant. He was sincere and humble. And he made her feel happy. He'd never criticized or goaded her. He'd only encouraged and comforted her through all the many frightening troubles of the last few weeks. He'd risked his own life to save her and her brothers. And knowing herself as she did, that she would love her husband with her whole heart and support him in every way she could, she found this man, of all men, worthy of her love.

Delia and Sir Geoffrey made their way, hand in hand, to the healer's chamber to find Edwin. They had said little since their audience with the king and future queen. But Delia knew the first thing she wanted to do was tell Edwin the good news.

Inside the room, Edwin lay on a narrow but comfortable-looking bed with his face to the wall.

"Edwin? We have such wonderful news," she said softly as she approached his bedside.

He turned until he was lying on his back. "Delia?"

"It is me. And Sir Geoffrey is with me."

Edwin pushed himself up to sitting.

"How are you feeling?"

"Better. What is your news?"

He seemed to be trying to balance himself. Her stomach sank to think how awful it must be as a knight to lose his arm.

"The king has exonerated you and all our brothers."

"And you, Sir Geoffrey?"

"Yes, me as well," Sir Geoffrey said. "And I will even get my father's title and inheritance."

"I am very glad to hear that." And Edwin did look glad. His brows went up. "Do they know who killed the coroner?"

"They know exactly who. We found a witness when we went to Bedfordshire. And we know that Parnella and Sir Geoffrey's uncle, the Earl of Yelverton, were behind it." She decided not to tell him just yet that those two had also murdered their father.

"Would you like to get some fresh air?" Sir Geoffrey asked him.

"That is a very good idea," Delia said. "I know how much you hate being indoors. Some air will do you good, especially now that we know we are all safe."

Edwin's expression did not change. "No. I do not wish to get any fresh air."

His morose appearance and tone of voice filled Delia with sadness and a desire to help fix this melancholy in her oldest brother. He surely would not fall into despair. Not her strong, capable, courageous Edwin. *God, help me to help him.*

Two weeks had gone by and Delia and Edwin were home again at Dericott Castle. She was in the front entryway observing how the light snowfall from the night before had covered everything in a perfect dusting of snow. She was thankful she had finished the last two sweaters for Gerard and Edwin while she and Geoffrey and Edwin were at the abbey waiting for the rest of her brothers to join them. But she also remembered the tears that had flowed while she was knitting Edwin's, knowing she'd be knitting only one sleeve for his.

All her brothers were back to their duties, and Geoffrey had returned to his family's ancestral estate, managing to get things set to rights after taking it back from his uncle, who had disappeared with Parnella and Cedric. It made her melancholy to think of her innocent baby brother being raised by Parnella and possibly Geoffrey's uncle. What would become of him? Delia would probably never get to know him at all.

But her soon-to-be husband sent a courier every two days

with a new letter. He'd even written her a poem. It was witty and made her laugh, as well as moved her to tears with its declarations of love and adoration for her. She'd never thought of him as a poet. He said it was his first poem, and as such, he had begged her not to judge it too harshly. But she loved it because it came from his heart.

Through the window she saw Edwin slowly making his way up the front steps. She rushed out to him, as he still had occasional trouble keeping his balance.

"Let me help you," she said, taking his arm.

"I don't need help." He said the words in a soft tone, but they stung just the same.

"I know you can do it on your own." Had she offended his masculinity? His sense of independence? "I'm sorry, Edwin. I didn't mean to—"

"No. It's all right. I just don't want you treating me like an invalid."

"I wouldn't treat you like an invalid unless you were an invalid."

It was a weak jest, and it didn't break the scowl forming on Edwin's face.

"I may only have one arm, one hand, but I don't want you feeling like you have to take care of me. I can care for myself."

"You are so grumpy now." They were walking up the steps together, side by side, but slowly.

"I am not grumpy." But even Edwin's tone belied his statement. "It is good that you are going to Bedfordshire soon to marry Sir Geoffrey—Lord Strachleigh. You always did want to take care of people, and I am not accustomed to being taken care of."

"It must make you angry when people assume you can't do things for yourself." She tried empathy instead of caregiving, since he was so opposed to that.

"It does. It makes me very angry." Edwin hadn't allowed anyone to cut his hair lately, and it fell into his eyes like a shaggy mane.

"You're as gruff as an old bear." Perhaps a little teasing would break him out of his mood.

But Edwin said nothing as he went inside the house and started up the stairs, probably going to his bedchamber, where he spent a good deal of time, more than likely brooding over his ill fortune.

"Don't be sad."

Delia spun around. She hadn't realized anyone else was in the entryway.

Mistress Wattlesbrook took a step toward her. "He just needs time to adjust and accept this. He will be well."

"I hope so." Delia sat down on a bench against the wall, and Mistress Wattlesbrook joined her. "But it hurts me to see him so downcast. And it's all so unfair." Speaking the words out loud brought her down even more than when they went silently through her thoughts. *Unfair.* It was such a heavy word.

"What is unfair, my child?"

"The fact that my brothers were falsely accused and had to be imprisoned in the first place. If they had not fought to escape, they would be dead now. And as unfair as all that was, it was even more unfair for Edwin to suffer the consequences of someone else's evil actions."

"But everyone suffers one thing or another in this life. Are you saying that Edwin's unfair circumstances are more unfair than everyone else's?"

"Yes." But Delia thought about it. Many people had much worse circumstances than Edwin's. At least he had been exonerated by the king. That was very fortunate. And all her brothers were alive and well. That was also very fortunate. Perhaps she was being ungrateful.

"What about Parnella? She did this to us, and yet she and that evil Lord Yelverton have run off to the Continent and have escaped any consequences for what they did to us, for murdering our father and Geoffrey's father and causing Edwin this pain."

"That does seem unfair, it is true."

"And Sir Elliot may have been dismissed from the king's guard for what he did to me, but he is still free and being supported by his family. His father is a marquess and very wealthy."

"There are many unjust things in this world, I will grant you that." Mistress Wattlesbrook nodded as she stared straight ahead. "But does it help you to dwell on the unfair things?"

"What do you mean?"

"Does it make you feel any better or change things to get angry about the unfairness, to stew over it?"

"No, of course not."

"I believe there is a passage in the Holy Writ about learning from our trials and tribulations. Do you recall reading that?"

"Yes, I believe I do."

"Consider it pure joy, I believe it says?"

"Yes." Was God cruel to tell her to consider her trials pure joy? Did that include the trial Edwin was now facing? There was nothing joyful about losing his arm. And yet . . . perhaps all these cruel and unusual events they had been through were a way of helping them mature and grow and learn. When Larissa and Delia had spent a few days together at the abbey, Larissa revealed that she had gone through abuse at the hands of her sister when they were children, and her father had not been very kind to either of them.

Perhaps they all had a choice when they experienced unfair things. They could become like Parnella, who was cruel and selfish and would do anything to get what she wanted. Or they could become afraid and reclusive like Larissa, who rarely left her house and was sometimes nearly overwhelmed by fear. Or they could become like Geoffrey, who had determined to be noble and good and never do anything dishonorable after the terrible injustices inflicted on him and his sister by their uncle.

She had thought she could not live without her brothers. If they'd died, how could she have gone on? But she could have gone on. God would have been with her, and He would have given her the strength to bear whatever trials she had to face, just as God would give Edwin the strength to bear whatever struggles came to him. God had never left him, even though he had lost his arm. And Delia was very thankful he was alive.

Things might not always turn out so well. But Delia now knew she would be able to endure anything, no matter what happened, because God was with her.

"Do you think," Delia said, "that Edwin will one day feel as if his life is well and good? That everything turned out for the best?"

Mistress Wattlesbrook smiled. "Oh yes. Your brother may be angry and hurt, perhaps blaming God for not saving his arm, but he can be joyful again. Of course he can. The only thing that stops us from being joyful is ourselves."

"Ourselves?"

"What we allow ourselves to think." Mistress Wattlesbrook shrugged her shoulders and stood to her feet. "You worry too much, Lady Delia."

Delia must have looked as frustrated as she felt, for Mistress Wattlesbrook smiled.

"Forgive an old woman. No one wants to be told what to think or feel. But the answer will come to you. And it will come to Edwin. Our thoughts and beliefs cause us to experience either joy or bitterness, sourness or sweetness. It is our own choice."

Mistress Wattlesbrook started to walk away. Delia was left with the strangest feeling inside. It was as if she was seeing the future . . . and the past . . . and the present all at once. There was good, and there was bad, but perhaps what Mistress Wattlesbrook was saying was that she could choose how she would let herself respond to both the good and the bad.

And there was so much love to set her thoughts upon—love from Geoffrey as well as from her brothers and from God— that she had no excuse not to choose to forgive those who had wronged her and to focus her thoughts on the joyful things that surrounded her.

Epilogue

Delia stood in the warm sunshine of spring. Finally, the birds were singing again, the flowers were blooming, and the trees were budding. And she was marrying Geoffrey.

He held her hand all the way through the village of Dericott. The church had never looked so pretty, with its cream-colored stone walls and tall, square belfry, the checkered crenellations across the top, the arched windows and doorways. The sky was a perfect shade of blue, with layers of fluffy white clouds floating overhead.

Geoffrey—or as everyone else now called him, Lord Strachleigh—squeezed her hand gently and smiled with his eyes. He bent and kissed her temple, just as the priest began to speak.

Could her heart be any fuller?

Her brothers were there, all of them looking more handsome than ever, if that was possible, with such striking expressions of goodness and nobility on their faces. Even Edwin did not look as morose as he had all winter.

Geoffrey's sister, Amicia, had arrived from the Continent. She was so lovely, both outwardly and inwardly, that Delia couldn't help but hope she might catch the eye of one of her brothers. She was only sixteen years old, and far be it from Delia to interfere. Such important matters were not her business to meddle in. She would leave it up to God to choose her brothers' wives, as well as her new sister's husband. She had to remind herself often, since it was a big temptation to decide for them who would be best.

The air was crisp but not too cold, and the sun sparkled in her new husband's eyes. God had been so good to her. She'd thought often about the unjust things that had happened to her and to her brothers, but perhaps she would understand someday why He had allowed events to unfold the way they had. For now she would just be thankful that they were all alive and that those who wished them harm were far away. Joy no longer seemed as fragile as it once had.

She had once believed that her happiness was dependent on people staying healthy and circumstances being good. But now she felt that joy was not so easily broken as long as it was bound together with love and hope—love of God and good people in her life and the hope that she would always have love, both to give and to receive . . . "*on earth as it is in heaven.*"

As she gazed up at Geoffrey, she vowed to love him as perfectly as possible, and to receive his love with as much gratitude and openness as her heart could manage.

Coming June 2021

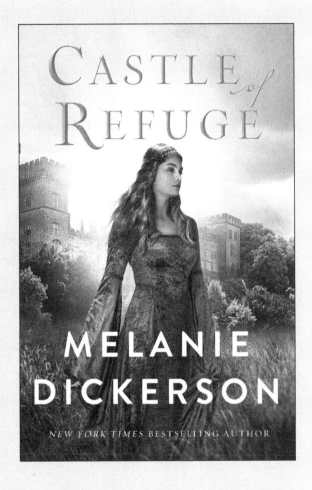

CASTLE *of* REFUGE

MELANIE DICKERSON

NEW YORK TIMES BESTSELLING AUTHOR

The power of love is brought to life in this retelling of "The Ugly Duckling."

THOMAS NELSON
Since 1798

ACKNOWLEDGMENTS

I want to thank my agent, Natasha Kern, and my publisher, Thomas Nelson and HarperCollins Christian Publishing, for all they did to make this new series a reality, and for continuing to believe in me. The people at TN—my editors, Kimberly Carlton, Julie Breihan, and Jodi Hughes; the marketing and publicity people, Kerri Potts, Matt Bray, Marcee Wardell, Margaret Kercher, and Paul Fisher; and Amanda Bostic, who is the guiding force—feel as much like friends as business associates. I am very appreciative of all of you and all you do for my books.

I also want to thank my friends and family who helped me brainstorm as I worked through the plotting of this story, including my daughters, Grace and Faith Dickerson, and my niece, Morgan Lee. Again I want to thank Natasha, who not only helped me think of plot points, but whose pep talks were much needed in this season. Thank you so much.

And most of all, thanks to my delightful readers, who share my books with their friends and on social media and write me the sweetest emails and messages. God bless you all. Stay tough and keep believing that the best is yet to come. You can do anything God strengthens you to do. Always persevere, keeping your eyes on Jesus, and never give up. "Rejoice in our confident hope. Be patient in trouble, and keep on praying" (Romans 12:12 NLT).

DISCUSSION QUESTIONS

1. What was it about Delia's new stepmother that seemed odd from the very beginning?

2. What do you think were the reasons Delia felt such a loving attachment to her seven brothers?

3. Why did Delia hate Sir Geoffrey in the beginning of the story? How long did it take her to change her mind about his character, and why did she?

4. What made Delia decide to leave home? What was her plan for saving her brothers?

5. When Delia's brothers were sentenced, do you think her fear and desperation made her trust someone who was untrustworthy? Has fear ever caused you to make a poor decision? What were some clues, or warning signs, that Sir Elliot was not trustworthy?

6. Delia had a strong desire to take care of her brothers. How did this make her vulnerable to Sir Elliot's insincere offer to help her brothers escape?

7. Delia believed that God cared for her, but she struggled with what that meant. She knew it didn't mean that bad

things would never happen to her. So what does God's care look like, practically?

8. What was Sir Geoffrey risking by helping Delia's brothers escape? He hated the idea of doing anything dishonorable. Do you think he felt torn about helping them?

9. In this story, King Richard II was greatly influenced by his councilors. What kind of king do you think you would have been at the age of fourteen? Have you ever been influenced by others to do something you later regretted?

10. Delia struggled emotionally with the injustice of what had been done to her family. Have you ever been outraged at something unjust, such as being wrongly accused or punished by a person in authority? Have you ever stood up for someone being treated unjustly? Was Delia able to fully resolve her inner conflict about the injustice?

11. Larissa was able to overcome her agoraphobia to help save Delia's brothers. What fears have you overcome that were holding you back?

An Excerpt from
The Golden Braid

Chapter One

LATE WINTER, 1413, THE VILLAGE OF OTTELFELT,
SOUTHWEST OF HAGENHEIM, THE HOLY
ROMAN EMPIRE

"Rapunzel, I wish to marry you."

At that moment, Mother revealed herself from behind the well in the center of the village, her lips pressed tightly together.

The look Mother fixed on Wendel Gotekens was the one that always made Rapunzel's stomach churn.

Rapunzel shuffled backward on the rutted dirt road. "I am afraid I cannot marry you."

"Why not?" He leaned toward her, his wavy hair unusually tame and looking suspiciously like he rubbed it with grease. "I have as much land as the other villagers. I even have two goats and five chickens. Not many people in Ottelfelt have both goats and chickens."

She silently repeated the words an old woman had once told her. *The truth is kinder than a lie.*

"I do not wish to marry you, Wendel." She had once seen him unleash his ill temper on one of his goats when it ran away from him. That alone would have been enough to make her lose interest in him, if she had ever felt any.

He opened his mouth as if to protest further, but he became aware of Mother's presence and turned toward her.

"*Frau* Gothel, I—"

"I shall speak to you in a moment." Her mother's voice was icy. "Rapunzel, go home."

Rapunzel hesitated, but the look in Mother's eyes was so fierce, she turned and hurried down the dirt path toward their little house on the edge of the woods.

Aside from asking her to marry him, Wendel's biggest blunder had been letting Mother overhear him.

Rapunzel made it to their little wattle-and-daub structure and sat down, placing her head in her hands, muffling her voice. "Father God, please don't let Mother's sharp tongue flay Wendel too brutally."

Mother came through the door only a minute or two later. She looked around their one-room home, then began mumbling under her breath.

"There is nothing to be upset about, Mother," Rapunzel said. "I will not marry him, and I told him I wouldn't."

Her mother had that frantic look in her eyes and didn't seem to be listening. Unpleasant things often happened when Mother got that look. But she simply snatched her broom and went about sweeping the room, muttering unintelligibly.

Rapunzel was the oldest unmarried maiden she knew, except for the poor half-witted girl in the village where they'd lived several years ago. That poor girl drooled and could barely speak a dozen words. The girl's mother had insisted her daughter was a fairy changeling and would someday be an angel who would come back to earth to punish anyone who mistreated her.

Mother suddenly put down her broom. "Tomorrow is a market day in Keiterhafen. Perhaps I can sell some healing herbs." She began searching through her dried herbs on the shelf attached to the wall. "If I take this feverfew and yarrow root to sell, I won't have any left over," she mumbled.

"If you let me stay home, I can gather more for you."

Her mother stopped what she was doing and stared at her. "Are you sure you will be safe without me? That Wendel Gotekens—"

"Of course, Mother. I have my knife."

"Very well."

The next morning Mother left before the sun was up to make the two-hour walk to Keiterhafen. Rapunzel arose a bit later and went to pick some feverfew and yarrow root in the forest around their little village of Ottelfelt. After several hours of gathering and exploring the small stream in the woods, she had filled two leather bags, which she hung from the belt around her waist. *This should put Mother in a better mood.*

Just as Rapunzel reentered the village on her way back home, three boys were standing beside the lord's stable.

"Rapunzel! Come over here!"

The boys were all a few years younger than she was.

"What do you want?" Rapunzel yelled back.

"Show us that knife trick again."

"It's not a trick." She started toward them. "It is a skill, and you will never learn it if you do not practice."

Rapunzel pulled her knife out of her kirtle pocket as she reached them. The boys stood back as she took her stance, lifted the knife, and threw it at the wooden building. The knife point struck the wood and held fast, the handle sticking out perfectly horizontal.

One boy gasped while another whistled.

"Practice, boys."

Rapunzel yanked her knife out of the wall and continued down the dusty path. She had learned the skill of knife throwing in one of the villages where she and Mother had lived.

Boys and old people were quick to accept her, an outsider, better than girls her own age, and she tried to learn whatever she could from them. An old woman once taught her to mix brightly colored paints using things easily found in the forest, which Rapunzel then used to paint flowers and vines and butterflies on the houses where she and Mother lived. An older man taught her how to tie several types of knots for different tasks. But the one skill she wanted to learn the most had been the hardest to find a teacher for.

She walked past the stone manor house, with the lord's larger house just behind it and the courtyard in front of it. On the other side of the road were the mill, the bakery, and the butcher's shop. And surrounding everything was the thick forest that grew everywhere man had not purposely cleared.

Endlein, one of the village girls, was drawing water from the well several feet away. She glanced up and waved Rapunzel over.

Rapunzel and her mother were still considered strangers in Ottelfelt as they had only been there since Michaelmas, about half a year. She hesitated before walking over.

Endlein fixed her eyes on Rapunzel as she drew near. "So, Rapunzel. Do you have something to tell me? Some news of great import?" She waggled her brows with a smug grin, pushing a strand of brown hair out of her eyes.

"No. I have no news."

"Surely you have something you want to say about Wendel Gotekens."

"I don't know what you mean."

Endlein lifted one corner of her mouth. "Perhaps you do not know."

"Know what?"

"That your mother has told Wendel he cannot ever marry you because the two of you are going away from Ottelfelt."

Rapunzel's stomach turned a somersault like the contortionists she had seen at the Keiterhafen fair.

She should have guessed Mother would decide to leave now that a young man had not only shown interest in her but had declared his wish to marry her. The same thing happened in the last two villages where they had lived.

Rapunzel turned toward home.

"Leaving without saying farewell?" Endlein called after her.

"I am not entirely sure we are leaving," Rapunzel called back. "Perhaps Mother will change her mind and we shall stay."

She hurried down the road, not even turning her head to greet anyone, even though the baker's wife stopped to stare and so did the alewife. She continued to the little wattle-and-daub cottage that was half hidden from the road by thick trees and bushes. The front door was closed, even though it was a warm day for late winter.

Rapunzel caught sight of the colorful vines and flowers she had only just finished painting on the white plaster walls and sighed. Oh well. She could simply paint more on their next house.

Pushing the door open, Rapunzel stopped. Her mother was placing their folded coverlet into the trunk.

"So it is true? We are leaving again?"

"Why do you say 'again'? We've never left here before." She had that airy tone she used when she couldn't look Rapunzel in the eye.

"But why? Only because Wendel said he wanted to marry me? I told you I would not marry him even if you approved of him."

"You don't know what you would do if he should say the right thing to you." Her tone had turned peevish as she began to place their two cups, two bowls, pot, and pan into the trunk.

"Mother."

"I know you, Rapunzel. You are quick to feel sorry for anyone and everyone." She straightened and waved her hand about, staring at the wall as though she were talking to it. "What if Wendel cried and begged? You might tell him you would marry him. He might beg you to show him your love. You might . . . you might do something you would later regret."

"I would not." Rapunzel's breath was coming fast now, her face hot. It wasn't the first time Mother had accused her of such a thing.

"You don't want to marry a poor, wretched farmer like that Wendel, do you? Who will always be dirty and have to scratch out his existence from the ground? Someone as beautiful as you? Men notice you, as well they might. But none of them are worthy of you . . . none of them." It was as if she had forgotten she was speaking to Rapunzel and was carrying on to herself.

"Mother, you don't have to worry that I will marry someone unworthy." Rapunzel could hardly imagine marrying anyone. One had to be allowed to talk to a man before she could marry him, and talking to men was something her mother had always discouraged. Vehemently.

Mother did not respond, so Rapunzel went to fold her clothes and pack her few belongings.

As she gathered her things, she felt no great sadness at the prospect of leaving Ottelfelt. She always had trouble making friends with girls near her own age, and here she had never lost her status as an outsider. But the real reason she felt no regret was because of what she wanted so very badly, and it was not something she could get in tiny Ottelfelt.

Rapunzel was at least nineteen years old, and she could stay in Ottelfelt without her mother if she wanted to. However, it would be difficult and dangerous—unheard of—unless she was married, since she had no other family. But if they went to a large town, there would certainly be many people who knew how to read and might be willing to teach her.

"Mother, you promised someday you would find someone who could teach me to read. Might we go to a large town where there is a proper priest who knows Latin, a place where there might dwell someone who can teach me to read and write?" She held her breath, watching her mother, whose back was turned as she wrapped her fragile dried herbs in cloths.

Finally, her mother answered softly, "I saw someone in Keiterhafen this morning, someone who . . . needs my help with . . . something."

Rapunzel stopped in the middle of folding her clothes, waiting for Mother to clarify the strange comment.

"And now we will be going to meet him in Hagenheim."

Her heart leapt. Hagenheim was a great town, the largest around.

She tried not to sound eager as she asked, "Isn't that where you lived a long time ago, when Great-Grandmother was still alive?"

"Yes, my darling. Your great-grandmother was the most renowned midwife in the town of Hagenheim—in the entire region." She paused. "Someone I once knew will soon be back in Hagenheim after a long stay in England."

"I don't remember you saying you knew anyone who went to England. Is it a family member?"

Her mother turned to Rapunzel with a brittle smile. "No, not a family member. I have never mentioned this person before. I do not wish to talk about it now."

The story continues in *The Golden Braid*
by Melanie Dickerson.

ABOUT THE AUTHOR

MELANIE DICKERSON IS A *NEW York Times* bestselling author and two-time Christy Award winner. Melanie spends her time daydreaming, researching the most fascinating historical time periods, and writing and editing her happily-ever-afters.

Jodie Westfall Photography

MelanieDickerson.com
Instagram: @MelanieDickerson123
Facebook: @MelanieDickersonBooks
Twitter: @MelanieAuthor